better knowledge that their intimate paradise will remain suspended between the
past ten thousand human years and the
moment of complete annihilation, delaying
with memories, hopes, and dreams their encounter with eternity.

When everything has been abandoned
except the poisoned moon and even the
voice of all that had been crushed is still,
it is clear that Carpelan's world, exploding,
would have been worth keeping, after all.

VOICES AT
THE LATE HOUR

VOICES AT THE LATE HOUR

A Novel by Bo Carpelan

Translated by Irma Margareta Martin

Introduction by George C. Schoolfield

The University of Georgia Press • *Athens and London*

Voices at the Late Hour © 1988 by Irma Margareta Martin
Published in 1988 by the University of Georgia Press
Athens, Georgia 30602
All rights reserved

Rösterna i den sena timmen © Bo Carpelan 1971
Originally published in Swedish by
Holger Schildts, Helsingfors

Designed by Betty McDaniel
Set in Berkeley Old Style
The paper in this book meets the guidelines for
permanence and durability of the Committee on
Production Guidelines for Book Longevity of the
Council on Library Resources.

Printed in the United States of America

92 91 90 89 88   5 4 3 2 1

Library of Congress Cataloging in Publication Data

Carpelan, Bo Gustaf Bertelsson, 1926–
[Rösterna i den sena timmen. English]
Voices at the late hour: a novel/by Bo Carpelan; translated by
Irma Margareta Martin; introduction by George C. Schoolfield.
p.   cm.
Translation of: Rösterna i den sena timmen.
ISBN 0-8203-1008-5 (alk. paper).
ISBN 0-8203-1009-3 (pbk.: alk. paper)
I. Title
PT9875.C35R613   1988   87-27619
839.7'374—dc19   CIP

British Library Cataloging in Publication Data available

INTRODUCTION

George C. Schoolfield

A fact that often has to be explained to the outside world about Finland is its bilingualism: a minority, now reckoned at about eight percent of the total population, has Swedish as its mother tongue. Finland was a property of the Swedish crown from the twelfth century until the Swedish-Russian War of 1808–1809, when it became a semi-autonomous grand duchy in the Russian empire; before 1863, when Czar Alexander II was persuaded by the publicist and Hegelian philosopher Johan Vilhelm Snellman to grant Finnish equal rights in the governmental and legal systems of the country, Swedish had been the language of administration, commerce and culture. Elias Lönnrot's *Kalevala,* a compilation and reworking of songs about Finnish myth which he had heard performed by largely illiterate folksingers in Russian Karelia and elsewhere, had been a precursor of the change; *Kalevala* was first published in a shorter version in 1835 and then, expanded, in 1848. The appearance of the plays and then the great comic novel *Seitsemän veljestä (Seven Brothers,* 1870) by Aleksis Kivi may be viewed as the beginning of a modern literature in Finnish, a body of letters that grew rapidly. Comparisons may be made to the burgeoning of Czech literature (over against literature in German) in nineteenth-century Bohemia and to the Gaelic Revival.

As the century moved toward its close, Swedish speakers in

Finland began to know a feeling of isolation in what they rightly regarded as their homeland. Their ties to Sweden were tenuous; after all, many so-called Finland-Swedish families had come to Finland's coasts in the Middle Ages. The great authors of the golden age of national awakening, from the 1830s on—Johan Ludvig Runeberg and Zacharias Topelius—had written exclusively in Swedish and yet were keenly aware of their identity as Finns (or Finlanders, as they also called themselves). Indeed, the very Swedish they spoke and wrote was different, in pronunciation and vocabulary and even points of grammar, from that used in Swedish proper. (A similar comparison would be the Irish or American variants of British English.) In turn, for a time the country's Finnish-speaking majority nurtured a strong sense of mission, sometimes mingled with an inferiority complex: it was painful to be reminded that Finland's national anthem, "Our Land," had been written in Swedish by Runeberg, as the opening canto of a set of narrative poems about the war of 1808–1809, *Fänrik Ståls sägner* (The Tales of Ensign Stål). And it was painful too, somewhat later, to be reminded that the native tongue of Jean Sibelius was Swedish (and that he composed his songs, *par préférence,* to Swedish texts); Gustaf Mannerheim, who led the victorious White forces in the Civil War that rent the new nation after its declaration of independence from Russia (December 1917), was another Swedish speaker with a notoriously weak command of the Finnish language. Happily, the language strife in Finland never achieved the acrimony it did (and would) in other bilingual lands; the 1919 constitution of the Republic of Finland guaranteed the rights of the minority group in an exemplary fashion, and the Winter War of 1939–1940, in which Mannerheim himself became a symbol unifying the entire nation against the Soviet threat, brought about an effective close to public expressions of ill will between the language groups.

Finland-Swedish men-of-letters had contributed in some measure to the process of unification. The *Kalevala* had been translated as early as the 1860s by the librarian of the University of Helsinki,

Karl Collan; in 1912 the poet Arvid Mörne published what remains one of the best brief studies of Kivi's *Seven Brothers;* and, among the modernist poets of the 1920s and 1930s, there was evident either a stance of neutrality in the language question or an active effort to bridge the linguistic gap. To be sure, these authors—Edith Södergran, Elmer Diktonius, Hagar Olsson, Gunnar Björling, and Rabbe Enckell—were determined not to let themselves become hypnotized by exclusively national problems. Their horizons were larger, and their hopes of influence beyond Finland's borders were fulfilled to the extent that they radically changed the face of lyric poetry in the whole of Scandinavia. Recently, Bo Carpelan has remarked that an award of the Nobel Prize to Rabbe Enckell during that poet's last years would have been a fitting recognition of the enormous contribution the Finland-Swedish modernists had made to the literature of the North.

Certainly, the strength of the minority literature has been in the lyric, just as the strength of Finnish-language literature has been in the prose narrative, from Kivi on to the middle of the present century, with Pentti Haanpää, Väino Linna, Veijo Meri, and their contemporaries and successors. A good deal of conjecture has been devoted to the possible cause for the Finland-Swedish lyric gift (and a concomitant inability to write successful novels); a theory often offered is that the members of the minority have been compelled to introspection by their lack of a broad social context. Putting a witty point on the matter, the critic and novelist Merete Mazzarella has proposed that much of the actual conversation carried on by Finland-Swedish authors is in Finnish, and so the dialogue in their books is often artificial or stillborn. As it were, reality has belonged to the majority, and the realm of the unfettered imagination (described in a very personal language) to the minority. Another factor is the cumulative weight of the literary tradition; Runeberg wrote only a handful of prose tales, never read today, but his lyric and epic poetry has a permanent place in the canon. Topelius and Karl August Tavaststjerna, Strindberg's friend and contemporary, were, to be sure, indefatigable writers of narrative prose (and Topelius, like Runeberg, was quickly translated into Finnish, melting into the majority literature as a Finnish author *honoris causa*); but their lyrics may be their more lasting contribution to letters. The modernists were lyricists above all else; only Hagar Olsson did not try poetry, instead composing brilliant criticism and much less brilliant novels. (Easily the most vital Finland-Swedish narrative prose produced by a modernist was the "woodcut in words," *Janne Kubik* [1932], of Elmer Diktonius, who was totally bilingual; Diktonius claimed to have "thought" this book about a Finnish Everyman in Finnish, not in Swedish, and he later republished the novel in its "original language.") It was noted long ago that Finland-Swedish prose customarily leaned toward the prose-poem or the aphorism or close self-analysis (in the psychological novel or such autobiographical sketches as those of Enckell or another modernist, R. R. Eklund), rather than toward direct narrative; even today, so distinguished a novella writer as Solveig von Schoultz has felt obliged to state that she regards herself as primarily a lyricist.

Bo Carpelan was born in Helsinki in 1926, the son of a bank employee; the family bore a distinguished name, and the visitor to Suomenlinna-Sveaborg, the great eighteenth-century fortress in Helsinki harbor, will see Carpelan's Bastion, named after a military forebear. Contemporary circumstances were by no means so grand, however, and in *Gården* (1964)[1] Carpelan would reproduce scenes from his boyhood in a cramped apartment house, where he had become aware of the problems of the weak or the unusual child, as well as the gray lives of the adults around him. After finishing his studies at the Swedish Normal Lyceum, the oldest of Helsinki's Swedish-language boys' schools, he quickly made his literary debut with the lyric collection, *Som en dunkel värme* (Like a Dark Warmth, 1946), while at the same time engaging in literary studies at the university and beginning his long employment at the Helsinki City Library. The academic undertaking was completed in 1960 with a doctoral dissertation on the most difficult of the modernists, *Studier i Gunnar Björlings dikter,* a monograph Carpelan has modestly characterized as evidence of "how confusedly inspired [he was] by the New Criticism" in those days. (Between 1950 and 1964 he was also an active literary critic, writing for *Hufvudstadsbladet,* Finland's leading Swedish-language newspaper.) His library work led him to the headship of the department of foreign literature in 1964, a post from which he retired in 1980 when the Finnish government awarded him an "artist's professorship," affording him the leisure to devote time entirely to his creative work.

As soon as his debut book appeared, Carpelan was hailed as the great hope of Finland-Swedish poetry, all the more welcome because the little literature seemed to lack fresh lyric talents. The promising Christer Lind had died in 1942 at the age of thirty; Solveig von Schoultz was still best known for her autobiographical novels; Lars Huldén, destined to be the other leading figure among younger poets during the next decades, would not make his debut until 1958. What captured the reviewers' favor in the early collections—*Som en dunkel värme,* followed by *Du mörka överlevande* (You Dark Survivor, 1947) and *Variationer* (Variations, 1950)—was Carpelan's apparent desire not to be a mere imitator of the modernists. His language had a polished richness particularly surprising in a beginner, and his emotional intensity showed how close an adept of Gunnar Björling he was. In style, however, he did not resemble his mentor, who was noted—and sometimes notorious—for ellipses, apparent non sequiturs, and willful absurdities; critics remarked that Carpelan's chiseled lines and muted elegiac tone were in fact reminiscent of Rabbe Enckell. In addition, as Carpelan has recounted, he learned from Wallace Stevens and from the "image-laden" verse of the leading Swedish poets of the 1940s, especially Erik Lindegren—poets who themselves, as they set out on their careers, had been liberated from the constraints of rhyme and a regular rhythmic pattern by the example of the Finland-Swedish modernists. However, Carpelan never rivaled, or wanted to rival, Lindegren or such other Swedish "forties' poets" as Karl Vennberg and Harald Forss in difficulty or obscurity; throughout *Variationer*, a single central attitude is discernible—the poet's affection for a world of beauty, principally to be found in nature, a world whose serenity is ruffled by intimations of pain or loss. With his refreshing objectivity about his own work, Carpelan has been inclined to censure his first verse flights as "weighed down with symbols"; yet his lyric strength, even then, lay in his ability to present often complex emotional states lucidly and movingly, as in the four-line poem from *Variationer*:

> What is shadow? What is your longing?
> The silence's rain, the autumn's beauty,
> silver-gray mist over flaming trees.
> no persecution, no death.

That Carpelan took himself very seriously in these years is plain enough, but flashes of irony and self-mockery come to the surface in the prose-poems of *Minus sju* (Minus Seven, 1952): "the odor of snow, as of clean glass, is so imperceptible that only a reflection about it put on paper can give a notion of its almost non-existent nature." *Objekt för ord* (Objects for Words, 1954) seems to mark the end of the initial and most self-conscious period of Carpelan's lyric production; just as a sense of humor had let itself out of the bag in the prose-poems, so a sense of what might be called visual objectivity appeared in the new collection. Like the young Rilke, Carpelan strove to learn to 'see,' and, like Rilke, he practiced upon *objets d'art*, as in the suite "Upon Observing Some Old Flemish Masters":

> She is aware of the sufferings she will meet.
> In her white ruff she keeps her calm, nonetheless.
> Her childish hands rest too, touch us therefore
> where we lose ourselves in details, remind us of
> our childhood, of the future—like the master himself, unknown.

A second phase of Carpelan's lyric began with *Landskapets för-vandlingar* (The Landscape's Transformations, 1957). Now the poet, who before had talked primarily to himself, presumes a community of experience with his reader: poet and reader are joined as they watch the approach of death:

> You press through shattering vaults, death,
> Someone calls you but your way is not changed.
> You draw near through the smoke of the twilight.
> Untransformed you stand at the goal of your task.

Or, more cheerfully:

> The morning wave ripples dew-fresh
> against the white sand's solid cloth
> and the foot ascends so that, cooled by the sea,
> it may feel the beach-line's warmth, concealed in memory.

The poem expresses the kind of bliss everyone has known at a vacation spot. Two years later, in an unexpected branching-out for a poet who had seemed not so long ago to cherish a refined exclusivity, Carpelan published his first book for children, *Anders på ön* (Anders on the Island), about a little boy's growing awareness of the paradisiacal island where he vacations with his parents—a little boy who bears the name of Carpelan's son, born in 1957.

In *Den svala dagen* (The Cool Day, 1961), Carpelan achieved a tone unmistakably his own; here he demonstrated, again and again, the art of the unforgettable line—for example, "redan för dig är vårarnas sorl förbi" ("for you, the spring days' murmur is already past"), and "jasminen står dunkel vid porten som aldrig öppnas" ("the jasmine stands dark by the doorway that's never opened"), or "nattens skugga, den sista, rörde vid dig" ("the shadow of the night, the last, touched upon you"). The mode is elegiac; the restrained melancholy that informs so much Swedish poetry in Finland, from the baroque's Jakob Frese on to Runeberg and beyond, had found a new spokesman. Just so, the brevity of which Runeberg had shown himself the master in the two series of "Idylls and Epigrams" (1830,

1833) and which, more recently, Rabbe Enckell had fostered in his "match-stick poems" (so-called because of their tiny size and the sudden light they could give) was cultivated by Carpelan in poems that encapsulated a human fate in a few lines.[2] "Höstvandring" ("Autumnal Walk") is one of the best known of all Carpelan's lyrics:

> A man walks through the forest
> one day with shifting lights.
> Meets few people,
> stops, observes the autumn sky.
> He means to go to the churchyard
> and no one follows him.

At the same time, Carpelan continued his quest for a completely direct and open relationship to nature; a key line in *Den svala dagen* is "Sök inte i det stumma gräset" ("Do not seek in the mute grass, / seek the mute grass"). With the baldly titled *73 dikter* (73 Poems, 1966), Carpelan carried this stringency toward a laconicism that could momentarily become baffling for the reader; against his own sternest critic, Carpelan has called some of the poems almost incomprehensible. Yet there is no mystery about the following:

> Human being foregathers with human being,
> they are many in the burning cities,
> they are rinsed in oil,
> and arise again
> in someone's words, in fire.

The shadow of a cataclysm of the most awful dimensions had begun to fall over Carpelan's quiet, undramatic work.

As if in reaction against the occasional riddles of *73 dikter*, Carpelan's next collection—and his most widely read—was *Gården*, in which he summoned up the memories of his boyhood in a section of Helsinki called Kruununhaka, or, in Swedish, Kronohagen. Immediately appealing, the book—amid its several views of sordidness or even petty brutality—spins a web of family life, or family lives. Writing at a time when there was much outcry in Finland, as elsewhere, against the presumed falseness and evil of people over thirty, Carpelan showed how concerned he was with parents; the perspective in the book is that of a child, or rather, of a grown man remembering his childhood:

> The future was seldom mentioned.
> The day was enough.
> Saturday was best,
> father and mother as if they
> had been children,
> and I hear their voices
> like a hand on my forehead.

But this sanctuary ("Mother was reading, / and I followed, disappeared from the world outside") is threatened; another poem from *Gården* runs:

> I awoke when someone cried out in the courtyard.
> I awoke at the smell of gas: everyone lay dead, I too.
>
> I awoke when war broke out and my clothes were burning.
> It was quite still. Only father, snoring comfortingly.
>
> I awoke at so many catastrophes.
> It was like a training course for the future.

The children's books of Carpelan formed a consoling contrast to the nervousness revealed in *Garden*. In *Anders i stan* (Anders in the City, 1962), he had already given a sweet view of childhood with parties and pets and kindly policemen. Subsequently, in books aimed at young people, *Bågen: Berättelsen om en sommer som var annorlunda* (1968) and its sequel *Paradiset: Berättelsen om Marvins och Johans vänskap II* (1973),[3] he proved to the careful reader of his oeuvre how essential these other publications were for an understanding of his work. The main figure in the pair of stories is a mentally retarded boy, removed from the Finnish skerries to the unfamiliar and threatening life of the city. He is set upon by an unthinking gang, but somehow—aided by a friend (a more mature version of Anders in the books for small children)—he is able to cling to his memories of an island paradise, a realm of perfect peace human beings all too rarely know.

The anxiety which runs as an undercurrent in Carpelan's poetry comes to the surface, wholly, in the frightening rush of the novel *Rösterna i den sena timmen* (Voices at the Late Hour, 1971), his first narrative for adults. Anxiety appears again, albeit reduced to the threatened destruction of a single person, in *Paradiset,* where Marvin, the boy from the skerries, runs panic-stricken through the streets of a city he does not understand. In the psychological thriller *Din gestalt bakom dörren* (Your Figure Behind the Door, 1975), Ewald, a mild-mannered Helsinki businessman inclined to moral compromise of every sort, suddenly finds himself harassed by a double, who acts out patterns of behavior the original Ewald has suppressed. The threats continue in the detective story *Vandrande skugga* (Wandering Shadow, 1977), about a small Finnish coastal town at the turn of the century. On Nyvik's pretty surface, symptoms of decay and destruction appear: rats bob up in shop corners, mysterious fires occur (and a baby carriage burns, together with the doll someone has placed in it), a prostitute and then the town drunk are murdered. The book has a somewhat contrived happy ending in which the murderer is identified, the widowed police chief (appropriately named Werner Frid [Peace]) who solves the case finds happiness with the servant of an upper-class family (its head, the perverse Consul Reding, has committed the crimes), and it is hinted that, under Frid's benevolent eye, some social injustices will at least be ameliorated. Carpelan is scarcely the first to have observed the rotten microcosm of the idyllic small town; in Scandinavian literature, he has such distinguished predecessors as the Ibsen of *Pillars of Society* and the Knut Hamsun of *Mysteries,* and the plot of *Vandrande skugga* is easily seen through. What fascinates, though, about this flawed book is the persistence with which Carpelan juxtaposes the idyll, which obviously delights him in spite of the ills he sees, and its impending destruction. In a novel from 1907 by the Norwegian Tryggve Andersen, *Mot kvæld* (Toward Evening), a fjordside community quite literally experiences the end of the world one hot August. In *Vandrande skugga,* the end of a society rather than the end of the world is predicted; Dr. von Adler, the mortally ill physician, tells Frid as much during a summer festival at the town club: "Sometimes it looks to me as though the whole business were a colorful balloon, slowly pumped to capacity with poison gas, that sooner or later will get too close to a flame."

Even in *Jag minns att jag drömde* (I Recall That I Dreamt, 1979), where Carpelan again takes up the prose-poem form he had chosen for *Minus sju* a quarter-century before, he still cannot submerge his premonitions of disaster, however much he enjoys the playfulness the form allows and its opportunities for an imaginative and fruitful continuation of his long love affair with his native language. However, his dreams are not realms where the worst danger hides but essentially places of safety: "everything dreamt, and living only through the dream! Only a handful of people who lie quite quiet, dreaming each paving stone on Bath House Street, every tree which now sends out its aroma with white blossoms from behind dusty fences. And the roofs in the old houses that bend but still are not broken: after all, it is not the rafters that support their roofs but the dreams, the early dreams." Dreams, like islands, are places of the greatest happiness and, paradoxically, of the greatest permanence; it is only awful reality that will destroy them, or their dreamers. Or, as the waterbird says in one of the most enchanting of these prose-poems, gazing down into a sunken (and a dreamt) city, a *ville engloutie* in an underwater valley: "Can I say that what was once our sky is now our sea? Here is a silence that restores our worth to us and our dignity. Here is a purity that resembles the simplest of songs. Here is an absence of fear that gives peace unto our eyes and forms the basis for our system of light. Our city is fair, and when sometimes I rest on the rising streams of water and look out over the vale's shadows and glimmers of light, I know that I can find no better sanctuary. Perhaps, our vale is the only place our language can still live in purity."

The 1970s may seem to have been a time of concentration on prose, culminating in the dream book, where Carpelan could bring to bear his special talents that lay more in evocation than in narration. However, the decade also saw the appearance of two of his most convincing lyric collections, *Källan* (The Source, 1973) and *I de mörka rummen, i de ljusa* (In the Dark Rooms, in the Light, 1976). Putting together the former, Carpelan looked once more to the sources of strength (familial love, erotic love, nature, the very act of perceiving the beauties of the world) that mankind must have in order to exist; nevertheless, visions of destruction persistently thrust themselves upon him, as in the poem "Städerna" ("The Cities"):

> The cities stand with open walls.
> The unhelmed ships are led by the winds
> this way and that, and strike against the docks.
> The ferris wheel in the amusement park
> stands shattered.
> The goddess of Peace runs, blind and gilded
> she shimmers through the water.
> The fountain in the square is dried up,
> free entrance given to the embassies,
> ministries, banks.
> Doves and sea gulls are dead along the docks
> and gutters.
>
> And the people,
> where are the people?

Was this poem an afterbirth of *Voices at the Late Hour,* and were the worst fears now to be put behind the poet? In the collection of 1976, for which Carpelan received the Nordic Council's Literary Prize (1977), he tried to turn from the dark rooms to the light ones, taking pleasure once more in simple expressions of affection for persons, for places, for nature. Yet the reader may be aware of something ominous suggested by that most mundane of plants, the cauliflower. (In 1986, after the Chernobyl disaster, the cauliflower bought in the supermarket could well be thought to contain the seed of a distant but horrible death.)

> The cauliflower is a hard cloud.
> It is a brain substance,
> each branch part of a stem.
> It grows unseen,
> hidden in green leaves,
> then swells
> with sprinkles of soil,
> with a slight smell of poison
> as though eyes could grow blind
> or fill with tears
> but do not weep.

Is the vegetable also a nuclear cloud? Suggestive precision is evident everywhere in this capstone collection, which came out exactly thirty years after Carpelan's debut; in 1980, he made a selection of what he considered the best of his verses, *Dikter från 30 år* (Poems from Thirty Years), slighting the earlier lyric volumes to the advantage of the later—as might be expected of a poet rightly proud of the mastery he had achieved.

In the present decade, Carpelan has devoted much time to the translation of individual Finnish poets, especially Paavo Haavikko and Sirkka Turkka, and has prepared an anthology of modern Finnish verse, again in Swedish translation, intended to present this other side of his country's literature to the rest of Scandinavia. Unlike some Finland-Swedish authors of that now-distant time when the minority's members were wont to write tragically—or melodramatically—about its immediate demise, Carpelan and his colleagues are an integral part of Finnish cultural life; his undeniable *tristitia* comes not from a sense of belonging to a dying miniature culture but from his membership in mankind, a threatened species. His only book of original lyric poetry from the 1980s thus far has been *Dagen vänder* (The Day Turns, 1982), which pursues the contemplative course taken in *Källan* and *I de mörka rummen, i de ljusa*: thoughts on aging and the ages of man ("The third birth: into the silence, the backyard's Sunday, / unreal, waiting, a twist of smoke, / unseen"), thoughts on his own easy contact with the dead ("the day falls / as a beam of light falls / in a dream, the dead fall / smiling toward us"), thoughts on his longing which may well contain the essence of his poetics ("I long for a day / where light is spread thin like a blanket / concealing nothing, dramatizing nothing"). Even the threatened city seems safe for a moment in the poet's eye, if not in reality:

> And those who still see and hear beauty
> hold, for a moment, city, plain, and arch of sky together,
> the dogs of death are driven away and in silence
> a child's voice rises like a flower out of the light,
> an admonition, a sign.

A year after *Dagen vänder* appeared, a different creative tack was taken with *Marginalia till grekisk och romersk diktning* (Marginalia to Greek and Roman Poetry), an experiment in which Carpelan— lamenting the disappearance of classical training from the classroom—pays tribute to the firm diction and images of poets from Homer to those of the Greek anthology and from Lucretius to Juvenal. As ever, his own concerns shine through these glosses, or what he calls his "images, associations, aphoristic comments [and] lyric fragments": the importance of memory and of family continuity and, as ever, the final threat—occurring, strangely enough, in his reaction to the poet of transformations and of the art of love, Ovid:

> forests and waters stand mute—soon
> burned and poisoned all,
> and mankind, its life and dreams:

flakes of ash, blown away
by a blind and raging wind
Only one sun, one life
and there, beyond, transformation's law
Perhaps these dead oaks too
spoke once a time, foliage-fresh
as lovers.

The overriding artistic effort of the 1980s, however, has been the composition of *Axel* (1986), about the friend of Sibelius and Bo Carpelan's great-uncle, Axel Carpelan, to whom the composer's second symphony is dedicated. The book is a fictive diary, going from Axel's tenth year (in 1868) until his death in 1919. (Axel is a clumsy and ineffectual man, surely one of society's outsiders. Might it be suggested that Carpelan's 1982 book for young readers, *Julius Blom, ett huvud för sig* [Julius Blom, a Head of His Own], represents, in a very modest way, a preparatory study for *Axel?* Both the boy Julius and Axel are people who ultimately do not fit into society because they mean to march to their own drum, however much they are tormented by hypersensitivity—a condition that is crippling in Axel's case.) Axel should not be regarded merely as Sibelius's good and guardian spirit; the eccentric is a truly Carpelanian character, deeply in love with life and aware of its constant losses, forever afraid of disaster—in his case, the disaster of ridicule or rejection—but unwilling to close himself off from existence on that account. The novel also reveals Bo Carpelan's own affection for music, another of the "paradises" life affords. Unlike the Finnish poet Eeva-Liisa Manner (whom Carpelan has translated), Carpelan has written very little poetry directly about music, turning rather to the other arts of literature and painting for occasional *sujets*. Indeed, he has characterized his own process of writing as having a visual rather than an aural beginning: "To me, the writing of poetry is a listening with the eye, an attempt precisely to capture an experience, a vision, a mood." Speaking through Axel's diaries, Bo Carpelan has given music its due praise—this last paradise of his, supplementing the ties of blood and love and the ties of memory, supplementing the beauties of nature and the dream.

The original inspiration of *Voices at the Late Hour* may have been regret, or frustration, that movie audiences were unwilling to attend a film originally made by BBC Television, Peter Watkins's *The War Game* (1967). At least this is the way Carpelan remembers the genesis of his book; certainly, the novel has two specific cinematic allusions placed strategically within it, one at the beginning ("In silent films of the future, houses suddenly collapse like New Year's tin over a flame") and one near the end ("As in a Russian movie the whirling treetops of the parkway take time away, restore time, a road opens up and closes again"). Understandably, filmmakers were quick to respond to the nuclear threat and its awful fascination. Stanley Kramer's *On the Beach* (1959), based upon the novel by Nevil Shute, was a chronicle of final events in Australia, as the cloud of nuclear poison swept around the world toward the far-off lands of the southern Pacific; Sidney Lumet's *Fail Safe* (1962) examined the likelihood of nuclear mistakes; Stanley Kubrick's *Doctor Strangelove* (1963) gave a piercingly funny account of the events that could lead up to nuclear war; and Peter Watkins's documentary in its very dryness was the most horrifying of all. Oddly, the Kramer film, starring Gregory Peck, with its pleasant setting, its emotional entanglements, and its strange calmness, seems most to prefigure Carpelan's novel. Carpelan's reader may want to imagine *Voices at the Late Hour* as a film; with his prose, now rushing forward, now lingering, Carpelan suggests a cinematographic narrative, a tale principally told by the camera's eye. He even employs the time-honored film device of the flashback, as the Grandmother (and Tomas himself) recall her escape from revolutionary Russia, and her meeting with Hannes, who would become Tomas's father. Other flashbacks occur as well, to a distant or a more immediate past: Bert's recollection of estrangement from his father ("with his fine manners, his memories stuffed into garment bags, and his things which all bore his monogram"), Max's memory of his days in the labor movement, Helena's of her sexual development and the causes of her frigidity, Vera's of her learning about Tomas's brief affair with Helena, Martin's of being bullied in school, and so forth.

What intensified the horror of Carpelan's novel—or his film-in-words—for Scandinavian audiences was its very location in the Northern year, "amid the lovely greenery, amid the flowers, amid the wind and birdsong." It is June, just before Midsummer, the time of setting out for the country; Tomas, with his wife and son, has planned a pre-Midsummer weekend from a Friday to a Sunday evening that never comes. His mother intends to join them at his home—typically, for her, in a dress "perhaps a bit too formal for a trip to the country"; after Vera has finished her part-time job for the day and Tomas his legal chores at the office, the quartet will then proceed to visit his cousin Bert and Bert's wife Helena at the farm and will be joined there by Bert's sister Rosa and Max, her husband. Thus the family members mean to gather in the countryside, the traditional place of refuge and rest for Finns; the farm they will visit is closely related to the *locus amoenus* which plays so great a role in Carpelan's books for children and adolescents. The planned excursion—"the suitcases are already packed"—is turned into a terrified improvisation, the routine pleasure into the most awful experience of all. A strikingly large number of Scandinavian (particularly, Finnish and Finland-Swedish) novels or stories have their locales in the summer world, so different—so expectedly different—from city life. We may think of the summertime setting of many of Solveig von Schoultz's stories, from "August" to "Sea Sauna," of the very title of Johan Bargum's novel, *Sommarpojken* (The Summer Boy, 1985), or going back a little in time, of *Hem till sommaren* (Home for Summer, 1960), Hans Ruin's essayistic account of summer on a real island, "Härligö" ("Splendid Island"). Still another factor, a more insidious and sinister one, should be mentioned in connection with the weekend trip. The excursion to the country has been made easier, as it were, by constant rehearsal—like the beginning of the war itself. (We never know the cause of the war. Nor do we learn much about the bombing of the unnamed place in the north of Finland.) Families have long made their little trips, pilots have long flown their mock missions, technicians have long sent off their still unarmed missiles; practice gives facility, practice makes perfect.

The last evening on earth, the Saturday evening before Sunday's second explosion, the assembled members of the family do what is traditionally done on a summer holiday: they fetch groceries from the nearby town, eat, drink, talk, tell stories, play on the grass, splash in the water—all under the shadow of Friday's first blast. Little Martin thinks, " 'It's almost like Christmas, or Midsummer. . . . We are having a party!' He was filled with a strong, quick, sudden feeling of bliss." The family members persist in hoping, against their better knowledge, that the disaster can somehow be remedied; after Friday's explosion, Tomas harangues himself, using the persuasive anaphoras of a lawyer in the courtroom: "Tomorrow I shall regain all that I have lost. Tomorrow everything will be restored: the water and the air, the dawn and the dew in the grass, the faint whispering of the waves and the voices awakening and ringing fresh in the soft wind. Tomorrow the bad dream will end and the joy of reality will resume." And Vera, so firmly attached to her city home, wonders about the fate of their "Viennese chair" and remembers how they bought it at an antique shop and how the shop's whole loft was filled with such chairs: "They are probably there still—in the dark. We might go and buy some. . . . I wonder what they do when it gets night. All the pairs." Her reflections, momentarily turned childlike in their animism, continue into horror: "If there is a fire, they'll burn up in an instant. Will they feel anything when they are burning?" Tomas and Vera and the others cannot bring themselves to think their thoughts to a logical end. When Tomas and Bert (with Martin tagging along) go into town on Saturday afternoon, they see how volunteers are signing on to help in the stricken area in the north, and how draftees—thoughtless boys, still tormenting the fat youth in the unit—are dispatched to the stricken area; once again the visitors from the farm must conclude—and want to conclude—that the world has not ended after all: "There can be no mistake of such magnitude." Beset throughout his life by an indeterminate anxiety, a desire to flee ("Had he in childhood inherited so much fear that it was only now coming to the surface?"), Tomas decides that he must at last free himself from this burden, this anxiety "like some strange dust particles penetrating under his skin" and go north too, to confront the injured and the dead: "I must see it! I have to see those who are dying face to face, I have to see my own face! Yes, I know, I'm hiding behind words; I hesitate; I rush in two directions and may break, or become more assured." This positive act may simply be taken as a sign of Tomas's momentary triumph (an imaginary triumph?) over the psychological flaw from which he has suffered all his life; we cannot be sure. But we can be sure that he cannot persuade himself that life is over.

Everyone in the group at the farm must devise, or discover, some defense; they cannot really confront the ultimate "face to face." The Grandmother, after her melodramatic flight from Russia, has experienced Finland's Civil War of 1918 and lived through the Second World War; thus she simply tacks the cataclysm onto the list of disasters she has already observed and survived. In her life as in her calling, she has been an actress, putting experience at a distance, seeing it as a play in which she has had a role—out of which she steps at the end of each evening. (During the War of 1941–1944, she toured the provinces in J. J. Wecksell's historical tragedy *Daniel Hjort* [1862], a drama about the final stages of the "Club War" of the late sixteenth century, another terrible event which Finland survived.) Hearing of the disaster, she cannot help recalling the others she has seen. "It's the third time," she says, remembering the scene at the Finland station in St. Petersburg:

There was the same kind of anxiousness then, the same fear. We stood at the window of the railroad car and saw the women running with their skirts raised high, their feet swinging like black clumps, their hips like

xxiii

horses' hindquarters. They latched on. One fell and remained lying as if she wanted to go to sleep. Their voices mingled with the whirling snow. This was one of the last trains from St. Petersburg. All was swept away. I was a young girl and shy of life, of the touch of a rough sleeve, of people coming too close. . . . That was when I learned a certain indifference, a frostiness, a distance. I learned to sing and speak inwardly, inaudibly; I also learned the art of imitating, of amusing, of laughing.

For Max, nearest in age to the Grandmother, the defense is not quasi-historical, but quasi-philosophical; he has learned, in his long and turbulent life, the consolation of dispassionate thought, and he observes and dissects his companions: "He sees that Tomas is afraid. He sees that Vera unconsciously despises him for it. He sees how Bert is getting quieter all the time. He sees the little flames in Helena's eyes and under her skin. He withdraws." Touching Rosa, his mind slides farther, taking pleasure in the cool awareness of a transfigured moment to come: "I see, I feel, June is standing cool and waiting at the door out to the bay." And, although he cannot find a passage he looks for in Montaigne, he can remember a quatrain from the Silesian poet of the baroque, Andreas Gryphius:

> Mein sind die Jahre nicht, die mir die Zeit genommen,
> Mein sind die Jahre nicht, die etwa möchten kommen;
> Der Augenblick ist mein, und nehm ich den in Acht,
> So ist der mein, der Jahr und Ewigkeit gemacht.[4]

Cherishing his moments one by one, Max is aware that he will perish; after the quotation, the passage goes on: "Eternity, the stone and we who shall die . . . ."

Max has seemed to be a fitting helpmeet for Rosa, as she has been for him—he with his benign calmness, she with her jovial generosity: "Half his breathing is Rosa's," and half hers is his. With his hand, Rosa says, he gives her solace, and in their last moment of lovemaking she finds, once more, "the deep satisfaction she lacked in everything else save him." Max, then, is Rosa's defense, as he long has been. Nonetheless, even in the moment of happiness, Rosa too becomes afraid, while hesitating, like the others, to put a name to her fear: "The green blind beat against the window; a flash of fear went through her at the moment of orgasm." Not even Max can make the blind stay quiet, and Rosa's terror would be greater still if she realized that she, like everyone else, lies somewhere outside Max's innermost world, however much a part of him she has become; as he reflects about her, "the constant giver, always outwardly colorful, inwardly searching for security," he numbers her simply among the group that wants guidance from him, the youthful and wise old man. He cannot give it to them, nor does he want to: "they are all searching for security, and I am not their pilot; I observe them, I sit in silence, I speak in the same manner to all of them, the same way I speak to myself, and sometimes I ask myself: have I already died; was something irrevocably cut off, way back in my childhood, in the hard battle with poverty? My sole goal was the core of the rock." The self-made man, Max is hard at his core, unlike Rosa, whose hardness is only in her tanned skin; among the doomed sojourners, Max and the Grandmother are the most impervious to fear.

When the travelers from the city arrive at the farm, Martin—whose frightened and baffled eyes become receptacles for so much—sees "Bert's heavy shape. He carries a rifle. Past him pushes the dog, violently barking: soft echoes in the bright air. They have arrived." Fleetingly, Martin notices Rosa with her "broad fifty-year-old face" and her "broad hoarse voice" and is scarcely aware of Max, "her shadow and her husband . . . a thin line, a note in the margin, a grammar book in dirty tennis shoes." The child's attention belongs to the man with the gun and the dog; to Martin's innocent view, Bert—not Max—is the master figure. Yet Bert's strength is of a different nature from Max's, and seemingly more limited; he knows only the tangibles of life. Having come from a social stratum far above that in which Max began, he has defied his father, whose sterile posing he scorns, and has chosen a different father instead: "I was the foreman's child and ate his hard crusts of bread. Best to plow close, without causing damage, that I learned from him." Now, Bert is ready to defend his poverty against interlopers, and this readiness is his defense against fear. Yet we may wonder if Bert can offer much more, in the late hour, than his outward and praiseworthy steadiness; inwardly, we learn, he has been consumed by the unhappiness of his marriage to Helena. "Something in Helena reminds me of Mother. What? The hot skin, which so easily makes you sated."

If no bomb had fallen, the situation which the guests entered that Friday evening would nonetheless have a painful and inescapable tenseness. Tomas has told Vera about his fleeting encounter with Helena; she appears to have accepted the matter with calm self-assurance: "I knew that he returned to me still more yearning, that her heat concealed an emptiness, that her silence and frigidity were not a defense but a Nessus cloak, and that she would shrivel up without anyone's noticing it, shrivel up inside her beauty. She was not the one I felt sorry for—it was Bert." There are intimations, as well, that Vera and Bert are attracted to each other, or have been. At the table the first night, "Bert tried to catch [Vera's] eye; for an instant they looked through each other's pupils, then slid past while Helena was thinking: they no longer know each other, too much has happened. She felt not relief, but a hunger for a reckoning—to be able to take hold of her husband's and Vera's relationship, lay it bare, cut into it, slowly. Tomas's foot touched hers involuntarily and quickly withdrew."

Like the farmer Bert, Vera has a deep urge for security; in her case, it takes the shape not only of devotion to her home but also of her wish to be cared for (as she thinks of her mother) and of her yearning for some sort of religious faith. Instead of meeting that need, Tomas has infected her, and their son as well, with his own anxiety. As she trenchantly puts it: "In Martin, I am discovering Tomas's restlessness and fear, the same tendency to withdraw. I have learned from Tomas; I withdraw my hand." Tomas, in his turn, has charged Vera with "a lack of tenderness," and she thinks of herself as "a vacuum" (while quoting a line from Edith Södergran's poem, "Vierge moderne": "I am no woman, I am a neuter"). Helena envies Vera not for her husband, in whom she seems to have had no real interest, but rather for her son, Martin; Helena desperately wants a child—otherwise, as she says, she will burn up. A quality of eternal dissatisfaction attaches to Helena, a notion of having been dealt with unfairly by life. She takes an odd satisfaction in the thought that now, at last, life has dealt ill with everyone else as well: "she felt she was one of those people who, when they want some sun, are shaded by that single, solitary, tiny cloud to be found in an otherwise clear and cloudless sky." Now, thinking perhaps of the great cloud hanging over them all, "she smiled: she had progressed a bit." This insight—that misfortune plays no favorite—is Helena's wry means of deflecting terror. She has just had a hideous vision of her death: "she saw herself lying dead, thrown across a chair like a piece of clothing; her skin was glowing in the dark, painfully exposed to all eyes"—lines to be read as a contrast to Bert's loving words, once upon a time, about how she shone in the dark as he beheld her.

The ramifications of these several entanglements and desires, these failings of ordinary human beings, could lead—in a film-drama of Ingmar Bergman, for example—to revelations, to recriminations, and to hatefulness of the cruellest kind. Surprisingly, the generous Rosa comes close to such surgery with her observations on Tomas and Vera:

In spite of having narrow eyes in a puffy face, I can see well. I see this Hamlet who is playing his irresolute part without enthusiasm but with longtime practice. He steals the scene; his mother was queen once, on the stage as well. If you don't fall into the orchestra pit, you will notice the stage dust. Not as much on her as on him: that's probably why he became a lawyer. That Vera didn't notice the role within the role is probably due to her secure anchoring. Was due to. Even if Vera could speak with the tongues of angels, she would still be a black angel who had discovered a crack in the universe. From that crack all the crumbling begins.

xxvii

Rosa guesses correctly that Vera has seen through Tomas at last, and that their union is dissolving. Tomas seems to imagine that his wife is deceiving him (recall his fantasy early in the book that he recognizes Vera entering a stairwell, into which he pursues her, only to be stopped by a closed door, like a rejected lover). Vera thinks of a lone bird "searching for a resting place," and has, as well, vague sensations of guilt ("this is some vengeance meted out to me, and the others have to suffer for it"). Helena suffers from her "hot skin" and gnawing dissatisfaction; Bert from his awareness that he fails to satisfy her. Max lives in his isolation, despite Rosa's love, and Rosa suddenly perceives that everything is "unreal, shadowy and swiftly disappearing." Poor little Martin stands afraid at the shore, "his white legs in the lapping waves." The attempts of Vera and Tomas to reach out to each other all too often appear to fail, despite their good will. As they flee the city, she says: "Drive carefully!" and places her hand on his knee. "He is stuck in his whirlpool, his solitude, his escape attempts. My gaze glides over his uncommunicative face, beyond the car and along the road; it doesn't stop, it falters." Or, in another small scene, Tomas kisses Helena on the cheek as she stands at the sink, and Helena smiles—but "both remembered their encounter, their lack of success, the loneliness they shared." None of the people at the farm can be called happy. Maybe it is better that the bombs fall, the missiles come, before the adults turn from self-torment to the tormenting of others. But, surely, Martin should be exempt from this fate.

All the grown-ups must be aware of the little boy in their midst, and somehow protective toward him. Max speaks to Martin as though he were an equal—the only approach the reflective Max can muster. Rosa is jollier, if equally at a loss: "You have grown," she says and, to deflect Martin's thoughts from the danger, "Surely you don't believe everything you're told." Bert—a natural object for the little boy's attention—extends comradeship to him principally through the dog Star, and Martin is able to speak directly to this extension of the master: " 'Tomorrow we'll fish, swim, won't we,' he whispers into its ear." Helena, deeply attached to Martin as the child she has not had, looks at him and allows herself to see his terror directly: "Martin is standing in the doorway; he quickly lifts his eyes and she can see straight down into his fear," but she is able to give him only banal words of caring, about milk in the refrigerator and taking the dog for a walk in the morning air. As he leaves—walking out backwards, not wishing to break the contact—she asks: "Why should he die?" For Vera, the fragile child Martin is a source of strength, her continuation, and she seems incapable of imagining that he too will be snuffed out: "Martin lives in me; he is my coolness and my calm; he is the thing I have to rally around; he is my rejoinder and my role, my disguise and my body; he is all in me that is strange and hence familiar; he is Martin and Tomas, and because of them I have to chase away all catastrophes." Tomas plays with Martin on the beach, fishes with him, roughhouses with him; yet, as we know, his absorption in his own anxiety dulls his sensitivity toward his son as toward his wife. In the novel's penultimate passage, Tomas's brave gesture of signing up for service in the north is also a flight from his family—and is, moreover, the kind of dramatic gesture Rosa has accused both him and his mother of making.

Significantly, Martin is less important to the men than to the women. Play-wrestling with him, Tomas actually fights with his own anxiety; Max—who has lost a child, a fact mentioned only in passing and left unexplained—keeps him at a distance; Bert has Star as his surrogate. For Bert, the land itself is far more important than the child he will never have with Helena; on the porch on Saturday evening, he tells Helena that he, and the other men, have talked about "planting seed, new methods, about our mutual mother earth." He compliments himself on the georgic way of life he has chosen ("I have toiled on the land. I have been washed by the seasons like a man by waves"), and within him also lies the still more elementary urge of the discoverer, the taker of new land. He has a vision of something lying beyond, he says, "what I have always seen and never discovered." The reader may conclude, using Bert as a key to the pattern, that the men in the book form a triad: the supremely disciplined and intellectual Max, the intelligent but tormented Tomas, and Bert, the tiller and guardian of the soil and would-be pioneer. Furthermore, it is Bert who, despite (or because of?) the failure of his own erotic life with Helena, has a curiously primitive concept of the male sexual organ: he has preserved the memory of his father, senile and attempting to masturbate one last time, and it may be Bert who utters or thinks the phallic hymn, the address to "the ruler of the world with its screwed-up eye, you, cyclops," a valedictory from which woman is strangely excluded. But Bert, like Max and Tomas, is also a man of culture; in the mildly drunken conversation about the meaning and worth of life, Bert introduces the story of Zosima's older brother, Ivan, from *The Brothers Karamazov*, in which the youth accepts the imminence of his premature death with "rare joy." Tomas chimes in with a quotation from Dostoyevsky's novel ("if no more spring came, would you regret your life?"), and Max spins out the thread by recalling still more of Ivan's speech, "his declaration of love for life."

Carpelan may have made a statement about sexuality by means of the human constellation of his book: the men are more able to intellectualize their predicament (women do not participate in the Dostoyevsky conversation, save as the object of polite questions); the men are the thinkers and doers and are more self-centered. Conversely, the women want a being to protect, a child that will be their continuation. The Grandmother sees Martin as a repetition of her Tomas; Rosa does her clumsy best to be motherly to Martin; Helena, in her last intercourse with Bert, cries "we have made a child, I know it now, I feel it, it has to be so." (Bert, clear-minded, recalls what she has said and does not believe it.) Just so, the final little gestures of tenderness come from the women. After her last lovemaking with Tomas, Vera "moves closer to him," and, near the conclusion, even though she realizes he is about to abandon her and her son, touches his cheek. Just so, Helena thinks: "I notice that

I'm smiling and that Bert smiles back at me," and Rosa "turned around on her elbow, heaved her heavy body, looked with clear shining eyes at Max." The Grandmother, too, remembers her late husband, Hannes, and knows love's happiness again. Of the women, Vera—who has a child—may be the most pathetic. As she warms Martin after he has been in the water on Sunday and feels his "shoulders sticking out like those of a thin bird, like little wings," she has a momentary perception that he is, for her, the *puer mira-bilis,* the savior boy. Then she realizes that "his thoughts she knew nothing about; his expression was somehow averted." Her disappointment and her loneliness make the book's ending still more unendurable.

Probably because of the presumed ingrown nature of Finland-Swedish life, the family—small or extended—has been the focus of attention in the novel and the drama; the broad picture of a whole society is rare indeed. Even those novelists contemporary to Carpelan who have attempted the large canvas, such as Christer Kihlman and Jörn Donner, fall back on the family's interweavings. *Voices at the Late Hour* began as a radio play, with the genre's limited cast and intimacy; and the voices belong to the members, by blood or marriage, of a single family. There are no friends—only the strangers seen in passing along the highway or in the town, and the suspicious figures skulking about the edges of Bert's property. A certain paradox lies in the situation: the end of the world is portrayed not in a great city (early in the book, Carpelan mentions the bombing of Dresden), not in a comfortable small community (as in the recent American film *The Day After*), not amid a band of strangers thrown together by chance, but in a gathering of relatives at a weekend paradise, a classic setting of the little literature. A tiny entity meets the extinction of the human race according to its social tradition and practice, and its observer reports the extinction not so much by describing palpable horrors (the book contains relatively few pictures of actual suffering and death) as by directing his gaze inward, into his few characters.

The circumstance that *Voices at the Late Hour* is a book so typical of the literature and culture from which it springs does not in any way diminish its artistic and human importance; rather, it enhances this importance. Disasters, presented in their full measure, dull the reader's (or the viewer's) awareness of what in fact is happening; how often we yawn at the disaster-film! In *Voices at the Late Hour,* the reader's attention is riveted on a few people, against a single and lovely natural scene. If the family disappears, and nature around it, then any survivors will be reduced to the level of humanoids or brutes. Carpelan's world, exploding, is a human world, a world that would have been worth keeping, after all.

NOTES

1. Translated into English by Samuel Charters as *The Courtyard* (Gothenburg: Swedish Books, 1982). Anne Born's selection of Carpelan's poems in translation, *Room Without Walls* (London: Forest Books, 1987), also contains a number of poems from *The Courtyard.*

2. Carpelan gave proof of his intimate knowledge of the entire history of the Finland-Swedish lyric with his anthology, *Finlandssvenska lyrikboken* of 1967, which has remained a standard over the years. In 1986, together with the poet Claes Andersson, he brought out a sequel, *Modern finlandssvensk lyrik.*

3. Both books have been translated into English by Sheila La Farge. *Bågen: Berättelsen om en sommer som var annorlunda* appeared as *Bow Island: The Story of a Summer that Was Different* (New York: Delacorte, 1971) and, in Britain, as *Wide Wings of Summer* (London: Heinemann, 1972). *Paradiset: Berättelsen om Marvins och Johans vänskap II* (literally, The Paradise: The Story about Marvin's and Johan's Friendship, II) was published as *Dolphins in the City* (New York: Delacorte, 1976).

4. Andreas Gryphius (1616–1664), "Betrachtung über die Zeit" (Contemplation Concerning Time), *Epigrammata*, 1:76:

> I do not own the years that time from me has taken,
> Nor own the years that time perhaps for me will waken,
> I own the moment and, if it's kept well by me,
> Then I own him who made years and eternity.

VOICES AT
THE LATE HOUR

THE VOICES

Tomas, age 40

Vera, his wife, age 38

Martin, his son, age 12

Grandmother, Tomas's mother, age 69

Bert, his cousin, age 42

Helena, Bert's wife, age 38

Rosa, Bert's sister, age 50

Max, Rosa's husband, age 60

FRIDAY

The city is built of iron and cement, blasted into rock or perched on piles thrust deep into the soggy clay bottom; a tangle of cables and wires winds its way through the silent walls, underground, up cranes and poles between which roadbelts have been squeezed. In June the green parks float like mirages among the tall glittering façades. The streets blow the wind slowly through the darkening heat. Out of the sea rise the screams and wings of the gulls. From far above none of this is visible, not a single person, not a living detail, only the vaulted spheres and the light breaking against the misty clouds.

Gran

She is up so early; she tidied the room yesterday, she placed the newly ironed towel by the white washbasin; her eyes do not see herself but see in the mirror that her hair isn't quite in place; the water runs as if in grooves along the brown-spotted hands with long fingers. If you are listening, she is moving quietly, making barely discernible noises; then she clears her throat. Her years are on display on the mahogany shelf, dedicated to her as faded photographs. Early in the morning with its cool fragrance of mothballs, she pours coffee into the cup with the rose border and then sits with her hands in her lap listening for a moment: there, that was the newspaper. She gets up to get it, and all goes black for a moment. She turns on the radio after sitting down again; a sonorous voice says: ". . . exists in large parts of the world, and now a complication is feared which might . . . ," and she turns it off; her lips are moving: "mad." The newspaper lies untouched on her lap. She thinks through the day's program, sees herself getting up, notices the time (this happens in the dark but she sees it anyway), sees herself making the trip out and arriving when she was told to. She's already packed and has asked Tomas not to come for her; she wants to be there earlier, see the boy and Vera, maybe have time to rest awhile in the garden. She runs her hand over her dress; it feels quite lifeless. In the dim light the marigolds on the table glow like a silence or a greeting; she turns her eyes, but no one is there—only the flowers.

In silent films of the future houses suddenly collapse like New Year's tin over a flame,[1] suddenly sink step by step, and finally come to rest with a surface like polished soot. If I strain to hear, what is happening changes: dust swirls up, the roar won't stop; it does not get any louder but is loud enough to cover up the cries of those falling. With long lifeless nerve fingers my sense of disaster is feeling its way across eyes and lips, across landscapes that dreams create and reality will demolish. In the night the skin feels alien, rough, and dark.

Martin

Long threads are torn out of the sweater; they catch on the trees and form a spider's web in the early gray light. The houses whirl past. Martin's wrists are bloody; his arms move mechanically. It's the schoolyard, a circle of yelling voices. They form a wall; he is being pushed back and forth against it; he strikes out blindly at the open mouth, at the white splotch which is a face, breaks away and is suddenly standing in a silent park. All the noises settle down on the branches and shrink into birdsong. They are singing in the mist, and far away a woman stops and seems to be looking at him. It is Mother. Martin tries to call to her but cannot. She walks away among the trees, which are standing bare, autumnal. An old man walks up from behind him and stares at him. He is wearing a ragged black overcoat from which stuffing pours out like intestines or damp excelsior. His eyes blink, like a bird's, from the bottom up. Suddenly he is standing farther away from Martin, in the middle of the white path, under the sky which is black. From it emanates a shining light, like a pinhead; it rushes at him with tremendous speed; his body senses the enormous distance as dizziness in the optical nerve. The ground gives way. The light blinds him. The instant before it reaches him he takes a step aside, mobilizing all his strength. He starts to perspire. He opens his eyes, and the dream trickles away as if he were passing water. He sees the ceiling, the beams, the model airplane, the light beyond the curtain. All is quiet. Now he would like to run in to them but cannot. Suppose he is the last one alive. His hand feels lifeless; he places it under his hot cheek. He seems to see himself lying with his head pressed against the palm of his hand, knees pulled up, wrists aching slightly, eyes open. He sees the face, he strikes at it; everyone cheers. He breaks through the walls, which dissolve into clothing, shouts, school smell, echoing corridors. Someone holds onto him, but he breaks away; they step aside. He takes a step forward; they all step aside. Rolf moves into his path, big as a wall; he hits him and turns around. They all watch him, no one dares touch him. He shuts his eyes.

Tomas

He wakes up; it is quiet in the room, in the world—quite quiet, only light breathing. She lies with her back to him; from the boy's

7

room not a sound. He sits up slowly, takes off his pajama top, gets up, peeks through the venetian blinds: it will be a hot day. He goes into the kitchen, turns the burner on high under the water kettle, takes the teapot into the bathroom, empties it, places it on top of the washing machine. The cold water. The days that come and go. He is late and must hurry. The routine movements help. He drinks his tea standing up in the kitchen. Through the window he sees the verdure which now, toward the end of June, has begun to set and darken. He closes the front door quietly so that none of them will wake up. Why then is his heart beating so, why is he sitting motionless for a moment in the car, staring blindly at a white wall, an unfamiliar window, and hearing, as if at a distance, the news report on the radio and beyond the voice the steady rising roar of a thousand voices, a high dark tide?

Vera

She saw her eyes in the mirror, but they weren't looking back at her. She peered inside the pupil but saw only the surface, the skin, the fine lines around the eyes. Suddenly she felt like digging her nails into this skin but smoothed down the blond coarse hair instead. The routine movements of the hands continued. In a way she saw more clearly, but what she saw was alien—as if she had been examining herself in order to confirm a suspicion. What if cool water would flow down the bathroom mirror, as down the butcher's shop window, everything rippling in waves of water, in the folds of the watery curtain, all the flesh dissolved, the image wiped cool, wiped away by water, until nothing was left. She dipped her hands deep into the cold water, wiped her face brusquely with the soft towel. All was still quiet, a quiet summer morning. Everything was gliding past, and you had to hold on—to the movements, to the sink, to work, to the news reports, to the time, to the clothes; you had to hold on to warm skin, to a voice, to the children's voices, to

8

external things, to the trip, to concrete things. Was Tomas now standing there looking out the window? What was he thinking there in the city, caught up in the traditional, in the always dim high-ceilinged room? She had twenty minutes to get ready, get to her job. She was standing in a blue room, the walls were closing in around her, with slightly widened eyes she saw in the mirror her own image, the image of her eyes, like an echo. She left the room, turned out the light, picked up the newspaper from the hall table: SHARPENED CONFLICT LEADS TO WAR? Headlines, the words silent, isolated, just a sheaf of paper in her hand.

The streets were speeding along their tracks through the streetcar, coming together in a point which was torn off by the tall street corners. Disaster was closing in on the passengers who were looking the other way, out the fogged windows. Darkness was approaching like a station where no one gets off but where the streetcar makes a stop. On its way through the city the traffic crossed the sun's light and disappeared again in a glimmer, swallowed up by its own noise. Only closer to the sea did all movement abate. The sunlight was broken by the waves, the horizon by white sails. They were heading out, few were returning.

Tomas

He steps into the cool dark stairwell. Through the window on the courtyard he can see a black tin roof, blue sky, and the chiming of bells which, like the heat above the roof, is slowly penetrating into the cool darkness. The walls close in even more tightly. Followed by his own faint echo he mounts the steps to the second floor; there is a smell of floorwax; the staircase folds away beneath him; the elevator grille slides across the pale path of light from the entrance. He is quite thin and moves in the air like a drowning man until he stands

9

still. Someone is coming down the stairs, slowly groping along the banister—the old man, his face covered by black scales, unshaven; the small spectacles emitting a flash; he can smell the odor of worn cloth, of the heat outside, of a vague, worn-out, outdated, turned-away mechanism which is alien to him. They greet each other with a nod and pass; he can see how they become so dark that they turn gray like ashes or glow and fall apart. They remain silent and pass as if sharing the same fear; he continues up the stairs, feels the building in his palms, this solid old building with girders, stone, beams, heavy stone steps, handrails of oak, a crisscrossing pattern of hard, finely ornamented scuffed banisters, now hollowed by worms but on the outside still shining with dark veins; finely paneled rooms, stairwells, corridors, cool walls and stone floors, tall quiet doors, a built-in darkness, immovable. The day is standing shock still; only a gull screams, while making a white escape from the yard with the one green tree; the walls, the almost invisible waves of heat, which the years of frost, of planning, stone upon stone, step upon step, shut out, years without a word spoken, silence followed by silence, where even the boy's voice is sucked up by the averted, the digni-fied air.

The door closes; he stands in the hall and, through the open office door, sees the yellow curtain slowly moving in the breeze from the street. Miss Dodo is tapping away at her typewriter in the adjacent room—swift, metallic, suddenly interrupted sequences, steps, el-lipses, staccato chips from an iron file; now she stops typing. The day starts moving like a huge shiny wheel around its hub, around the hot sun; everything is just a figment of imagination, suspicion, misunderstanding, forebodings, feelings, shadows pushed into the corners. He enters quickly, opens the window wide, and leans out; everything is alive: the people of the city with legs he cannot see under their bodies, the cars driving past that look like painted sheets of metal. Everything is roaring, moving, changing, dividing, disintegrating—no, not that, no disintegration; on the contrary, everything comes together, moves in concert, fits limb into limb, in violent union, in variegated, sparkling richness, in new attempts, the sunlight paler than the curtain, paler than yesterday: a portent of stormy weather for the weekend.

He sits down; the desk calendar page has been turned over: Friday. On the table are the bottle of mineral water and a newly rinsed glass. He rubs his forehead with his handkerchief, runs a finger over the bone structure and down his nose: it all passes, quickly disappears, and remains the same.

Martin

Pale, quite pale, with its white ears back, quite still, white with a pink nose, hiding in the tall grass, it had jumped, disappeared; his heart jumped after. He wanted to touch it and reached out his hand in the dream—it was thin, Daddy's hand around his wrist, a white spot that could faintly be seen among the shadows and the tree trunks, a blurry white spot, oh so warm, it cuddled up to him, was quite close; he could feel the warmth of its trembling body. He curled up under the covers; his hands were moving in front of him; they changed into small scratching paws, into a stiff brown sideways-looking eye, a nose that quivered and sniffed; a soft dive into the quiet green grass, he was in the country. He opened his eyes and saw the sun breaking through the venetian blinds, a pale shine; it was the day of the trip.

He lay still and heard voices, far away, out in the garden. They disappeared; if he closed his eyes, they disappeared and all became quiet. Only the hands were moving; the warmth crept like a prone body inside his body, the sleepy warmth.

The images kept shifting, a darkness arose; it tore them apart. Close by someone was watching him, watching the animal, suddenly took silent aim—a bounce, a bloody streak across the white fur; it was hurled against a tree trunk, consumed, broken.

He sat up in bed, he could only utter a groan, like the gritting of

11

teeth; then he realized that he had been dreaming, that he was sitting in bed, that he was awake, and that the silence was filled with sparks and sounds, as if under water in the midst of an almost invisible school of glittering, swiftly turning, rigidly biding, suddenly streaming, disappearing, dizzily and abruptly turning, darkening school of fish, gliding into silence, as if removed from the scene, dead, summoned, gone.

In the early days of June the light still fell through the foliage like water, like the reflexes of waves against the shoreline, through the tops of the birches rocking and trembling; then they were able to sit together, in the morning before the boy awakened and just observe: everything close by, yet sharply and clearly outlined, lacking something of what in their youth they had seen in the changes of the seasons or the day. Here was a garden, here the familiar; and as far as the "beauty of nature" was concerned, there was a smell of dampness. They could not watch the play of sun and shadow very long; they had to leave for work. He woke up earlier and drove to work; she had another hour and sat for awhile in the still cool but rising heat.

Why do we remember Dresden in particular? Because of the senselessness? Because of the lost monuments? Or do we see right through the Opera and Zwinger, beyond the burning *Frauenkirche*, the burning bodies shriveled up by the heat, the gaping mouths, the hollowed eyesockets, everything incinerated, choked to death? . . . The street collapses into a hot cascade of rays; the eye cannot perceive it before the body is hurled off, out of our sight, our memory, out of the light of day, out of reach of the protective and tender hand, away from experienced life into the merciful, all-forgetting, slowly congealing, all-tolerating, all-permitting, slowly benumbing oblivion: the oblivion that carries the seed of the hate and the wrath, the seed of another future conflagration, a teaspoon of soil for the tree of hate; that oblivion which has no knowledge or experience, no skin or teeth, or the insight of killing. Why do we forget Dresden? Why do we grow slowly out of memory, without memories, into a new Fury? The skin feels hot; the eye stiffens in its socket. We are standing in soon-burning snow; we take aim; we hurl hard. This is just the beginning, the start, still just childish hate. But wait! Soon the blood will blind the heart, the heavens will be silent, the streets will be wide open, the churches, the castles wide open to us. The river flows mighty and calm catching the sunlight; the streets, people, squares, all life, all love, all memories are assembled—into a focal point.

The heat increases like a thin, ever-more-glowing thread at the core of the bone marrow, slowly lighting up the very skeleton from the inside. No one sees it; like white shadows in a black landscape the people move about beneath the gaze of the observer in the darkroom: soon midday.

Gran

Between the bed, the bathroom and the kitchenette there is a path with things no one sees but me. This is security as I visualize it, heirlooms or presents from Tomas, the boy, or Vera. They no longer remember them. With me nothing is forgotten. They will stay behind when I leave. They have all been lined up in rows, sorted into shoeboxes, into drawers; I have tied strings around them. At the time of the big fire I knew all had been lost. Smell of smoke, or smell of bodies; everything burned up. Hannes was in Karelia then. They saved the grandfather clock, which was singed. It's so light outside that soon I can get myself ready. In the dressing room also I had everything in order. I sat down the way I'm sitting now, in front

13

of the mirror, and saw through my eyes another face, something to work with, take away or add years. It can all be done with make-up. With eyeshadow, with wigs, with mascara, with greasepaint, you can obliterate a role, a few months, the evenings while Hannes sat waiting. I could see it: the room, the paraphernalia, the body and the skin, long ago. You go through your routine, build up your mask, your whitewashed face, the thick black lips, the eyes that always look so anguished in a clown's face, the clown face which always looks like a deathmask. In the mirror I can see the window and the front of the building across the street. "Sit down here." "Come to me." "Are you leaving already?"—all fragments, but when speaking with the boy they seem to fit together again, into a pattern I cannot decipher.

Martin

The boy extended his bare foot toward the hot sunsquare on the linoleum. The door to the garden stood ajar; from the bathroom came the sound of running water. He listened, still half asleep. All was pallid, as when an illness is taking hold or when someone turns away and retreats among the shadows, and we don't know what he is thinking or doing; perhaps he is only lying there looking up at the ceiling or perhaps he is dreaming that he is a child, walking through a cool dell at his father's hand. It is an early summer morning, and everyone is happy; laughing voices can be heard and the voice of someone singing, far away, a rare, rare melody, rocking all the anxious ones to sleep—and they all lie down in the grass, under the tall dark trees, and go to sleep. . . . The boy is as thin as a streak of light; he looks around and disappears soundlessly; a door opens and closes:
"Martin!" she calls, "are you awake?" Both listen for a moment for the voice of the other.

14

Gran

She stopped in the road to catch her breath. She looked at the scruffy trees, at the lawn, at the flat landscape visible between the buildings. She saw how the trees grew denser, how the lawns were overrun by a golden yellow glow. She saw herself walking in a landscape somewhere, saw herself as a child, saw how the sun suddenly set and all was still, clear, and lonely. She could already then see how lonely it was. There were no shadows, but the familiar roads and fields, the summer playgrounds, the dark thickets with their hidden trails were strange to her, and she felt a calm, liberating coldness spread through her, as if she were lowering herself, or was being lowered, into cool water. She saw the trees standing bare, robbed of their splendor. Everything was standing where it had been placed; everything was strange—she, too, so old, so far away in the twilight years.

Tomas

He was in an empty room; was there not an empty space inside him? Had he in childhood inherited so much fear that it was only now coming to the surface and now on the threshold of middle-age was taking possession of him, like some strange dust particles penetrating under his skin? Had he not always dreamed about changing the world, and since his first trial realized that nobody really saw him and that he had to act alone? What made it so hard for him to approach those closest to him, so that bitterly he felt how they were breathing out of step with him? There was in him an insufficiency masquerading as human love, a softness and an un- sophistication which was only emphasized by his few passionate, ardent, reckless successes in court and to some extent also in social life which was increasingly becoming a burden to him. What had he hoped for? Something else! Something quite different, the security of floating, life, revelation! Fettered by habit, he felt betrayed. What was he doing here, in this high-ceilinged room, this hot Friday? There was one place where he could live, receive love, but not here! and he thought: that's how we flee, that's how we use up our time, we in our age group, we who sit in lonely rooms drinking by ourselves or walk around with our well-worn scripts like splinters in our face, continuing to nurture a bitter hope, as when a flame recedes and stays away in the deep dark evening—and we hear laughing voices pass by. But we knew all along that it would be this way. All that was dead would remain mute; no miracles would open the sleepers' eyes, no words would like a flash of lightning rend the darkness, the fruitless dreams, the ballast of memories. And at the same time he felt how the silence, the solitude, held comfort, like the painful and cool touch of a calm, steady hand, as if someone had awakened and understood, reached out a hand and released him from his guilt.

"How wonderfully quiet it is here; not a bird can be heard, no cuckoo is calling, no owl hooting, no lark singing, no clock sounding, no church bells chiming, and not a single cricket chirping. . . ."
and this silence—does it exist, is it alive, can it still be sought, where is it hidden;
and even if it were alive, is it not too late? . . .

Martin

He closes the door and sits down on the yellow spindleback chair with his face toward the window; he can see the houses, the road, the trees, and the sky which is lighter close to the ground. The floor

16

and the walls make his room; he supports himself on his elbows. Down where the road makes a turn someone is slowly walking this way; it is Grandmother. First a tiny person, then slowly the clothes, as if only the feet moved but the arms were hidden. At a distance she seems to be looking at him. She can't see me, he thinks. What if one walked like Gran, bent, slowly . . . ; he leans forward. He is glad she is coming, feels greatly relieved; the light which was empty comes alive. He gets up quickly, takes the milk glass with its white ring into the kitchen. Now she rings the doorbell. No. Now. He walks through the hall shadows; they are pushing out of the wall, or one of the walls. The sun in the garden glints by in the greenery. No one pushed his way in before Grandmother; no one pulled the door open by force or forced him into a corner. He is free; the summer's heat hits him as he opens the door, and he smells the dry, slightly sweet scent of Grandmother, of overripe apples, of drawers opened to reveal little secrets, the candy, always the same, the face, wrinkled and unforgettable.

Vera

The lone bird flies for a long time searching for a resting place; throughout the night it circles in the upward floating air from the warm valleys carrying darkness on its wings. I see it at dawn looking for a resting place, watch it settle down and fold its wings, and from the branch of a dark fir tree stiffly and silently stare out across the wasteland. Then I wait, while the day moves on along its course, until the bird's eyes meet mine, its gaze becomes mine, until—as if by a gust of wind—the air is filled with screaming, demanding wild birds, his kin;
I see it take off, rise slowly above them, head north; they follow, more and more inaudibly, until I no longer see them; the window clears, memory's eye turns outward, to the mild warm June day.

17

Tomas

Suddenly in the street he saw her turning the corner. It couldn't be Vera. He ran the last few yards; it was her dress, her hair, her hips . . . she disappeared into a doorway, he ran after her. The sun cut through the still air like an axe; he ran into darkness. There was a door, a heavy wooden one . . . he pulled at it, stood with a racing heart in a cool dark stairwell. Steps could be heard, close, farther away. He ran up the stairs, two steps at a time; a door opened, closed; he fell down on his knees, stood up, leaned against the wall breathing hard. The darkness was interspersed with thin light spots, like organisms in a strange sea . . . someone opened the front door, pressed the elevator button. He held his breath like someone pursued. Weak light entered from the yard through a narrow window; he could distinguish a wall, part of the sky . . . ; when the elevator had creaked past the second floor he started down cautiously, stood for a moment studying the name register but found no names he knew, nothing familiar; there was a heavy sweet smell of . . . was it fruit, berries, honey, something being baked behind a closed door? A child called out something he didn't understand . . . a mistake, a total mistake . . . he pushed open the front door, stepped through the doorway into the street, and went on his way hugging the wall. Perspiration beaded on his forehead, and the shirt stuck to his neck. Back in his room he immediately telephoned.

Martin

Fear: it's rushing back and forth in the garden; it makes the leg itch, cuts open the skin, forces the hands into cramped fists; and all the time he is standing still; no one notices him; he stands in the shade and sees the pale sun. Through the open door the radio can be

heard—music like water running out of a mouth—and the grass stands silent and fiercely green. Grandmother is waiting in the kitchen with juice that in the dark looks like blood. He shades his eyes with his hand but sees nobody yet. Daddy still has another hour until he will get up from his chair, take his briefcase, and open the door. He is driving his car; he runs his car over the iron railing; there is a horrible crash; he is dead . . .
like a bird's chest inhaling hard, quite hidden in the grass, with thin wrists, with pale skin in spite of the sun, the blond hair shining, he thinks: "it isn't true, not true. . . ."
along the road Mother is approaching in her blue-and-white-checked dress; he rushes to meet her; she takes hold of him and lifts him up, swings him around; the cool fabric smells newly laundered; green trees and white houses swirl round and round in great relief.
It's quiet, and there are no other people—only she and he—walking home together. He senses that she is tense; she holds his hand hard; the mouth smiles but not the eyes; he pushes it out of his mind, he laughs, he talks, he knows he is doing it; everything lives and moves on separate planes, colors, streets, trees. He sits at the table and hears her voice, far away.

Vera

So she has again returned from her part-time job behind the glowing curtains with a fruit pattern, her skin has stuck to the purse handles; she has returned again, dreaming of an ice-cold shower, food, Martin, the already-packed suitcases. Grandmother with crooked wrists: she looks at her own, almost flaming red. From the purse come sounds; someone wants out, wants to surge out; the leather shines in the sun shining in through the bus window; the asphalt flows by glittering with fine grains of sand, the sky almost blue-black through the sunglasses. She is there, has been sitting there almost forever; a kilometer is a year, ten kilometers to home, light and shade. She wipes her forehead and notices the wrinkles; someone is staring at her neck; this is foolish, senseless, unthinkable; a sudden cold sensation makes her shudder; this is only the beginning; she opens the newspaper and reads without reading, dissolves into the newsprint. From a window ajar a mild salt wind blows in from the sea that is covered in haze and heaving like a slowly rising arch, a shield, a big glittering birthing belly.

A boat cuts a silvery white swath; muffled voices are carried past, and her hands now rest in her lap, the eyes gazing past the waters, the islands, and the slowly ascending seafowl;

life fenced in by sheetmetal and rubber; by gusts, oils, fumes; by four walls, glass, and metal;

by warm skin;

she turns around to look the stranger in the eye, but no one is sitting behind her; it must have been someone else,

someone else who has found something to complain about or report on or has found some detail amiss, a run in the stocking, a loose thread, anything ripped by mistake or worn down, handles that have worked loose, leather burst at the seams, nothing in perfect shape;

above the sea an ever grayer and paler haze and the cool water running, filling the skin and the hair, slowly cooling the face with the high cheekbones, the closed eyes, the broad warm mouth; it's coming closer, as if it could speak. Tomas hears it, looks up for a moment at the photograph on the desk, then down again the moment the bus comes to a standstill;

he has returned to his work in the dim room. From the bar down at the street corner pop music can be heard like a muffled echo; it makes him think of stockings stuffed into the horn of an old gramophone: that's how it was—The Firebird flowing out, in flames, dying, shining,

spreading its wings over everything and everybody!

20

Tomas

Outside there is still a clear wind that follows the grassy slope to the top. From this height the sea looks like a wide open space. I have stood there, alone, my mind blank, simply happy; now a shadow, a spot on the sleeve can put me off balance, and the free wind roams the yellow streets, chained, like a dog.

Gran

There is someone still there—a shadow, a door through which no one passes, an old face, the tendons in the neck, the tremor of the head; everything is shaking, stirring up fine dust, a smell of dying, of cloth and loneliness, of secretions,

old grandmother like an old piece of furniture—no, like part of the room, just watching, waiting: won't he be home soon? The boy seems worried; so does Vera. The sun flings a sharp green glow up from the lawn and fills the air with earthen smells, as in big, lush, well-tended cemeteries, the one at Åbo with so many, many, all silent now, disintegrated, or with residues and remains in urns, coffins, where the wood has rotted away, the cloth decayed, no more headrests, no more open mouths,

if one might close one's eyes, feel how light the body is, yet heavier, heavier than all else on earth; every year weighs twelve months, every month has its customary pattern, the square she walks, out of the dark into the sunshine and back into the dark again;

in her own room there is no sun; a cool yard echoes in her dark room; from the kitchen penetrates the smell of coffee,

here everything is different; she is ready to leave, has her things around her, close by her feet; the suitcase has settled there and looks at her with affectionate eyes, the purse she got for her sixtieth birthday from Hannes; there was quite a crowd, coffeecake, of no consequence now; the hand runs over the old hair combed neatly

21

back, like a worn-out wig; the dress with the white lace collar is very beautiful, simple and becoming; it looks good on me, an old lady's dress, perhaps a bit too formal for a trip to the country.

As it grew lighter the houses receded in closed ranks, separated silently from the dark façades across the street, let the early sun slowly gild black roofs and rotating chimneys, sparkle briefly in windows that coolly reflected the blue sky, the first rustle of a treetop. . . .

The invisible voices could not be heard; only a solitary tired shift-worker turning on the radio while sipping his coffee caught some strange noises where there should have been silence, some excited voices, foreign words that slid past and disappeared into the June silence.

Where the decisions were being made the air was dense and somber. The radar shield emitted an incandescent glow; out of the air above the rock where the corridors had been blasted, a high dizzying sound penetrated the communication receivers and the sound screen and reached those silently waiting.

There were so many cities, so many people. Each death had its antipode in life, and she who lay looking out the window in the small provincial town felt—was it happiness? She was happy without any foreboding, saw that it was a clear morning, and then the pains resumed. Right at the moment of delivery all the lights went out; in a blinding white light houses and trees collapsed soundlessly, the lake went up in steam, death met birth and each knew not of the other's existence. Farther south it was several minutes later when the sirens went off, just when the shockwave turned life upside down.

Blast. Blast off the face, the lips, the skin, the skeleton, the eyes. Pick the moment: during lovemaking, during birth, in the sudden light.

22

Or even better: in everyday situations, in the midst of a phone call, while giving the newborn a bath. One day the sky is clear, it smells of earth, it's cool among the forest trees, spots of sunlight, a brisk breeze at sea, white sails: blast! Blast out of the dark the stem of all living beauty, raise a cloud swiftly, mightily, soundlessly like a single spreading, overshadowing, eclipsing, all-overturning brain, silently observing in an eternal breathless tumble, a brain-shaped cloud, unendurably white-white glowing toward the outer edges: blast! Blast away the petty revolutions, the laughable handguns, the fists, the passwords, the gaping mouths, the shows for snobs, the shrouds of the poor, the hysteria, the silence; yes, blast the very silence into outer space, toward airless space; make everything spin, spread far and wide, fly: blast. Never gather, never join, tear asunder! Explode! Start with the tiniest things, the closest, warmest relationship, the child, the family, the circle of friends, the job, the organization, the community: blast! Cut up, divide, learn. Tear, poke, recover your wits, talk with the like-minded, ridicule the enemy or ignore him, look straight ahead, straight in, throw light into every dark corner, break down any hesitation swiftly, be confident, occupy the scene, use the slogan: blast! Blast off the face, the lips, the skin, the skeleton, the eyes. Then move on to bigger things. Learn, teach others, teach the children, forget about the old, teach the malleable ones, cut out the rigid ones, leave open the wounds! Blast!

Here the fantastic starts happening—up here at Mrs. Mellsten's on the top floor with windows on the city and the mountains, and the entire lake blue as a child's eye, resting between vast forest lands. Mrs. Mellsten is justifiably proud of her view and of the half-recessed balcony where it is too hot to sit when the sun scorches the black roof that surrounds Mrs. Mellsten on all sides. She stands on the balcony shaking out the embroidered tablecloth she received on her sixtieth birthday from her good friend, and on the cloth is

embroidered in cross-stitch a goblet with yellow and red flowers—
you can catch a quick glimpse of them now and then above and
below her short, broad, tanned upper arm. Mrs. Mellsten suddenly
stops shaking the cloth; she has seen a shining object falling from
another shining object—one airplane crashing and one which is
not?—she just has time to reflect; she may be the only one to notice
anything odd before the air is yanked away and the lake is transformed into steam and Mrs. Mellsten's tablecloth is blown far away
in the sudden intensive white light, the tremendous roar, the sudden silence when everything is tumbling, charred and crushed, or
is hurled aside, and the rays like the leaves of a huge sunflower
slowly spread past the mercifully dead, the ones in shock, the
burned, the moaning, the crawling, the crouched and silent, or the
ones groping along, blinded;
surely no one could have believed it; it's too fantastic, it just
couldn't happen here; there was no reason, especially in June when
it's hot anyway, burning hot, and still hotter farther south in the
capital.

Tomas

I was on my way home along the expressway. Sometimes I have the
sensation of driving unconscious, a dizzying moment of darkness.
Habit is the greatest danger. I had crossed the bridges; the water
was glittering dimly yellow in the hazy sun. In the north I saw an
odd cloud. The radio was playing bossa nova when the car was
suddenly, as if by a hand, pushed to the left, toward the center of the
road. Terror made the landscape lose all color for an instant. I stood
on the brake. I heard the side windows shatter. Ahead of me a
motorcyclist lay in the ditch, his wheels spinning; his helmet emitted a flash. The heat cut into the skin like a wound. On the other
side of the road a bus had run into the ditch. You could hear
screaming. The only thing moving was the motorcycle wheels.

Now it's started, I thought. Now it's here. It wasn't an unfamiliar thought and hence so awful: it hollowed me out, made me feel sick; I opened the door and threw up on the charred yellow strip of grass; there was a strange smell of rust, rust and phlegm. I had caught up with my fate; I had arrived. I was unhurt. The boy! Vera! I straightened up and turned on the ignition: the car started immediately. Someone was waving; like sleepwalkers, people were starting to crawl out of the bus across the road. I backed up, put the car in first gear, and drove off. The wind tore at the inside of the car. I felt my cheek smarting; there was blood, a narrow cut. A crack in reality, in the here and now. I drove through the terror and the confusion. There was a woman with a child; she shouted something, raised her arm. I drove past all the remains; everything was dead anyway, everything still green but dead.

Gran

The boy is running in and out so anxiously that you have to follow him with your eyes. Tomas, too, ran like that as a child; it starts to worry you; you stay worried for years: how will they manage, how will they be able to take the knocks and the blows, to manage in spite of that softness, the thin joints, the fear, and the sensation of being cold, freezing . . .
"oh, is that so?
Come, let's go out in the garden and have a look."
"Don't pull at me so hard, I might break," the boy imitates her. She laughs her dry birdlike laugh, parrot's laugh, pushes up her shoulders; the bony face is crisscrossed by wrinkles; the brown-flecked hands have a firm grip on his face, which is resting against her bony hip like a huge pale egg, a real fairytale bird's egg; she warms it; they stand in the midst of leaf shadows as if the years were standing still or dropping all around them;
he is late;

25

his wife lights a cigarette for no reason, perspiration beads on her forehead, something chafes;

there is a tremor, the light shudders; they are on their way in; the boy falls flat on his face into the room, Grandmother after him, and they are knocked over; the glass explodes in big hard over-another-sliding sparkling metallic smarting blows;

it is hard to breathe; everything stands for a moment at zenith, silent, biding, for an instant, like the redhot tip of a needle pointed at the optical nerve;

then things start crashing,

in the kitchen the cigarette burns a hole in the linoleum; Vera is on her knees; she has known this, no one has suspected it;

they are alive; the boy screams, Grandmother moans; she gets up and runs to them, pulls them inside,

in the kitchen a faucet is running, it suddenly gurgles; the water is slowly strangled.

Tomas

Perhaps they are still there, perhaps they will still step out, perhaps they will suddenly be captured by the hidden camera: he with the thin dark hair, standing in the doorway, he shouts something: "Quickly! We have to leave!" And his mouth is open, always the same restless nervous anxious life, forever issuing orders to leave, as if he were trying to cross a threshold which isn't there, push through doors that are standing open, escape from things sitting there in bowls, on tables, keeping a sharp eye on him: the fruits on the table, the broken glass all over the carpet or his mother hurrying out of the kitchen and yet standing still, in my picture: the thin joints, the same birdlike fragile life;

and there, close to him, his wife looking him in the face, who turns away and hastens without haste, whose hands have already arranged everything; she wipes her forehead with her hand.

The boy! Where is the boy? "Martin!" he calls and his voice almost breaks, but the boy comes quietly out of his room and quickly puts his arms around him; thus they are captured, remain in the photo; I take it, I look at it; it's blurred, it burns slowly, hardens into a wall of ashes which falls apart . . .

no, it's alive, they are alive; they speak, they touch each other, as if to make sure that they are alive; they hurry off, dragging heavy suitcases into the car; there is a smell of metal—burnt metal—and burnt wood, as in empty backyards where nothing grows anymore, where old machine parts lie rusting; that's how it felt, that's how it smelled: the grass quite dead. People were running around their houses in the pale June sun; nobody heard what they were shouting.

The little seed is growing in the vast darkness. It seems as if someone were walking around in a forest with a candle. The light roves about but finds its way. Benches, the bare floor, a corner. There someone receives the seed and holds it in his hands. It burns with a steady flame, its sprout crooked; it grows! Everyone in the house holds his breath; there is no sound but the water dripping from the dark well-pump in the yard. It resembles a male organ. Out of the seed slowly emerge a head, crooked extremities, two blind eyes, and the belly with the twisted stem. It is surrounded by small hairy protective leaves: you can feel them if you lightly touch the tip of the seed. It is quiet in the room, but outside the wind starts blowing, oh how it blows; the trees are bending, the window panes are bulging, the rising water is trying to get in; suddenly everything gives way on a high, shrill, chiming note: the darkness wells inside. It sucks the seed along, carries it outside; it's daylight and the sun is shining through the whirling trees. In the eye of the hurricane the water level sinks, the seed is submerged, gets stuck in the wet soil. A flower, a person is standing there. He looks around, he lifts his hand: it moves, it gropes for the light, it rises. Everything is so bright that the eye can see for miles around: all the land farmed, all the houses silent and newly painted, all the trees with whispering foliage. From very high up, slowly, a streak of darkness now descends. Many people stand among the trees, some of them already prone, shading their eyes with their hands. Now it is high noon and the shadows start to lengthen. More and more people come out of their houses, as if expecting visitors. They turn their faces up: there! there! Like an even, swelling sound the objects, the roads, the landscapes surround them. Around the sun there is a big wheel; they do not see how it is slowly turning. The oldest ones fall asleep, bent, heads against the dark tree trunks. From them the darkness is emanating. It trickles like slowly running water over the roads, is sucked up by the air and meets that other darkness which has been descending faster and faster. When they meet, there is a sound like something shattering, perhaps in outer space: all those waiting take a few steps back, but they can't even see their own hands in the dark. Behind them, in the dark, a faint light is discernible, approaching quickly. It burns through the silent rooms, through the tree trunks, through the fields and the contours of the figures. Black now becomes white; the picture is obliterated.

Do not trust the white plaster wall: it is covered in braille, full of signs. At high heat they slowly emerge, first only as shadows, then as ever clearer, sharper, and darker forms: imprints of fists, backs, mouths pressed against the silence, sometimes entire faces in profile pressed into this mute mass, seemingly unable to reply. In the end they all glow, as if they were trying to tell us something, as if they wished to convey a message, as if they were branding themselves into our skin, or as if the wall were one gigantic skin surface, hard, tense, close to the breaking point, now slowly returning to its silent white unspoiled condition. This wall amid the lovely greenery, amid the flowers, amid the wind and birdsong.

28

Gran

It has begun. It's the third time. First there was the Civil War,[2] and
Daddy had weapons hidden in the kitchen woodbox. Someone had
made him put them there. Snow was whirling around the city
squares. I was a girl then; I sat at the window and saw people
running. The Russian sailors wept after shooting their commander;
he was young; they pulled him on a wagon. During the Second
World War we went on tour and played "Daniel Hjort." Our breath
looked like smoke coming out of our mouths; the airplanes sang on
a high note up in the wonderful deep sky. Tomas was little; he was
running in among the trees and back again; summer came and they
all started getting killed, one after another; what was the point? But
this, this is big, it is incomprehensible, it is some disease of the
blood, under the skin, a fear so great that the mouth cannot make a
single sound, cannot speak a line. It would have been better to die
before it happened.

The gas ovens are outmoded, the cattle cars stand empty, the camps
are falling into disrepair, weeds and dust cover the fields where
mass killings used to take place; the regime is antiquated, the
mechanism no longer socially acceptable. We are living in a super-
efficient technological society; no one dispatches these trains anymore, no one keeps camp diaries in the same slow painstaking way
as thirty years ago, no one attacks—just the shiny rocket head; the
firing mechanism is automatic now; no one does the firing, no one
can be blamed, no one takes sole responsibility; we are all responsible, no one stands alone;
the bodies lie charred and discarded, or move as if in a cramp, in
shock, with eyes open or closed, in rows; the few doctors and
nurses are also succumbing; many limbs show changes as the skin
reflects unknown processes and spots break out or travel, spread;

the light flutters or goes out, the heat expires in the exploded radiators, limbs are twisted in the strangest positions—"he just stiffened, remained that way. . . ."

Twilight, summer night, summer dawn; morning comes as usual, the train is standing still, the cattle cars are empty, the road is deserted; only in the city can you find odd, slow, secretive, backward, febrile or befuddled activity; in the alarm center in the rock shelter stand the living, the clothed, the shaved, the active ones, the observers, the privileged, the decision-makers, the half-baked semi-murderers; they have done their utmost without enough sleep; exhaustion does not keep them from doing their duty; while watching the radar and long-distance TV they swallow strong hot black coffee, fruit, bacon, bread, all still uncontaminated and nutritive, nutritious.

There is something wrong with the air purification system; the repair crew is trying to prevent a leak; the radiation gauge has not yet sounded the alarm, but the air suddenly seems to be filled with still more darkness, a gust of wind, from the streets, from the squares, from outer space, from the dead;

like a greeting it penetrates, like a soft touch, like a mother's touch, as if someone were touching their lips. In the parks the trees stand bare or with black leaves; almost everything is in disorder, razed, spread about: shattered glass, bricks, plaster, ashes, broken trees, animal cadavers, broken vehicles, cars, buses; nobody has the strength to clean up here; how messy we leave our temporary abode; no one comes to clean thoroughly, no one rings the doorbell, no one stands there with a shopping bag, no one takes out a mop, a bucket, a vacuum cleaner, rags, scouring powders; there is of course no water; it's dark in the bathroom, pitch black! When you turn on the faucets, they only gurgle and scream as if a thousand devils were crying in deathly anguish; they are useless. Moreover, the children still lie in their beds, mother is on the floor

30

halfway to the kitchen, and the roof trusses are broken; you can hardly move about, much less wash. Father sits strapped in his car, but the car is in the ditch, it lies there quite forgotten. Water has been hurled into the fields; there is a low continuous sound like wind, but there is no wind, as if with a weak, even breath someone were trying to resuscitate—what? the ground, the mountain, every broken flower, the animals and nature, the human being with his mouth open?

Oh, it is persistent, this invisible wind; it finds its way down into the mountain caverns, finds those who have looked for shelter there; they can't get any deeper down or farther in: their nails aren't strong enough; their boots, their riding britches, their bellies, their uniforms, their blind eyes are in the way; there is no peace in this silence, no real silence; as long as there is life there is hope; as long as the situation is under control there is a situation and control, there is life, the life of the growing nails, of the growing hair, of the skin where the changing spots are like the shadows of a strange vast foliage, a gigantic treetop, a crown, a corona, the life of the dried saliva, the calm growing life of mechanized death, the life in the silence that soon will be a silence, in the object that soon will become an object, that will have been used up, in time which soon will be eternal and inviolate, like a forgotten landscape that no one has ever seen.

Tomas

We can't leave it like this. We have to leave it like this. The windows are broken; anybody can get in. Would you prefer to stay until you can no longer get away? Is there any sense in that? Think of the boy, think of—well, everything. Do hurry. There is nothing of value here. We'll pull down the shades and nail them shut. Take along the most important things, I mean out of your drawers. There is hardly anything here. Why are you crying? This could damned well be

31

expected; odd that it didn't happen sooner. All the garbage, all the promises, all of it . . .

and this, it's no longer ours, don't you see how it's staring back at us, how it hates us, how it never had anything to do with us, these things, all this property, all these gadgets, all the mementos . . . Take! Take! For God's sake, take!

And you, what are you standing there for? That's no good; you have to be quick, look around quickly. Someone's coming, we do know him; he'll break down the doors and won't listen to us; no, we certainly won't stay here—hush! What was that?

A voice out of the transistor radio suddenly cuts into the silence, says a few unintelligible words, is erased again: a roar or a whisper, which? We don't know; the sound level might also be a fault in the transmission; perhaps everything is much quieter, much calmer, much smaller, much softer than we have imagined, more alive, feel here, quite alive . . .

He puts his hand there, against her bosom; they stand still for a moment; they hear the boy calling from the car. She goes out first, then he; he no longer sees the room, closes the door quietly, from habit, sees them looking up, their pale faces, those three whom he loves most, after himself, or as much as himself—he doesn't know which. Everything looks unnaturally sharp, as in twilight.

Nobody can find the holy family. The star points into outer space. The man, woman and child climb into the car back-first, the grand-mother head-first. All that remains of the forest, and it is a consider-able amount this far south, stands in mute astonishment creating its own silence. A whisp of blue exhaust fumes is barely discernible in the air. Gone, gone, are rest, respite and peace! And the grass that didn't get mowed, the bicycles still leaning against the wall, the eye still focused on what was and now seeing the light changes, the broken connections with the world, the memory which faintly picks up words uttered long ago, that same morning, when they still didn't know anything, when all the birds were singing in their usual places and the skin wasn't somebody else's skin. Those dreamed to death.

Tomas

She is wearing a sunbonnet as protection against the heat. She says that the bus drove into the ditch. They all crawled around like ants and the kids were screaming. Then she walked the last few kilometers. Now she is here, holding onto the car door. She wants to clean the house; it's cleaning day. Her eyes are stiffly focused on me; I have to look back at her, turn her around and send her back; we can't take her along. There is no space for her. She repeats, "it's cleaning day." I start the car, but she holds on. Her face, big and heavy, leaning down at the car window, and the hair combed back, and the wrinkled white hat resemble a fried egg, over-easy, floating in the pale hot air as if her head had nothing to do with her body. Perhaps it doesn't. "No," I say, "not today: it would be best to return home or go to the country, not back to the city." "Where?" she asks. "Where? To whom do you mean; I don't know what's happened." She looks to me for an answer. I have no answers to give. I have to disengage her hands from the window frame. "Don't worry," I say. "We will come back as soon as the situation has calmed down." I start the car and drive off quickly. There is complete silence in the car. She stands there looking after us in her big light-colored dress. It has red stripes. The broken glass glitters; there is an odd echo of voices: all houses are temporary, unfinished, not closed, not open, everything in a semi-coma, white or with black gaping windows, and over this or emanating from it is a smell, the stench of a rotten sun.

The still unscathed forests are cut down by the fiery hurricane as if by a scythe. It happens with a quick sweeping motion, slowly aimed. No human voice is heard. The hills are burnt bare but prevent the worst shock wave from spreading freely. It is as if a flame from below were corroding the earth's thin crust: the smoldering edges turn gray and fall apart. All the moaning is but a weak echo as if from a radio with the sound turned down late at night after the children have gone to bed.

Tomas

He had felt like hitting, pushing away that face, tearing something to pieces, giving up everything, exposing himself or some secret birthmark, and no one, no one would say anything; everything would take place alone. At this thought his hands gripped the steering wheel as in a cramp, and a body growing rigid inside his own wrapped itself around his back. He had felt like shouting to her, "get out of the way you damned hag; no one cares about you!" and his mouth was still forming the words when in the rearview mirror he saw his son, the long bangs hanging down over his eyes which were looking past him out at the road, and he was unable to interpret their expression.

Vera

Thin legs, bony, wearing long itchy stockings; they were growing inward, through the lanky body; those years I was always cold, it seems. Even as now: this is some vengeance meted out upon me, and the others have to suffer for it. I see the road rushing at me, lush greenery; it wells past in large chunks, forests melting together, fields lying bare, all of us being shakily carried along. "Drive carefully," I say and place my hand on his knee. He doesn't answer. He is stuck in his whirlpool, his solitude, his escape attempts. My gaze glides over his uncommunicative face, beyond the car and along the road; it doesn't stop, it falters. On the bench by the sauna hut a butterfly sat down; what brought that back? its colors glowed, we were kids. The boy—I forget his name—tried to hit it with a piece of board. It swirled off, down toward the ground; he threw himself on it, it fell apart, the wings were torn to shreds, the body twisted; I threw myself at him, clawed at his eyes, the world went black. The heavy body glides into the water, the eye closes, dust swirls up, the skin with flaps and folds; it could be liberated, to stand quite still in a sunny room as once I'd stood. Is not the room still there, the feeling, the innermost, untouched one? Any farther back I cannot reach. Perhaps it's a blessing.

A soft warm rain started to fall; the sparse rain made dark spots on the dusty leaves along the roadside, and across the land was the oppressive moist smell of earth, of grass, of hay which has slowly settled and begun to ferment in dark barns where only a glimpse of daylight reveals the flimsy walls and their gray boards. No one sees them; the cars rush past roaring and screaming, trees fly past, overturned or standing silent; it is noon and the heat quivers above the hot hood of the car which has been turned partway onto an unfamiliar forest path. They eat some of the food they have brought along, four people sitting in silence; they look around as if being pursued; the boy takes a few steps into the woods and is called back. Very high above them are three thin white streaks from the planes that rush away from the sun into the whirling yellow clouds, southward. They don't even take time to clean up afterwards, as they always used to; forgetting the plastic bag, they hasten back into the car; it is red and shines. A squirrel by the edge of the road suddenly leaps diagonally at the car, which tries to avoid it. The squirrel leaps back. It looks to the right, then to the left; inside it has a thin glowing lamp, a mechanism which drives it in a zigzag pattern past all chances. It sees a light and takes off. It manages to get between the car wheels. It is nervous, or nervousness is in its nature. The left rear wheel crushes the grayish-brown body. It had no chance. Or did it? No one can ask it. There are people with the quick and shifty, yet rigid, eyes of a squirrel. But those eyes are hidden, even to themselves.

Gran

"Oh, you are waking me up too early," she said. The window shades were down, glowing dark green against the summer sun. Everything in the bedroom was white. Hannes sat down on the edge of the bed with the silver tray; the glasses had a soft sheen, the bottle contained champagne. "Wake up!" "I am awake, darling." "Here, have some." She took the glass; it was cold, tapering, like a cone. She bent her head backwards; the skin felt quite soft and smooth. The chandelier with its rainbow sconces was like a rainshower, a cool rain in the morning twilight. He wore a mustache, which felt rough against her throat. Outside the window the cook was talking loudly; the words, the dialect, were mysterious, and she stroked his hair; it felt rough, dry, as when he lay dead, so long ago. She opened her eyes; the boy was sleeping with his mouth open against her knee, with beads of perspiration on his brow. Cloth, veins and wrinkles, all that was left of her, and no perspiration, as if the eyes and body had wept enough and run dry. What point is there in this, she thought? What point was there then, when Hannes was alive and we knew nothing about anything, nothing at all? Her mouth pouted; she couldn't articulate; the words were merely mechanical movements. I am old, I won't survive this. It's like sand, sand or ashes, in the dry mouth, cataracts in the wide open dry eye.

The mass of people is fleeing but remains, immobile. Like insects! It is just a photograph of another mass, a black mass of ants coming out of the ground or struggling down into it—ground-ants with heavy black hindparts, so many you can't catch them, can't get hold of them. The mass of people in the photo has been frozen in the leap, limbs tense, almost grotesque, legs thrown forward or backward. The wounds are not visible; they remain gaping or concealed under the black clothes. Those who are falling do not reach the ground; the dead are dead, the dying cannot die: they remain with rigidly staring eyes, extended fingers, hands pressed against the abdomen, leg sticking up in the air—a dance of suffering for which the Photographer wins gold, gold, fame, praise! He sucks his mustache full of anger and pride. Everything, everything depends on him: the whole technique of black/white, the blood you cannot see; it could be a shadow, a splotch, a face, perhaps part of a wall, the wall he dreams about, the wall with imprints of backs, the backdrop for those he is lining up to photograph. Everything remains in black or white; that way you know where to find them. Here, here they are throwing up, moaning, falling, here they have their faces torn apart. But all is quiet; the picture must be cut down, the configuration made more effective, black and white, shadow, light, all is absorbed into the mass without a trace, into the running little figures he loves, he feels for, as long as they serve his cause, the pattern, the screening technique. Make it grainier, retouch; no, the cries cannot be heard, the silence cannot be heard, nothing can be heard from this entire mass which is sinking into the ground, is plowed under, covered with dirt, mixed into the soil. Wait, they are coming back. Mass limbs, mass hearts, bodies *en masse,* the suffering collective of children, collectively, death.

Martin

In half-sleep the thoughts shake in concert with the monotonous rocking of the car. Treetops float past. Yesterday, no, a couple of days ago, I can't bring it back, hold onto it, it's too hot. She cut her wrists, red streaks; it makes you shiver the way cold glass does, the body contracts. Daddy was telling about it. It happened unobtrusively: blood seeped into the water, calmly and quietly. The blanket against his mouth, the saliva makes a damp spot. Close to the ground the grass is yellow; the animals moving about are gigantic, the dung beetle like approaching death. Invisible things, animals on the move that can't be seen, the taste of rust or blood on the lips, hot skin against the mouth. Someone takes to the air on wings above them, like a bird of prey; far below he lies pressed against Grandmother's knee; he glides off, is gone; forests, fields, shadows tumble over them.

Everything follows its path. From among the trees the stream of cars is being observed by someone who sends reports ahead. Cogs fit into cogs, the machinery begins to function, the call to serve branches out to those trained and less trained, cars start quickly from back yards with flowering apple trees, men in suspenders stand in airless administrative offices telephoning; from the wiped-out center the rings spread through the air, across the land, along the roads; in white rooms the cupboards calculate with sudden twisting jerks and blinking checklights the likelihood of . . . ; doors are closed on meetings where in a cloud of billowing smoke faces are negotiating, moving, being shuffled like a pack of cards. Everything follows its prescribed path, the waves theirs and the silence its own, the light its curved path and the darkness its own. Summer, summer is here. The swallows hurl themselves at the sky like projectiles, almost invisible. Smell the greenery, feel the wind from the sea, see the white wings, the white clouds, the white, white clouds!

Tomas

Tomorrow I shall regain all that I have lost. Tomorrow everything shall be restored: the water and the air, the dawn and the dew in the grass, the faint whispering of the waves and the voices awakening and ringing fresh in the soft wind. Tomorrow the bad dream will end and the joy of reality will resume. Tomorrow the water will feel fresh and salt against the clean-scrubbed skin, and when I turn on my back and float on top of the water I shall be looking into pure endless space, and it will be strange. On the shore stand Martin and Vera waving to me. The reeds bend, the water glitters. The child crouches down to look at the ants—how they rush along the ant path, how they stumble and struggle on with enormous loads— and he takes a piece of wood and stirs up the ants and crushes a few of them; they twist, and the back of the body curls up and sideways as if in pain. Tomorrow everything will repeat itself; tomorrow everything will be regained, or lost.

Vera

In a cold snack bar, on metal stools by the window covered with moisture. Surrounded by hard indifferent voices, youthfully inso-lent, exaggeratedly noisy. The girl with the multicolored apron, the cheese sandwiches on a catafalque under the plastic dome, the cheese curling up at the edges, the butter thick on the dry slices of bread. There, along the dark street with three-story houses, the balconies like matchboxes, their mirror images indistinct, only dark outlines. He came and sat down across from me. He picked up the teaspoon, pressed the teabag down into the cup; the color slowly spread. He was young, and we weren't yet married; the cold light shone like a sun; we could carry on a conversation just by sitting silent or by saying unimportant things: everything took on another meaning. I went home with him and stayed; he lay heavy on top of me, and we looked into each other's eyes. We moved quietly so that no one would hear. All the time, all the time, we were becoming closer. We opened, we closed all the doors. Our sleep was quite even and tranquil, our breathing like carrying on a conversation.

39

Gran

She sat in the car making faces. At first they didn't notice. She was old and had the right to expect consideration. First she made a face like the cleaning lady's, curled up her lips in a confused smile, opened her eyes wide. But the others saw only a contorted mask, as if she were having a stroke. Then she made a face like a child's. She had to close her eyes to try to recall what a child looked like, the image groped its way through the skin and face very hesitantly. But what they saw was the face of someone close to death. "Grandmother," said the boy looking at her, "are you asleep?" She didn't answer. "Let Grandmother be; she is tired," said Mother. Grandmother sat with her eyes closed. She fashioned the face of the man behind the butcher's counter, who had pouting lips and eyes that suspiciously bored into sausages and shiny dark liver. Some secret passion tinted his face red. He almost fell on his face into his meats. "Stop; I think Grandmother is feeling ill," said the wife. The car swung out of the line of traffic and raised a cloud of dust along the hot dry shoulder. On both sides stretched yellow fields. Grandmother opened her eyes and met her son's eyes in the rearview mirror. She made a face suitable for them. She moved her mouth, as if chewing. "I got hot," she said. "All of us could use a break," he said. They saw car upon car rushing past. She opened the car door and stuck her feet outside, took a few deep breaths. In the increasingly tired and sickly sunlight the forest's edge was black, as from soot. Two crows flew screeching by. "There must be water nearby," she said. "It smells like it." "Look," said the boy, "cornflowers! May I pick them?" He pushed his way out, and started tearing up the plants in great haste. She turned her face to the sun and closed her eyes. She made a face like a shield. When I am dead I will have my prettiest face, she thought. The prettiest, the smoothest. She pushed aside the thought, suddenly terrified, anxious, abandoned. "We had better go on," she said. The hands moved anxiously in her lap. The boy was standing still, shading his eyes with his hands, looking north. There it looked as if night had fallen.

Along the road burned-out or yellow areas suddenly appeared, as along railroad embankments where the heat and smoke from the rushing locomotive has burned off the green; in the air itself, in the birdsong, there were burnt areas, not silent but empty, where twilight did not dare enter, only the sudden darkness. They saw them all but did not talk about them. The ground seemed to be the fur of a leprous predatory animal which now, nailed up on the wall, was starting to fall apart.

Vera

Do you remember the antique shop where we bought the Viennese chair? Do you remember how dark it was in there?
What about it?
Oh, nothing. I just happened to think of the storeroom; it was in an old wooden building, up a steep staircase to the attic; through a trap-door in the ceiling dust was streaming like—like a stream, a narrow stream down over the chairs, chairs in pairs, wooden, old and worn, with peeling paint . . .
and all in pairs, always two, next to or on top of each other; some were hanging from the beams in the ceiling, in twos; the whole attic, the dark was full of them. . . .
They are probably still there—in the dark. We might go and buy some. . . . I wonder what they do when it gets night. All the pairs. All with four legs.
And if there is a fire they'll burn up in an instant. Will they feel anything when burning? Many were of a wood so hard that a knife wouldn't make a scratch in the hard, polished, wood surface. Others seemed held together merely by spider webs. Old peasant chairs, rococo and Biedermeier imitations. It smelled there as it

smells in old houses, like some perfume, a bit sweet. Or smelled. Now of course hardly anything is left.

Why should there actually be?

Indeed, why?

Tomas

What did the left hand say to the right one? Nothing. Could anything be heard outside, from the outside world? Only the wind beating against the windshield, the car engine, the grandmother's low voice saying something to the boy; he didn't reply. The road was full of silence; it glistened in the sunshine which now flowed out like smoke over the silent landscape. They met few cars; some had already turned on their headlights. The words on the radio could not be deciphered; he turned it off. He told himself: this is just an ordinary vacation trip. We are driving straight through a misunderstanding, or a nightmare; on the other side await tranquillity, silence, the familiar scenes, the sea. It was a coil of thought like a fine coil of smoke which slid past and was gone. There was a smell of burning rubber. "It smells of burning rubber," said Martin. "It must come from the outside," said Tomas. He was seized by a quick cold sensation, which tugged at the heart and the eyes: suppose . . . He slowed down, woods and fields slipped to the side, a motorcycle patrol roared by in black and white; at the top of the hill four jet planes glided in formation beyond the forest's edge, without a sound, swiftly. He had not seen them; there they were, gone with the speed of fear, with the taste of metal. It was there, all around them, everywhere.

Vera

They went into the woods and the boy threw up. The high straight pine trunks maintained secret contact, shut out the roar of the traffic, allowed the fragrance of bilberries and swamp slowly to rise and blossom out in shy bloom in the heather. Nothing but forest to be seen. Mother-in-law sat down on a stone. Vera lay down and, seeing them, ignored them for the moment. It was quiet, tranquil, like a ray of light between the trees, crisscrossed by shiny white insects. I long for water, to be able to undress, take a dip, be surrounded by coolness, sink with open eyes and live, hidden . . . ; she closed her eyes and opened them again. The smell of resin was like the brown smell of a clean wild animal. She looked in the direction of the road: Tomas was leaning into the car, straightening up, arranging; he stood up, looked to the right, to the left. She called to him. He stood for a moment turned toward her; she could not see his features but knew them by heart. She put her arm around the boy's bony shoulders; he leaned on her like a colt. She saw the man wave. All, she had experienced it all before—the stillness, the trees, this place. "Come, come," she whispered softly into the boy's ear; she didn't speak to him, nor did he hear her. That's how it is, she thought. We are all dying. Forever. "We'll be there soon," she said softly to the boy. "Soon. Be patient."

They dash off from school like twittering birds; the white feet leave not a trace in the dust of the road. Three weeks later the key squeaks in the old-fashioned lock; it fights back but yields; the silent classrooms echo, the blackboards are scrawled full of flowers and "Happy Summer," the yellow curtains hang limp in the heat and do not move the air, which smells of dust, chalk, and paper. They are dressed in leather, and under the helmets sweat pours out. Two hours later the roadblock is in place, the cars are channeled into the yard, the line starts to build. People wait in high-ceilinged rooms with wooden benches or desks; they are silent or speak in low voices. Toward evening the crosses of the window frames look black against the stiff lush greenery. They sit there for hours; Martin sleeps at the end of the bench, like an object left behind, useless, an object placed there, his mouth open, the breathing barely discernible. A feeling of helplessness sets in, like some secret pact; the hands move nervously; a loud voice is questioning, shouting;

someone gets up; people crowd at the door to the interrogation room, where some rotund local official holds court in his shirt-sleeves, his hair disheveled. Martin lies immobile, the blue jacket folded under his head; the three of them sit silently or speak only a few words. The twilight moves from the woods into the yard and stays. A whistle flashes in the sunset, shrilly; the sun itself, ablaze beyond the flat landscape with its blue shadows, is reflected in the school windows; they burst into flame. Those crowding inside do not see it.

Gran

The world goes black and then gets bright again. Tomas said some-thing; I replied, but what? If I push my sunbonnet back, they might think I'm drunk. Old people who are drunk move about like rhi-noceroses. It's exhaustion. If I were to stand up and spread my arms like a bird and then fall down on the floor, we would soon get out of here. What an ugly floor. What an ugly lamp. I say to Vera: "This is how it was during the Winter War;[3] we just stood in line waiting, for everything." She nods; her eyes become uncertain, her mouth tense. She has developed some wrinkles. I ought not to have said it. This isn't war. But the clothes are getting heavier and heavier, more and more wrinkled. Yellow curtains with yellow walls. Where are all the children now? Martin is sleeping as if he had a fever. Now that the sun is going down it will get cooler, cool as in the cemetery where Hannes lies. It's not him lying there. But I know he exists.

On center stage the man, the wife, and the sleeping son. The old woman takes a few steps closer to us. On the stage there are many supporting actors; they get up or sit down, crowd by one door, enter through another; now and then the door opens, and someone exits, quickly, with papers in his hand. The old woman takes a few steps closer to us. It is evening; light enters through the tall old-

44

fashioned windows. Suddenly the old woman reels over. She falls beautifully; in the theater they learn to fall gracefully. The man jumps up, and they support her head; is she dead? They are shouting something—to us? Someone is getting water. The higher you sit the better you can observe the entire machinery, the scaffolding. Her head falls back. The wife wakes up the son. He rubs his eyes, he leans against her, she has to prop him up. Is she really dead; is the show over? What now? Are you saying that they aren't actors, that they are amateurs, that they are watching us, that we are the ones sitting on stage, even though we don't know it! No, they aren't watching us. They are alive, their mouths move, they perspire, they touch each other or barely move. It won't get any darker than this, not in June. First the old woman is carried out. Then follow the son, the son's wife, and the grandson. Few take any notice of it. Few will notice it, he thinks; it is like turning a heavy mirror on yourself, like dying, leaving your body and observing it. It's hot; he leans his head back, thinks for a moment, and then says to her, the mother: "Yes, go ahead and do it." Indeed, she was an actress once. Father lived alone for many years. The old woman moves a few steps closer to us. The light grows dimmer.

Child, why are you crying over the dog that died? Are you crying over your parents? And you, why don't you speak? Are you sitting silent, do you keel over just like that? A firm gaze, an honest handshake, a quick reply, a sound mind, a sound body: children, have you forgotten what you have been taught? Have you forgotten what the teacher told you? Is this your way of showing gratitude? You do not answer. Are you refusing to live? That is unforgivable.

Martin

Martin had a dream about bread. When he was little they lived above a bakery. The smell of crisp bread floated up into his room. It was blissful, the butter melting on the warm buns, the cocoa and the sticky bread, freshly baked—it all became a warm secure habit. The crust yielded to the bread-knife in a fine rain of crumbs. The bread was hot; he almost drowned in it. Someone came and felt his forehead; he was sick, lying in the livingroom; everything was quiet and cool. There was only a faint smell of flour and warmth, a faint recollection of someone bending over him. It was early morning, and he was on his way to kindergarten. The sleeves were too short. He tugged at them; they came loose and were torn; underneath was only red skin, like that of the woman in the bakery with a white apron and white cap like a nurse's. She placed the buns on a board; the mild sun shone upon them through a milk-glass window. The air was warm and still, sweet, as if filled with fine dust. He wanted to be deeper down, closer to her, to sink into the dream, into the bread; red spots erupted on his skin.

There is a moon, which makes the twilight heavier. Across the meadows white fog is drifting. He has turned on the headlights; with whitening speed, gravel and road flow under and off; soon they will reach the ferry; they can sense the water, smell the oil and mud, see the long line of cars with parking lights turned on. The surface of the sea is calm, curving up at them. The ether is filled with a faint singing sound, like a swarm of mosquitoes one cannot pinpoint. It penetrates the eye, the skin, and waits in there.

Gran

There was the same kind of anxiousness then, the same fear. We stood at the window of the railroad car and saw the women running with their skirts raised high, their feet swinging like black clumps, their hips like horses' hindquarters. They latched on. One fell and

46

remained lying as if she wanted to go to sleep. Their voices mingled with the whirling snow. This was one of the last trains from St. Petersburg. All was swept away. I was a young girl and shy of life, of the touch of a rough sleeve, of people coming too close. Then I looked them in the eye, and everywhere I discovered fear. They ran across the snowy fields like black insects, small cockroaches; they fell as if clubbed and soon could not be distinguished in the dark. The blazing icy sky was reflected in the house windows. That was when I learned a certain indifference, a frostiness, a distance. I learned to sing and speak inwardly, inaudibly; I also learned the art of imitating, of amusing, of laughing. Hannes saw through all that. I wonder if we will be driving past the cemetery. Probably not. It's dark, it's windy. Wind, stage wind, dust and darkness.

She walks carrying an old butter churn. It has been in the family since Great-Grandfather. So has the farm. It was close to town. The butter churn covers up most of her body and forces her to bend backward. Her peeling face peeps out, the neck turned sideways so that she can see past the churn—whatever there is to see. She walks along the road and occasionally falls into the ditch. She crawls out like an insect. She drags the butter churn along like a life-raft. Her eyes look straight ahead. There is not a living soul to stop her until she gets to the crossroads where a red tractor blocks her way; no trace of the driver. She remains standing there. She holds the butter churn as if it were her child.

Vera

This is how I used to listen to the living water. During summer nights I listened to the lapping of the waves. Then as now the moonlight glittered on its ever-darker path. I was alone, but protected. Was I? Was I not protected by a sense of security within myself? There was not, there never was, this contact with external things, with "nature," "beauty," with roads and landscapes, with beloved objects, with friends and loved ones. I constructed it all. One after another the threads are being torn apart, as if scissors were cutting into a ball of wool; and from inside this ball of wool there suddenly drips—blood, a thin rill. No one sees it. Also what I want to say is cut short. Once we get there I must be able to speak, to say, to get close: "I am no woman, I am a neuter." How bitter, how different. I am a vacuum. In the dark I see light; it doesn't reach me.

Tomas

If only this fear which is in my palm and which I press against the metal railing of the ferry as we stand closely pressed together looking out across the smooth waters,
if only it were so strong that it would flow into every vein like a congealing solder, straighten me up, steel me, make me cool, make me calm;
if only this sound from almost-invisible stars—this sound that cuts through the roar of the engine and the gasoline fumes, the pulsating water, the cramped people and their cramped words and thoughts—would suddenly swell, sweep away the faint mist along the shores, and like a truth penetrate our eyes and make us nameless, anonymous, consecrated to death, calm,
and hence we could gather together in agreement, comfort, and love one another, be close to one another; and nothing—no fear, no ill deeds, no catastrophes, no fire or heat—could touch us anymore,
as if there were only one single language, the most direct one, the most intimate one, among all of us;
so that through fear we might find peace.

Martin

The way a pale honey-yellow shimmer from a sun you cannot see falls into a silent room, lightly touches the floor, the old upright piano, illuminates "Almqvist's Songes"[4] open on the music stand, quickly glides on, as if it were not the sun at all but a searchlight imitating the sun, a decoration already dismantled, that no one remembers anymore . . .

as late on a quiet December day, the Christmas tree stood there, with its thick dark-green branches; scarcely anyone noticed how it shone; it was watered and kept alive. Yet life was still of one piece, full of wishes that were often fulfilled; there was someone standing in the lighted doorway, who then entered, bent down over him; he pretended to be asleep; from the TV came sentences veiled in mist that he did not understand; the image dissolved . . .

The strong wind lashes the water; the ferry is having a difficult time; spray hits the cars and the boy who stands by the railing. It is pitch black; the evening light shines on the slippery wet surface, on the big plate surfaces; the water flows by. He leans forward, feels Father's hand on his shoulder and hears his voice: "We'll soon be there." "Are we going to die?" "What nonsense." "But if a bomb falls on us?" "It was a mistake. Everything will be all right." He pulls the boy toward him. What do you do; how do you protect yourself? No skin will serve as a shield. Those who died far away are here now, their eyes rigidly fixed on a blood-streak low in the sky.

Someone must kick and beat on the one who wants to give up. By stabs and blows he must be forced to live. Someone must find the weak spot, the shinbone or the back, or the thin skin between the fingers. You must act resolutely and stubbornly before the person dragging behind collapses, staggers off the road, and remains lying there. They must at least be made to crawl on. Kick them along.

Make them feel pain through all the layers of apathy. Get them to safety. Get them away. Pain—that's the only chance. Otherwise they'll remain lying there—across the road, in the ditch, or against a wall which may topple any minute. Abandoned by the world. You must drive them back, get them to function. Don't let them die. The one who focuses upon the life of another forgets his own pain. The one who wants to sleep is lost. Walk, walk on, hit the one who is half asleep, do violence unto him until he screams "stop!"—until he looks at you with bloodshot eyes and pulls back, and you know that he will live.

Tomas

She will steal the show from us and play her at-death's-door role long after all the actors have left the stage. From her I have inherited this feeling of unreality, or the feeling that much is of no importance and can only be dealt with by frowning. She wipes the frown off; with me it stays, if not on the face then in the eyes. Vera who can see it does not understand. On the other hand, she is right in calling the old woman headstrong; we all know that. If much is unreal, we see it in a special light; and sometimes—often, as far as I'm concerned—I get frightened. Then I lower my voice, then I move more slowly, then I see through the rearview mirror how she rubs her wrinkled cheeks with her thumbs, the long bony thumbs I held onto as a child. I reach out my hand and place it on Vera's thigh; she takes it softly and puts it back by me, looks at me and says: "Sleep and you'll see that everything will turn out all right." "In my sleep?" I mumble. "As for children," I add, but I am speaking to myself. Someone puts his face in through the side window and says: "Perhaps it would be best to keep the windows closed." "We can't, it's too hot, the boy can't sleep," I say. "Just to be on the safe side," he says. He has been repeating the words a hundred times; they are lifeless, paper with faint writing, something indistinguishable in

50

the everlasting twilight which never changes into night. "He is right." Vera has turned toward me but I cannot see her eyes, only the pale face.

Martin

They think I'm asleep. I keep breathing the same way. If I screw up my eyes I can see their heads. I can hear everything. We are aboard the ferry. Some child is crying; the ferry shakes and thumps, but the moon glides across the window and stays there, then slowly turns. Those who live up there, can they see us? "Are you awake?" Grandmother whispers. I close my eyes quickly.

Gran

The ferry floats out into the pale night like a group breathing in unison; dim lanterns tremble in the silently flowing water. Who is the badly burned woman lying under a blanket in the rear seat of a car from the north? Some military guards stand in a group conversing in low voices. I see what I want to see; that's quite enough. The ferry is weighted down; it has taken on more than its limit. The opposite shore lies mute in the pale light; the sky is still faintly red after sunset. The year weighs twelve months, every month thirty days. Years and days whirling away. I tell the boy: "Try to sleep when you have the chance." "Aren't you going to?" he says. "I need so little sleep anymore," I say. The motor's throbbing is like a heart, a mechanical heart in the moonlight. I can hardly feel my own. "I am old, I might die if you touch me." My mouth twists into a smile; I laugh inside; it's no doubt a hoarse laugh, like what you would expect from an old bird with stiffly blinking eyes. I am an eagle in a straw hat. Not even the night can affect me. I am one of the elements: this has been the secret of my life. A bitter element, light and bitter.

51

Tomas

They may have dinner ready when we get there. The boy is tired; we have to put him to bed right away. Who isn't tired? Do you think . . .

I don't know. You know, I've always expected the worst, no, not expected but accepted the eventuality, been on my guard. . . . Yes, and been scared. Have you noticed? You, you have had nightmares; I have touched you, but you never noticed it. Keep your hand on mine. I find it difficult to drive for long at night, even if it's only a summer twilight; I seem not to know exactly where the road goes. Also, the clouds are low, almost black. But above is still a thin rust-colored cloud layer. I wonder if it . . .

Can you get anything on the radio?

Only confused voices.

Only disturbances.

Only the sleepers; they rush up or float past, in their feathery garb, with claws, with open mouths, with broken necks, with stiff limbs, in the ultimate silence of the tortured, with poisoned limbs, with all the pain of the tortured, without release, nails dug into the skin, skin bared, limbs slit open, the fire reaching ground level, the martyrs, the mad, the innocent, the children that keep dying, with bloated bellies, with emaciated bodies, you consider them samples or remains—all images that for a moment whirl through his consciousness . . .

when we get there we will sleep, just sleep, rest, that's all we can do, rest, wait.

The wind bends the dark trees but is inaudible.

Martin

Martin is shaking along across a field of snow. No, it isn't snow, it's ashes that whirl up and settle on the eyes and lips. It gets dark. The

52

feet stiffen, they slit open in grooves which emit pitch or blood. This quickly congeals. The trees and water are like mirages, metallic. Out of a black treetop suddenly flies a swarm of black screeching birds, as if they were the leaves themselves. They dart down and up; he crouches; they stop, abruptly. The car has come to a halt; it lights up the wall, the door, the rose border. Martin sits up; the door opens and a soft yellow light pours out on the steps and is cut off by Bert's heavy shape. He carries a rifle. Past him pushes the dog, violently barking: soft echoes in the bright air. They have arrived.

Martin

She is sitting in the kitchen; the broad fifty-year-old face dissolves into the semidarkness, and the small eyes shine alertly beneath the plucked eyebrows. In her hand she has a jar of cold cream; a shiny silk blouse glimmers on her broad shoulders. She takes hold of the boy's chin as he stands in front of her and twists the painted mouth into the semidarkness, and the small eyes shine alertly beneath the plucked eyebrows. In her hand she has a jar of cold cream; a shiny see all her adventures which, in a broad hoarse voice, she has related to him and his parents beneath the low-hanging lamp at home, far away. "Surely you don't believe everything you're told?" she asks. He shakes his head. He feels his ears ringing, the light dimming and getting brighter again, sees how the lines in her face tremble as if consumed by a strange excitement, how her upper arms move as if they belonged to someone else, some alien person, filled with secret voluptuousness. They are all standing in the kitchen; the night is black behind the windows. Aunt Rosa's husband enters from the livingroom, her shadow and her husband; his tall thin figure bends toward them, and his burred voice underlines, pauses, stresses, underlines again: he is a thin line, a note in the margin, a grammar book in dirty tennis shoes; his pate shines. "What are you doing with the gun?" asks Tomas. Bert replies in a low voice: "Already there are some characters sneaking around that I don't want on my property." He turns around heavily. The dog is standing at the door; its eyes have purple glints and look dead when the light hits them. The boy notices and calls to the dog; it comes to him with the characteristic gait, the choppy half-rhythmic wavy motion down the shiny black back, and sniffs his hand. He pats its head and holds his face close to its warmth: "Tomorrow, tomorrow we'll fish, swim, won't we, won't we?" he whispers into its ear. Someone has turned on the radio; everybody in the room falls silent. Only the voice of the newscaster, slightly more high-pitched than usual, repeats, broadcasts: "critical complication . . . the U.N. Security Council has demanded the quarantined area . . . no more than seven thousand dead"—words, sentences, like the violet-and-blue dancing color spots behind his closed eyes. He can smell cinnamon, warm buns baked in the oven; he is back; he can feel the taste of security; inside it are no words, only colors, smells, overflowing riches—close, as in dreams, forever shifting, like the water sprays of fountains, like a slowly growing, singing, flowing but motionless waterfall.

SATURDAY

Helena

The chapped knees, the mud up the calves, the feet turned in, the too long shorts, all the children nobby, precocious, or retarded; the white bangs, the big ugly peaked caps and the suspiciously peering eyes underneath; children who stood rooted on the spot until you threw a bucket of cold water at them—then they flew at you or took a step back, unable to express themselves, got out a few words: "bread," or, "Dad is sick," or, "Ma says to say she can't come clean tomorrow." They were ashamed of the gift of speech; they ran off with hard quick steps, their feet beating like drumsticks, their fists swinging. They dreamed of breaking the long-distance record merely by straining, broke down and fell panting in the nettles, grew up under unspoken threats, oscillated between shyness and wildness. Suspicious, burdened by feelings of inferiority, on the point of exploding from superiority, they walked in silences only alcohol could break; they drank with the bottle pointing to an ever-murkier sky, grasped panting at female flesh. It soon passed; they were captured or let themselves be carried off to less and less familiar rooms with a chair, a table. They fought their way through these, while someone slowly slipped a tie around their necks and led them; or they fought their way through on their own, trimmed their nails, lay like corpses, with cold sweat on their backs. Then they forced themselves out into the woods, ran around as if in a fog, reached the goal, staggered past it, beyond it, into life, or out of life—they did not know. They picked themselves up, became rigid, looked around. There stood their children; their knees must be covered up, their fists opened; what must they do? what? They had never learned tenderness; they could get close only in the dark, touch the wife's face only on the sly. You had to understand their plight mutely, be humble, not speak too much nor be silent, be prepared. The child jumped back avoiding eye-contact, the mouth: I don't know, they didn't know, they lived in the dark, inside Bert, she could sense it; the boy with the hard chapped knees withdrew, bunched up, a hard crust of bread in his hand, moaned in his sleep, barely grown up, his grandfather a farmer, his father a landowner, he himself a farmer, land, everywhere land, and rocks.

Tomas

He reaches out his hand and holds it above her mouth, does not touch her. He feels her hot breath; his wife is asleep; the room is quiet. He withdraws his hand as if she had singed him. He turns over and lies with his back to her, stares with open eyes out into the room. A wave of fury makes him pull up his knees, clutch them with his hands. Every object, every chair, all the clothes, all the shapes, the shadows, the sunshine, grass and trees, voices, the voices of children, every living thing and all dead things that live in every cell—all this someone, some unknown someone, someone totally unknown to him can annihilate, destroy, burn up, dissolve, erase: in an instant, like a shining, burning consequence of refor-mulations, countermoves, debates, commissions, conferences, al-liances, pacts, interventions, speeches, parades, promotions, de-motions, handshakes, experiments, investments, limited wars, counteractions, escalations, investments, devaluations, revalua-tions, mobilizations, maneuvers, border incidents, attacks, coun-terattacks, humiliations, persecutions, this entire damnable dirty pattern of lies and clumsy attempts to cover up the predatory instinct, the death wish, the encapsulation, the skin, the nails, the sweat, the hate, the hate. That's the way he is. Nor can he escape it. He stares at the wall as if it were the walls of Jericho. But it isn't. On the wallpaper the delicate flower garlands on a light blue background resemble snares, rigged up against an eternal summer sky to catch unsuspecting rabbits. He turns on his back and feels his heart beating. She too has turned over, and he knows it. "Vera," he says. He turns and looks at her, and she opens her eyes and looks into his. They are close, closer; he can feel the hot skin of her neck against his lips, the sleep, the soft unfamiliar familiar body. She whispers, "someone might come," but neither hears the words; he closes his eyes, he pushes into her, she makes space, is soon filled with acid moisture, it's hot. He raises himself for a moment on his elbows. He sees her face which bears a severe withdrawn expression; perspiration shines on the upper lip. She keeps her head turned away, her legs arched high above him; he starts thrusting, and she raises herself, as if they were filled with fury, yes, now, like an act of violence, an explosion in the flesh, a moan, a blindness, a death, indeed a death, a fulfillment, a tearing asunder, delight or pain, delight and pain, loneliness, yes, union, sweat and this skin, this cheek he knows, which he touches with dry lips, the eyes that never rest, that watch and watch; she straightens her legs, he lies on top of her, light as a feather; he raises himself up on his elbows, he is the same height as she, he glides out of her and rests on his back next to her; it's quiet. After awhile she gets up and leaves the room; the door closes. Through the half-open window he can hear birdsong; he listens: there is a flutter, it recedes, it is no more, only the light, the room and his closed eyes, no thoughts, nothing, nothing.

The heads of grain are moving slightly back and forth in the morning light because no one sees them. Their stems, long and tensile, dissolve the gray light and catch the first rays of the sun. The roads

57

twist white and cool through the woods. Far far away they are starting to disintegrate; the woods begin to mutter and scream, the fields start to moan, people are lying still, with burnt skin, no longer moving, or are wandering aimlessly, hanging onto the arms of the rescuers, talking and talking, or staring down in silence; morning surrounds them with its soft winds, its still-warm waves. Here, farther south, the crows begin to screech; someone wakes up and thinks: "they ought to be exterminated," turns over, goes back to sleep in the cool clear June morning.

Helena

She wakes up early and listens: it is a clear calm day. Bert is fast asleep; leafy shadows quiver on the yellow curtain and on the blanket. There is a slight wind; the curtain moves in the dim light. She lets her body sink; with half-closed eyes she recalls the same motions, the same sunshine, the same yellow curtain long ago, in her childhood. She got up, washed in the bowl with the green flower pattern. There was a bit of fine sand at the bottom of the water pitcher, just a few grains that whirled up as I poured the cool water into the bowl. I dipped my hands in the water, cupped them and washed my face. This was in the summer of '44; I was ten years old. Daddy was at the front. The old villa was concealed behind heavy dark greenery. The radio on the round hall table was playing patriotic music. From the kitchen garden wafted the smell of wonderful food dreams. When I waded out in the bay the water closed around me great and pristine. What coolness! She turns over, looks with blind eyes at the simple pattern of the wallpaper, soft wavy lines, yellow on gray. She thinks: now it's gone, it's disappearing, and she lies there listening. The house is full of guests—Tomas and Vera (Vera!) in the hobby room, the boy with them, Rosa and Max in the guest room, all of them turned away from yesterday: it no longer exists; the morning unravels in shadowy rooms. The kitchen door

58

squeaks slightly when she goes out into the garden, dips her hand for a moment in the rainwater drum, lets the water run along the underarm; the verdure is patchy blue, the air has a faint smell of rust or putrefaction. She runs her hands over her hips, down to her lap. Don't you see how I am about to burn up? Give me peace, or let me give birth, mature and give birth . . . but the words are lifeless. She has said them too often; they do not belong here, in the fermenting, flowering, trembling world of grass and flowers, of leaves, of the wind among the leaves, of the skin, still warm after the short deep sleep. She goes back in, sits down in front of the bathroom mirror and looks at her thin pale face, the dark hair combed back, the pleading anxious eyes roaming all over her face. Suddenly she turns abruptly. Martin is standing in the doorway; he quickly lifts his eyes and she can see straight down into his fear. Now she regains her calm and says: "It's a lovely morning. There is milk in the refrigerator. You can take the dog along if you go out." He nods and walks out backwards. He might be her son. She sits still for a moment and hears his voice calling to the dog. "Why should he die?" she thinks. The boy escapes, throws himself in the water and becomes indestructible; he is permeated by coolness; it makes him invulnerable. He wades to the shore and raises his arm. His skin shines; she alone can see it.

Bert

He dreamed he saw his grandfather stop in front of him, or the farm. He came from far away: he had that expression; he was a total stranger. The thin wrinkled neck was sticking out of the always shining white shirt collar. Life seemed as if pressed out of a cannula there. Shadows glided over him, cool and deep. In the shade women in long gowns were standing at tables. Someone was swinging a tennis racket. Were they his or his father's eyes that scanned their bodies, their hips in the old-fashioned gowns, their flat chests.

They are laughing but he doesn't hear it, only sees their faces; then the father leaves, abandons it all. He runs after him but the road is muddy. He steps down again and again in the plowed furrow; it is an old-fashioned plow pulled by a horse, the way he had first been taught. It's autumn; the trees are bare. In the road ahead stands a group of silent people. They step aside. Father has stopped, his back bent. He takes his arm; everything gets heavier. When he looks at his face it is only a white splotch, a windowpane toward the fields in the bright June morning. He lies with his eyes open until he can see: that's how it is, he is awake.

Gran

From the girls' school there was a view of the women's prison beyond the park. A wooden bridge led there. Screaming rooks inhabited the walls. She had a wide-brimmed straw hat with a white ribbon. Sometimes the prisoners walked by; they had long striped skirts. Once a woman stopped; she shouted something to them and made a gesture they did not understand. There were narrow streets with wooden buildings that burned down more quickly than the slow fire-brigade could put out the flames, or there were silent gardens where she and a girlfriend used to sit on a white bench, drinking raspberry juice. Far, far away they were sitting, holding hands, and the houses were falling as soundlessly as light screens all around them, stirring up a bit of dust, as if from horses' hooves. The janitor came out, his face coarse and bristly, his small eyes almost boring into her; she tore and tore at it. Under the face, like under dirty wallpaper, was revealed another face. It gazed at her with such kindness. Her hands were closed in hard fists when the boy touched her shoulder: "Grandmother!" She woke up as from a faint. "Grandmother cried out," he said. The room was unfamiliar, with none of her things; she looked at him, barely recognizing him. "Thanks for coming," she said. Aged and shrill the voice floated out of the half-open window. She reached for the water glass, did not look at him; she mumbled something to herself; he didn't catch what she was saying.

They can be found far from the center of the explosion; they may be lying halfway in the water, halfway on land, on their backs or curled up, bent or stretched out, in the bright morning sun, as if sleeping or placed there by force.

Max

He goes into the library and takes down Montaigne but can't find the place. His skin and the paper: the same rough surface, the same dryness. Half his breathing is Rosa's. He is unobtrusive; he disturbs no one. He has accompanied Rosa on her trips, has paid for them; he takes care of all business discreetly but skillfully. He is ten years her senior, but nobody would guess it. He sees the countermove before the opponent does. What he dislikes most are the enthusiasts, those little truth-sayers, those busy bees who straggle like sleepwalkers from flower to flower, those masked aesthetes who write about machines in order to legitimize themselves, find an anchor: mere hot-air balloons. He has exported and imported machines. He knows the mechanism of Rosa. He knows everyone's place. He tells himself: this is undeserved. No one will find out. They think him somewhat ridiculous. That suits him. Only for brief moments does he feel something like sudden joy—when the light suddenly changes, or it gets dark. Then he can offer candles. He sees that Tomas is afraid. He sees that Vera unconsciously despises him for it. He sees how Bert is getting quieter all the time. He sees the little flames in Helena's eyes and under her skin. He withdraws. Sometimes he and Rosa discuss in a low voice those who live around them. He doesn't say a lot, never too much. He speaks to

61

Martin as to an adult. Then he withdraws, into himself, where he can be alone, undisturbed. While Rosa is bustling he can afford to be quiet; he never perspires. "Work! Work!" she used to whisper, "don't you ever perspire?" Never. He understands rocks, he knows their names, he tracks their veins. People and rocks: the same stuff.

Gran

I usually wake up early, but now I am rising to the surface as if from a dead faint. I am old and light; I float on the surface like a cork with many furrows. I am lounging on a red couch; wearily I wave my arm. Leave me! Don't bother me! I turn my lily-pale face toward him, but no one is there—only the door, the washstand, and the silence. I raise myself up and sit on the bed. No one sees me, but I see them all. They break up into lines of dialogue; their skin is stretched tight over the cranium. Martin was just here, but I guess I frightened him and went back to sleep. So much dry hair, dry skin, loose skin, you have to collect along the way. You are forced to show your liverspots. Living is hard, dying I know nothing about, except that I was with him, accompanied him, was away but was with him as he glided off, in, under that ugly ugly altarpiece.

The speech passed through metal microphones, through amplifiers and dispatchers, was picked up, passed through receivers, metal parts hot from electricity; the voice now swelled, now thinned out into a fine silver-white streak; graphically it might have looked like quick, successive green waves, reacted as quick leaps on a graded scale with a red warning signal. The speech could be made to swell, to roar forth through large rooms, or to sink down to a voice from far beyond the galaxies audible in small dark rooms where someone is lying sleepless. The speech selected from among its clichés and fed them into the aperture for oral communication. Lips were pressed together, parted again. Between them the speech was squeezed together and swelled again around vacuums. It said: "Critical complication." It informed: "The situation is under control." It condensed: "General alert." It passed through the receiver human beings but left its deposits: rust and metal particles as tinges in the blood, solidifying salts that made the voices of the dying indistinct, caves where you might crouch, facts where you might hide your head. The speech had no eyes; blindly it stared out across the devastated landscape. It could not dream nor change, only bury itself inside its own repetitions, its endless accusations, its eliminations and liquidations, its anti and super, its megaton and nuclear mutations, its guerrillas and GIs, its acronyms, distortions, dissimulations, its word monstrosities, its basic sentences, its slogans and appeals, its fetishes and documents, all the fragments that calmly, treacherously and matter-of-factly flowed out of a transistor radio on a kitchen table where two men sat, not seeing each other, drowned in the bog created by the voice.

Rosa

In spite of having narrow eyes in a puffy face, I can see well. I see this Hamlet who is playing his irresolute part without enthusiasm but with longtime practice. He steals the scene; his mother was queen once, on the stage as well. If you don't fall into the orchestra pit, you will notice the stage dust. Not as much on her as on him: that's probably why he became a lawyer. That Vera didn't notice the role within the role is probably due to her secure anchoring. Was due to. Even if Vera could speak with the tongues of angels, she would still be a black angel who has discovered a crack in the universe. From that crack all the crumbling begins. I who at times can hold onto my face only by pressing my small fat red hands against my cheeks, I know what that means. Once at Port Said I looked straight into the eyes of the diver hanging onto the side of the ship, down below. He knew what I was worth and what I was after. And I knew what he was after. It leaves a bitter aftertaste which can be washed away with whiskey. You gargle and spit it out again. As far as the boy is concerned, his loneliness irritates me. I perceive it, I feel it, I reject it. Only in Max can I accept it. In Bert it is so well hidden, so deeply entrenched, so smoothed over, flattened out, grown over that he can blame himself: you don't bury mines at such depth un-punished. He might explode along with her, his wife. It's only dry crackle, unchanneled restlessness. Life demands fatty substances, mirrors and faces like mine, in order to adjust itself. What counts is the distance from the eyes—to the mirror image. That's it.

Martin

He stopped. He saw that part of the foliage was in sharper focus, more mysterious than the surrounding part which was lost in transpirations of greenery, billowing immobile congealed streams of leaves and shadows. There: his heart jumped. Something moved in there; branches were bending, there was rustling, the enemy was spying, taking aim; it saw him. Hot dark spots erupted on his skin, he was done for, he couldn't get a word out. He stood absolutely still; now one must inhale, fall to the ground in sudden surprise and roll over, down, out of reach, outwit the assassins, expect the vio-lent whiplash of a smarting bullet, have a horse ready, jump into the saddle, flee. The sun scorched his back; someone was watching him from inside the shining bushes cascading in red. No one will learn about this; no one can help, no one. The world went black before his eyes. He took a half step back, then saw the boxer gliding out of the wall of death; it stopped and looked at him. "Star!" he shouted, overcome with fierce joy, and the dog ran to him. He pressed his face against the dog's neck; it wriggled and poked, drooled and sniffed; it was both soft and hard, and its eyes under-stood everything, picked him up like a mirror image which disap-

64

peared farther and farther into the dark recesses of the pupil's melancholy and cold shine.

Vera

Behind the flowering bush suddenly made wavy by the water streaming down the window glass the face of a woman or a young girl appeared and spoke to me, and it must have been me when young. She looked at me beseechingly, she wore her hair like me, but she was very pale, with smooth, almost glowing skin. She smiled at me from a distance I could measure by lowering or raising my eyes; I did not know whether I was dreaming or awake. She spoke my name: Vera, Vera. I looked around. Tomas had arisen. The room was dim, as if located deep underwater; water reflexes played before my eyes. I was lying the way I had that time. At the hotel was a headwaiter who often on sunny days would stand under the orange marquee at the entrance and watch the people go by. He fixed his eyes on me, watched me without making a move. The lilac dress chafed at the neck, and the heat made perspiration break out on my forehead; up in my room I lay under the cool sheet and saw the ceiling, the cornice and, in the tall mirror, part of the door which opens to reveal a black unexpected depth. The skin dissolves; the body is weighed down by its own weight, deeper and deeper down. He is the one observing me and I am unable to move; he will attack me, kill me, possess me, change me, mix up my limbs and tear my skin with his sharp nails. I am naked, as he can see, and that's why he contorts his face; it is his nakedness; he is unshaven and has a heavy surly protruding lower lip. He looks at me and I look back, straight into his eyes. I force him step by step out of the room; he leaves behind a smell of cooking, he disappears, he never existed. I got up, I was grown up, I moved my limbs freely, no one could touch me, no one could come really close to me anymore; when Tomas is lying next to me and I hear how fast his heart is beating, I am astonished that he can feel such passion, and that I can do it, somewhere, outside, in the room I live in. As if a weight were on top of me I turn on my side and look with open eyes at the door. If someone were to open it, break it down and step inside, I would be ready, or indifferent—no, not indifferent: Martin lives in me; he is my coolness and my calm; he is the thing I have to rally around; he is my rejoinder and my role, my disguise and my body; he is all in me that is strange and hence familiar; he is Martin and Tomas, and because of them I have to chase away all catastrophes. They do not exist; nothing else exists but this room, the sunlight, the voices, and my soundless breathing. Was that a scream? Was it he? Stay calm: if I stay calm, the world, the objects, the rooms remain in balance, the light is distributed, trees are trees and my skin is my skin, it is my skin, my skin.

During hot weather mass graves are the only solution. There isn't enough protective clothing, but the air force cooperates with blood plasma shipments. A box of Geiger counters lies forgotten at the roadside, dust is flying, no one can get through the roadblocks, but the area is difficult to control; in the dark, in the woods, along the shores you can see movement, hear weak voices, moans, the mobilized troops have their orders but don't like to go near the wounded. You feel most sorry for the children, many of them quiet or moaning weakly, under blankets, on the ground, throwing up, having cramps. They have been placed in rows in the shade along the wall. Flowers are growing there, jonquils still in bloom, but soon their time will run out, they have already withered, burned to a crisp, quite dried out.

Max

It was at the time when one's skin seemed covered with blue marks and cuts. Everywhere sharp kneecaps were sticking out from under

66

too-long shorts. The men reeling around in the parks had dirty cuffs. In shady spots the snow stayed until June. Quite untouchable, I walked through the corridors resounding with disinfectant; I couldn't even get close to myself. Only in books I occasionally found something reminiscent of myself, a joy of recognition. That was fifty years ago, fifty years of daily rising, of friendship and politeness, of facial expressions I could not decipher—not mine, always those of others. Nothing has been difficult since I left school. There I learned how the skin can be made insensitive to blows. Those marks will erupt later, inwardly, and only Rosa has seen them—or has she? The mechanism of a complicated machine, the detail that fits into another detail without knowledge of the total picture, blindly, programmed: what fascination, what dead perfectionism. My discoveries, produced in transient hotel rooms during quiet hours of the night, are dreams tamed into slaves, and I myself have unknowingly become a slave of my ambitions. I see what I want to see. I do estimates, I measure: sunlight, distances, forests, this smell of corrosion or of forest fires. When Tomas passes me on his way to the kitchen I say, "Have you had time to visit the grave?" and I see him jump. "The grave?" "Yes, your papa's of course." "Oh, that one. No." He disappears and I think of Hannes, his restlessness and gaiety, his way of telling a story with his hands, and the way they later shrivelled up, became yellow. He was twenty years my senior. Men born in the 1890s are all dead, almost all, and their adventures: as if life were full of things that could be changed, or of self-evident things, commonly agreed upon things—honesty, zeal for work—how they became part of the clothing, the body language, how they were thrown off during nightly orgies, how I didn't understand those men, yet inherited from them features which I have had to fight against, spots to be rubbed out and torn off: a distant era, school distant too. I still remember how the pointer hit the desk, how the pale faces turned simultaneously, how it was like emerging from darkness into light when the exam was over. I remember the years of training in Manchester: filthy streets, work, work, and at home, in the silence, the philosophers, the pre-Socra-

67

teans, and Montaigne. It was like creating a protective wall, a bastion with wonderful, deeply glowing colors. When Rosa entered my life nothing was broken; I could follow her, fit her into the patterns I had created. Her slanted eyes, her sharp eyes, her quick tongue, her laughter—we were an unmatched pair, said those who didn't know of our silent contacts. And the alienation between us, the cool within the heat. The same cool I feel in this beer bottle I am holding in my hand as I hear the house waking up, the shadows shorten, and the hot day rise like a haze above the fields.

Helena

A light reflex from one of the planes in the formation is hurled down from the hazy gray-blue sky. The sound is the same one I recall from that time. Then all the trees were standing still, frost-clad, black against the dizzying sky. Many planes, a single resounding note signifying death. The air defense sent out its fire like oddly muffled white puffs of smoke; no snow fell, the frost gave the blue a silver coating, the landscape was at rest or held its breath. I was six years old. If someone, a little girl, now stood holding my hand and looking up at this single sound which reaches us only after the planes have passed, if in her eyes, in her touch I recognized the same fear, the same delight, the same excitement, or heard the voice among the hard wintry trees, "might I die? tell me!" like throwing oneself down a precipice, or standing still, burning up and vanishing forever . . .
They say to me and I say to them: "what was that, whose planes were they, what is going on?" And I look at the morning view, the dark oak on the slope down to the road, the kitchen garden that needs watering, the greenery that must remain green, Bert's face which remains his face, the hair with the cowlick, the childlike neck, the sharp line between suntanned skin and the almost sickly white: no, he doesn't want transformations, alterations, or changes;

68

he wants the colors that belong to each season. He wants to be sure that I stay the same, but I cannot; I change with every touch, like Tomas—I recognize that expression, that secret delight, that fear. It's like a smell or an emission from the ground, from the leaves— the smell of dandelions, hot and damp, like a thin smoke that blurs the outline of the forest's edge, distances the birdsong, makes the skin hot; he sees me or he sees me not.

Gran

Never to be born. To die young. Not to drag these years along, not to get sick, not to become bored, not to grow old gracefully, not to remember—rooms you sat in when young, hot summers, years which slowly got colder, apartments that grew darker. Old age brings along its own smell, no matter where it goes. It lives in my closets; I no longer notice it. I take it with me outside; the trees are so very green; all those I address speak so fast. From where I sit I can see the road the wagon rolled along, the juniper we passed: it's dry, it hasn't a dark blue shadow anymore, it stands upright but is dead. They are running hither and thither. Sit in the sun; don't look straight into it. Still the colors look washed out; everything looks brownish, as in old photographs, all the pretty pictures of my youth with short skirts, eyes looking seriously at something outside the picture, or in landscape views, views of cities, like etchings: a narrow alley, steep roofs, the snow and lonely lanterns, someone walking softly, speaking softly, aging softly, dying softly, without shouting, without cold sweat, without fever, heat, without paralysis. . . . A friendly city with small lighted windows at dusk, gardens that fill the gateways with distant, dark cool greenery, small towns where life is standing still, where perhaps no one is living— there we'll go, the boy and I, hand in hand, first through the dark gateway, then he almost tears himself loose to get to the garden with the rare flowers. They are in bloom; they spread a fragrance of—a

69

heavy fragrance, a smell of decomposition, no, of—silence. Silence. Let's go in there and stay. It's cool in there, with a few glowing-red poppies, a table is set and someone in a white dress is bending over it. But her hand, her hand is trembling; she is unable to pour, she trembles; she is so youthfully dressed, but the face, oh how ugly it is, wrinkled and ugly, toothless, sneering. Here, too, she exists; she lives here too, in this lovely garden. The boy must have become frightened and run into the shadows. I keep looking for him; moaning, I crawl on all fours. He has disappeared and it's getting dark; the old gaslight is lit but only spreads its light over the huge lilac bushes. As in the cemetery with its heavy fertile soil. Far away, deep down, as if looking down from the third balcony, the stage badly lit; someone moves about down there and disappears. Perhaps the director; only a white face remains, resting against a red divan like a gravestone. The footlights are turned off, one after another; the skin grows darker; the entire theatre is dead.

Martin

There was an old man; he collided with a truck and the wheel ran over his head. He had a yellow helmet that burst. His face was quite flattened, and grey mucus oozed out of his brain. I pushed my way out of the throng of curious onlookers and went home. I sat as I am sitting now and saw hardly anything before me: various kinds of things. My skin was smarting. Dad says to me: "all will be well." Sometimes I see them, quite distinctly, their voices, their faces, their teeth; I understand what they are not talking about and what they are hiding. Sometimes I don't know what they are hiding. I stagger as if someone were hitting me or leading me through totally un-familiar rooms. Aunt Rosa, what is she doing here? What is Uncle Max doing here with her? I move my lips, I let her touch me. Everything has started to come apart; there is an ugly unfamiliar smell; my arm smells of hot sun, and green isn't green but yellow. If

70

I take everything out of my pocket, I feel much lighter. Peas, a piece of string, an eraser, two hard one-mark pieces—with them I'll buy something that will last forever and ever, always. I know what they are up to. Today when Mother touched me I felt as if I wanted to tear off my arm, run somewhere, back to yesterday; I don't want to grow up, I don't want to die, ever. The dog runs to me, it lowers itself on its forepaws, its rear end is up, it wants to play; we run in zigzags and someone is after us. We run in under the low apple trees; everything is in bloom, shining. As if scared, Star is running like a wild beast in the grass; I see its eyes, it wants to bite, it wants to jump at my throat, hang on; I throw myself aside; we stop running, both of us panting. The grass is covered with sweat. I dip my hands in the rainwater drum at the corner of the house and rinse my face. I dip both my arms into the drum. My face floats on the black water; it is in pieces like the faces of all the others. Then I hear churchbells far away; they are like a pendulum, which puts everything in place.

Tomas

A moment before the music starts the imminent bars can be perceived like a distant echo. A moment after the picture is moved you can see the gray outline left behind. A moment before birth a voice can be heard saying: "no, I don't want to be born!" A moment after death the image of the dead person still moves, a hand drops, a foot kicks a chair, echoes and reflexes. Behind me walks a shape that penetrates my body, follows close at my heels, has its eyes pointed at mine and through mine into the world. A moment before speaking I can hear myself speak inside this stranger's skull. I see the dark leaves of the raspberry bushes around me, I see my clasped hands, I hear my voice repeating: "Let there be no war, let there be no war." He sees my lips moving. He is no god; he is the bystander. Let me become him, let me be him. He steps inside me, takes me to cool rooms, lays me down and sinks me into deep sleep. He wipes my

71

brow and supports my head. He gives me a drink and then gives me a shove. I fall down on my knees; it is damp, with a rank smell of earth. I get up quickly, I leave and he watches me, doesn't follow me—except with his eyes. The fundamentals of civil law. If I thought I was alone in my study—no, somewhere in my childhood I have already heard that voice, seen that shape, felt someone fit his limbs into mine, his gaze into mine. Events shift like ripples on the surface of the sea; we stand watching them, we jump into the water, we call out, we thrash about; look, we have changed! changed! And there is someone standing on the shore; he places his foot on our hand—a glimpse of daylight, of light, then we are whirled along, unchanged; we shatter, do not change. He gets up and leaves; the boy runs after him; the trees, the grass give way. Then through the deep silence a lark rises, begins to sing, as if nothing had happened, as if nothing had happened but everything had changed, a bright, high-pitched song, almost like a scream, almost like a great joy, above the field, in the almost light-gray June sky. "Tomas!" his wife calls, and he stops, turns around. The boy catches up with him; Tomas clutches him close to his breast as if he were the one seeking a safe harbor. Martin struggles free; wave upon wave of colors, movement, sound come at him.

Bert

About growth, soil and crops they know nothing. You have to stand free, like a tree in wide open spaces. Now and then the earth gets black, is scorched; everything looks like a photo negative or begins to glow: I know that. My imagination has had years to learn agility, to plow close to the bedrock. The screeching gulls follow in the furrows. Spring—then everything is cool, and I am alone. Father with his fine manners, his memories stuffed into garment bags, and his things which all bore his monogram; I watched him from far away, from the attic window, from the cow barn. I was the foreman's

72

child and ate his hard crusts of bread. But to plow close, without causing damage, that I learned from him. Mother was almost un- hurt when she died, suffered only from a secret disease, a death wish, away from the cold, the faultless life, the brutal formality. I only remember her as a shadow, a silent lap, a hand that touched me and quickly withdrew, into illness. From windows and holes in the wall I observed him. Like a peacock he strutted off, on "inspec- tions." Soon it will be breakfast time. Something in Helena reminds me of Mother. What? The hot skin, which so easily makes you sated. On the edge of the ditch there is suddenly a dead bird. It seems unhurt. It is a sparrow hawk. It has probably been poisoned. I kick open a hole in the ground, place it there, trample earth over it. In the west a dark cloudbank can be seen; the only sound I hear is the crickets'. Cricket. He played that too, they say, while he was in England. Naturally. His refined sweat, my sweat—the same dis- tance, after all, to the things quite clearly seen. Come close to me: always I am the seer, the absent one.

Rosa

In the park with the shady foliage, the dimly shining paths leading farther and farther in, the sudden glowing cascades of rhodo- dendrons, high tree trunks like the skin of exotic animals, there among the silences the springs, the black still water into which you might glide down, disappear without a trace, and from which your heavy body might never be recovered. . . .
Rosa was walking there with her father and mother and observed the clouds gliding like dark lavender membranes across the eve- ning sky, and the sun shone through the cracks in the clouds, showering the gray sea visible between tree trunks with its rays, coloring it silver-white. . . . Outside the labyrinth with its dense dark-green hedges they met the young man in riding britches, wearing gold stripes; attentively he guided her in among the path-

ways. The spurs, if he had spurs, jingled softly, like violent waves against a hot dry sandy beach. The evening sun cast its reflexes; a small dagger swung at his hip; dust settled like a fine membrane on his boots. . . .

She started to run; panting, she rushed between the narrow high walls, heavy with shadows and darkness; a pale moon rushed inside these same borders which outlined the sky in ever-new patterns; she wandered farther and farther astray. . . .

He, too, lost his way. They ran panting, he somewhere close by; she stopped, he also stopped suddenly; her chest heaved and sank; someone was trying to push through the hedge, a hand, cuts in the skin, white gloves covered with streaks of blood. Just then the first flashes of lightning rent the sky, the roar of thunder wiped out the bright evening light, and she turned around, ran back, found the exit; there was the pungent smell of totally open, strangely glowing flowers; Father and Mother had disappeared. . . .

She heard his voice: "Rosa! Rosa!" and turned around and waited. She knew what she would do, she knew her body's need; she was standing alone, she could never again be alone. Night fell.

If you don't know which road to take, stop. Stand still. Notice the shadows, the shortest of the day. Out of their shade you look toward the house. Through the window you can see them moving about or sitting in silence. The wind, too, has stopped tearing at the treetops. The sunlight falls across the road like dust after someone has walked there. Sniff the air: a strange smell is wafting in; it is unfamiliar, carried in from far away; it penetrates the mucus membranes and approaches the optical nerve—like a very light haze, like tears. The hot sandy plane flows by; there has once been snow here, everything has been cold, white, full of freshness, glittering sun, crystals, frost. The door is ajar; they are all sitting in the kitchen with their legs like a row of pillars; they move them, it is dim. Animals with a familiar smell, they are strange, they change. Avoid them, pass them by, slip like an optical nerve through the door to the room where the dogblanket is; lie down, arrange yourself, settle down, close your eyes. They won't get up, they don't notice you. They have guests: others are speaking through their mouths; someone takes a step forward and merges with them, steps inside their forms, fits his limbs inside the stranger's limbs, his hands inside the strange hands, sex organ inside the stranger's sex organ. Everything must fit, every strand of hair must merge into its counterpart, every gaze must quickly capture the gliding, quickly changing countergaze; the gestures must be captured and arrested in order to continue where they had ceased; the knife, the fork, the bent head, the clothing and the skin. They did not assemble, they were here, they were shadow and body, a shadow body and yet skin, nails, mouths, sweat, emissions. They had not been there, now they sat assembled; for an instant these strangers sat assembled, passed one another bread and salt; in the livingroom the old clock struck twelve fragile strokes. That's when those others took the last step, stepped inside their limbs, took over their eyes and looked out into the room where the light was streaming in above the sink. This is how they sat: Grandmother against the wall, next to her Martin, next to him Vera, his mother, next to her Tomas; across from them, starting at the wall, Max, his wife Rosa, Bert, Helena. Grandmother and Max in mutual agreement: they passed the plates to each other when needed, they did not insist; perspiration glistened on Grandmother's lined face; Max sat silent, just looking at them. Martin reached for the milk glass; his mother looked at him, the hair, the thin beautiful childlike neck. Bert tried to catch her eye; for an instant they looked through each other's pupils, then slid past while Helena was thinking: they no longer know each other, too much has happened. She felt not relief, but a hunger for a reckoning—to be able to take hold of her husband's and Vera's relationship, lay it bare, cut into it, slowly. Tomas's foot touched hers involuntarily and quickly withdrew. He had lain quite still, she recalled; she could barely hear him breathe, only the silent tears, like those of a lonely child; it affected her painfully, her womb contracted. She drank, in long voluptuous gulps; the spring water tasted faintly of earth; it was clear, as if nothing could ever change it, as if it burst forth from a secret source which could never run dry. What if she could quench her thirst for good, make herself whole, overflowing? Vera smiled at her, said something; she replied, ran her hand over her hair. Tomas remembered that gesture; he had repeated it with his own hand. His upper arm touched Vera's; what was there to brood about? They were here, they could not change the world, nor the course of the day; there was no fear in the grass, nor in the sunlight or in the landscape around them; it was forever changing, shifting. The trees no longer stood where they had been standing; they also grew unnoticed; the flowers wilted; far away in the bay was a sound like a fisherman's boat. It was possible that the anxiety existed only here, in him. What if he stopped, gathered his thoughts, talked to those he loved or respected? They could sit like this and share. In the next room the clock had just struck twelve, high noon. The words interlaced and separated; they were hardly even signals, light tensile supports for the silence they were building up, the endurable silence. Those who had penetrated into their bodies were looking out through their eyes; their mouths opened and closed, soundlessly, like the child's who is half asleep; they spoke silently to themselves and loudly, at times shouting, to one another. But there was something alien here, in the folds of the clothing, in the habitual movements, in the fear or in the relief. Bert felt as if he were walking behind his childhood plow, how the earth beneath him yielded and resisted, like volcanic soil. Cousin Tomas, he thought, you are scared; and immediately he had a bitter taste, like a quick nausea, the iron taste of fear in his own mouth; he held onto it—the same feeling he sometimes had when Helena looked at him with expressionless eyes, as if she had already decided their fate, didn't want to go on anymore, as if she had con-

76

demned herself: infertile, living only in sensuality, focused on filling a vacuum. From the steaming plates odors were rising: the
slightly sweet floury odor of the potatoes, the fresh sunny taste of
the tomatoes, the soft terse mixture of onion, spices, cloves and
salt in the pickled herring. They all knew them; it was like a
feeling of coziness. The thoughts moved around these smells,
hands stretched out toward others, secret spots appeared on the
yellow tablecloth, someone lighted a cigarette—it was Rosa—
ashes spilled. In the middle of the table stood a dark-blue vase
filled with daisies; in Vera's memory they recalled the porch of her
childhood, the cool shadows, Father's voice from the garden, the
way everything glowed or sank into the light summer night. In
those days they had almost all their meals outside, even when the
rain was lashing the small panes of the glassed-in veranda. "Vera!
Wake up!" her mother called, but she sat daydreaming, looked
through the garden down to the bay and out to the sails gliding
farther and farther away. The flowers smelled somehow too soft,
too warm, too faded; they smelled like poverty. But here, among
them, the flowers were almost ignored, glowing faintly, no, not
really glowing, just standing there, with their rough light-green
leaves like fine sandpaper, like skin. She noticed Rosa looking at
her, assessing her; she was in her eyes earthbound, rigid, heavy: it
had nothing to do with her body; she could not follow Rosa's
twisting trails, her colorful adventures, her violent mood swings.
The broad features, the rings, the tanned skin, all the exotic. Oh,
poor thing, Rosa thought, my skin is like leather, it can take anything—except perhaps his pity, his caresses, his (Max's) silence.
She had learned from him to keep quiet, to look through her eyes
down at silent streets, the invisible empty roads, the lonely lanterns, the stranger's steps, the blows, the screams; she knew them
all, the silence following the blows, everything empty and abandoned, the wind through the trees and their compressed
darkness; it would soon well out and attack them. It was not
surprising: catastrophes as well as joy lived like gusts of wind in

77

her; that's how it was. Like the music's echo before the music begins, the presentiment of the music which never catches up with the music itself, the voice that has already begun to speak, has already revealed—they clothed themselves in their words, their skin. Martin was looking at them; they were bigger than he. They talked but yet sat silent. He remembered how his maternal grandmother who was now dead had moved her mouth, not a sound came out, it chewed and chewed; silent tears were dripping from her eyes, she wept when she saw him, he didn't understand why, felt embarrassed. She died; he never saw her again. Was she now lying with her mouth closed deep down in the dark, looking through the earth up at the trees and the sunlight pouring down like water between the leaves? His upturned face with the smooth skin, and hers, the old woman's, where the lines forever lingered like the cracks in a mountain wall, where the years had made a landscape, a beach where the water slowly flows and ebbs among sharp rocks; in the clear water the fish are standing still, moving neither upstream nor down, opening their broad jaws. It is fall, the water cool already; there is a smell of leaves, as in cemeteries where leaves are being burned; it is the silence following the steps of some lonely wanderer. Nothing to seek, nothing to find. The eyes move under the wrinkled eyelids; they think it's suspicion, but she has turned away; the uncertain movements of the hands actually recall the boy's. It was all long ago; she follows like the eddy quietly following the startled water, the immobile eddy which suddenly stops: the day strikes twelve with fragile strokes across the wide water; the sea lies calm. Then snow begins to fall softly, on top of all the dead: they are lying discarded, crumpled up, bloated; they die with each breath, by the hand of others, or forgotten; the shots can hardly be heard here; none of them listen. They are sunk in the eye of the storm, surrounded by a whirl of clouds and snow; the half-open mouths are not visible there, the limbs stretched out in cramp, the children, the once-mighty men, the once-smiling women, and all the old people, with shaking hands, they no longer tremble, they are lying still, frozen. While we sit here eating they are dying, while we sleep they are dying, half the globe is plunged into darkness, the water runs like blood there, no one sees the signs of spring, no one can smell the melting snow: they are starving to death, breathing with their eyes rigid in total silence, in barracks, on wooden cots, laid out in rows, or on the half-overgrown roads. It isn't snow, it's sand covering them up, some primeval sand that comes from nowhere and has covered up everything, covers up everything; someday, he thinks, soon, it will look here the way it does on the moon, only the ruins will be standing, they will no longer be "mighty," there won't be any language. Somewhere beneath a mountain someone receives an order and straightens up; the ice-cold light from the ceiling fixtures cuts shadows in this face unfamiliar to us. He passes on the order over the intercom, he quotes the code number, he is doublechecked; no one carries sole responsibility: we are responsible. We eat, love, are born and die without having seen the rooms in which our future is being prepared. He walks through a corridor, he enters the headquarters, they stand up, they are always on the alert; all the controls have been adjusted, the light from the television monitors is flickering, the lights of the panel resemble the starry sky, still more beautiful; everything is in order, three minutes remain, it has been aimed, it is a holy moment, they feel themselves the leaders of mankind, its defenders. Perhaps one of them interferes, throws himself at the other two shouting (we cannot hear what he is shouting); they overpower him, he tries to kick the main switch, he succeeds; the room is sunk in darkness but does not die, the room doesn't die, the television monitors sound the alert, the alarm is sounded, they have to postpone for a few minutes, postpone; there is always someone to carry on, all the situations are under control, it doesn't happen, the hand approaches the control panel. In the next room they sit in silence; it takes place in silence, no one sees that spring has arrived, or early summer, how the earth is pushing up its first blades of grass, its first flowers, how high the sky is, how the dying are dying and the unborn are being born. From far away, from the arteries, the subterranean chambers, the first attack wave is launched, the first self-guided missiles. A handful of men are tensely studying a map of the world, the electronic brain; they live, they breathe, they have eczema or stomach trouble, they grow, their nails grow, they are alive, they are unaware of it, they are plagued by nightmares, they can't recall them; once they were children, it's in the past, once they sat at a table eating, it was summer, they were talking, passing dishes to one another. He sat there and out of their reach created this world of horror and emptiness, this disgusting fantasy, these images of fear; was there not fear inside him? What facts did he have? He had more than enough facts. More than enough is not enough. He looked out the window: the day turned over, it started slowly sinking.

All of them are sitting at the table with the bright yellow oilcloth, as if in bending their heads they had totally yielded to their fates. They look up as I enter. Perhaps they cannot see me clearly where I stand in the doorway. I want to gather them all and take them to the door. The day has reached its midday height and is extending its shadows. Slowly they fall longer and longer across the green lands. But it's odd: seen from inside the kitchen, the familiar slope, the trees and the steps down to the garden, the air, everything is toned down to a pale lavender twilight where people move about dark. The dog, already standing outside, turns its head and looks at us, pricks up its ears and sniffs. How dark it is even though it is the middle of the day. The old lady goes down the stairs first; she barely looks back, as if her goal were near; she gropes with her hand for the concrete rail and finds her way down the steps to the garden. It looks as if she were wearing black. "Don't touch me," somebody says, one of the younger women. In the kitchen everything is quiet; a light from the north window is reflected in the cups and glasses; the boy isn't around. I would like to speak to him, or just touch him; he may be the loneliest of all. A man and a woman linger in the doorway, turn around and return inside the house. The skin, the eyes, now I see it: they are all wearing makeup, nearly white like clowns, and dark wigs; the bitter lines are gradually softened by the sudden twilight, but their real faces I cannot make out. A motley crowd, not a group, not a gathering. And the old lady is their leader. She divines by the most secret signs. The man over there is transforming earth into dreams: he holds seeds of grain in his hand; he looks at them as if there were enough light and time. Along the road twisting around the field a big dark wagon is moving, more like an animal than a wagon. They see it roll past; it makes no difference to them! I point at it and ask the woman standing next to me: "Is that the one you've sent for?" She doesn't answer. She bends down. There stands the child, the boy; he holds her hand, hides behind her, is nearly concealed by her. I squat and reach out my hand toward him, but he pulls back. "Don't be afraid," she says. "It's nothing." Nothing! "Surely you recognize me," I say and smile at him. He looks straight into my eyesockets but doesn't see me. I beseech, reach out my hand. Suddenly it brightens; the day returns as he struggles free and rushes out into the meadow, starts to chase the dog that runs past him, turns around, panting, runs in circles around him. The light permeates me; my bone structure slowly disintegrates. No one sees it, no one acknowledges me; they all go on with their gestures, their calls, their leaps; the trees move in the wind and the leaves glitter in the brightening air. A hard high sound, like that of a water fowl, carries me off.

Rosa

After the meal they went up to their room. They needed to say nothing to each other. She took off the necessary. He lay down beside her. My old husband, she thought. She saw his thin face quite close; he was lying with his eyes closed. "Wait," she said. She had become slower as the years went by; she turned away from him and carefully applied the petroleum jelly. When she turned to him again, she touched his penis, the persistent, the familiar, the knobby one. Quite soundlessly he pushed inside her; "lie still," she said softly. She looked down into his face as into something familiar, forever escaping, aging and unchanging. She supported herself on her hands, moved cautiously as if she were rocking herself, and him. So old, almost like children. No, she wasn't old; she felt her limbs get tense, how quickly she came, as always, and how he gave her the deep satisfaction she lacked in everything else save him. The green blind beat against the window; a flash of fear went through her at the moment of orgasm, like taking a gulp of water several times and then gliding off into sleep. For a moment she lay with her head against his stomach, held onto his penis which still was stiff, touched it with her lips; but he guided away her head with his hand and said, as if in sleep: "No, I'm too exhausted." It was quiet, the others had gone out into the garden. "Max, will we survive?" she said into his ear. He opened his eyes, looked into hers. His face was lined, like hers, it was young and lined; she needn't demand an answer from him. From the garden the boy's clear voice could be heard, along with the dog's barking. They both looked toward the window and listened. She had to close her eyes, but the hot tears kept running, slowly and silently; he had to wipe them off with his hand.

Martin

It is sunny and warm. The haze smells of mud from the bay which is not visible. The grass rushes past my feet; the dog is panting and makes an abrupt turn. Dad watches with a white face, perhaps he doesn't see at all; he can get angry suddenly, suddenly run his hand over my hair; he is silent, his shirt sleeves rolled up. He lifts me up, he twirls me around, he runs with me, I yell. I get frightened. He wrestles with me, we roll around in the grass. "Martin!" Mother calls, but we pretend not to hear. I sit down on top of him. He looks at me as if scared. The dog comes to us and pokes at us with its nose, then lowers itself on its front paws; the rear descends. It gets quiet. A bee is buzzing. "Ask Mom to come here," says Dad. I motion to her. She comes and sits down next to him; he puts his hand on her knee. I take a long straw and hold it in my mouth. "I think the situation is quite serious," Dad says. "It was probably not just a temporary mistake. We have to be prepared for . . . big difficulties," he says. "You know what that means, Martin. It means we have to try to stay calm. It means we have to stick together." "Is everything going to be poisonous?" I ask. "Then we will die." Dad looks at Mom and says, "No, I don't think so." Mom has a blue blouse, her arms are pale, her hair is dark. "I think it's necessary to drive into town," Dad says. "Bert and me. They close at three on Saturdays; we still have time to shop, and perhaps we'll find out something." "What," Mom asks. "I want to go along," I say. "No," says Dad. It's hazy green, everything: the slope, the dark forest, the road which is light brown and goes in and out of the ground, past rocky mounds, behind the barn, over the hill with the juniper. "Take him along," Mom says suddenly. "You won't be gone very long after all." I see small streets, wooden houses, the square with the three stalls selling potatoes, vegetables, apples. I see the harbor with the motorboats and the harbor park with the weeping willows, the water glittering like their leaves. A taste of salt is on my lips. They are speaking with each other. I get up and go down toward the old apple tree with its small sour fruits; they will pop out later in the summer, now it has just flowered; the branch from which you can swing curves down knobby and silver-white; I take hold of it, extend my body, swing slowly in the air. It's warm; I see a thin white streak of smoke in the sky, then I hear the sound, but the plane is so high up I cannot see it. An upstairs window opens; Aunt Rosa looks out. Far away a great swarm of bees seems to be standing still in the air, filling it with shrill buzzing. All stands still looking up, and nothing happens. Then the tree slowly seems to become frost-covered, because of this sharp light; the entire landscape takes on the appearance of winter when frost develops and the sky is full of very thin white glittering twigs. The sky goes almost black, the trees look like a fairytale landscape when night falls and the children cannot find their way home. What if suddenly a deer or a unicorn were to rush out of the woods? It stops, it raises its head, it turns its head and looks straight at me; its eyes are black and shining. I stand still; I am scared and can't make a move. It is as if snow were falling and the world dead. "Martin!" someone calls, "Martin!" It's Mom. Air rushes into my lungs; I turn around and run. The sun is shining, the sky is pale blue, the dog runs to meet me, everything is moving, running, forever, forever.

There a tree stood. There an entire forest. There the suburbs started. There was the bus stop. There was the entrance to the hospital. There was the provincial prison, a wall surrounding the entire complex. There, beyond the park, was the cathedral. That over there! That was the water tower. And there, farther away, the oil refinery. That bare spot, it was the central park. From this spot here you have the best view. It's good that it's here, so you can get an overview. Look over there; all that was water. The big square was more or less straight ahead of us, over there. There, that was woods. See, this wasn't such a small town after all.

Gran

I can't remember everything, but quite a lot, more than they would ever believe I remember; the more I tilt my face and look like that cleaning lady who screwed up her eyes and always stole one thing or another from me . . . I don't remember what. Then she died, and her children never came by anymore or looked in; when they were little they used to play on the lawn which was green. Like now, when it's hot and I'm resting, I stretch out my legs cautiously, feel with them. It was long ago, but I do remember how it started getting darker in the theater, how the lamp sconces were shining quite dimly at the first balcony, at the second, at the third . . . and the faces like small slices of bread down on the stage; they look up; there I stand and surprise them: "I'm not dead," I'll shout to them, I shall. As when children are playing and Martin is with them, he always runs past me and only tags me lightly. I am the jerky movements that continue mechanically after something has died, after something grew tired and I lay down. It is dark in the room; only the curtain is light against the window, washed and newly ironed like a dress I had; I was standing in front of the mirror fixing it; he bent over my shoulder, and the skin was quite smooth or wrinkled. Everything happens quickly, drops out of sight, is jerked away, closes its eyes: to rest. It is almost as still as a tomb, as if I didn't exist and I were lying here, not so long ago, with my thin wrists, spotted like some kind of paws—leopard, mink—perhaps the biggest part of all: Countess Troubetzkoi in—what was the name of that play? They were dressed in tails; I was sitting on a red sofa in a white dress; in the glass sparkled—no, it wasn't champagne on stage— some kind of soft drink; if Hannes had offered something like it in private I would have struck the glass out of his hand. We were riding wrapped in soft furs; there were deep blue shadows between the trees, farther and farther away. His face is barely visible anymore, it too enveloped in the blue shadows, as if in white material, as if in a shroud; then it's all gone, only the wind touching it, we who were just born and soon will be lying here facing out into the room as if I were expecting somebody; no one comes, no one need come: they don't know I'm afraid of being alone, afraid of the inescapable, all those demolished streets, the broken furniture, the noisy crowds, the drawn blood, the scratch marks, the dead with their slanted open mouths, stiff eyes, all the snow, all that congeals,

85

slowly burns up and sinks down into darkness, down into darkness, quite inaudibly down there. Only the swallows' calls, as if they were flying right through me, off, off, with my hand under my cheek, as if I were lying still on the bed and were not sleeping at all but were merely quiet, away, far far away, away.

Tomas

While I am playing with Martin the picture is arrested and we are caught in our movements that continue: I can see myself moving and standing still, entrapped. Just for an instant, a second, a silent stab deep inside the brain: then the game goes on; fields, woods, the air rush by. As if death were showing its respect for life a short while still. But there is so much I have yet to do! In the now-very-quiet study, in the bottom drawer, among the old court records from the time of Dad's bankruptcy, in a black pergamoid briefcase is something I have been creating secretly, the manuscript of my unfinished story, a text gradually growing fainter, thin sheets of ashes that crumble at the least breath of wind—like the surface of the sea, the sea we can all sense beyond the woods, between the tree trunks, the sea which touches inland with a thin finger-joint and with its voice makes the tree leaves move softly, as if they were hearing from a distance what is speaking at the innermost core of my being, a continually shifting, continually renewed thought slowly and gropingly phrased into words, words added to words, stones added to stones, plants pushing up out of the ground, the sand that shines and shifts in the water, the coolness that envelops me under my closed eyelids . . . but there is so much I have yet to do. I have not yet had time to attach my optical nerve to my eye, I have not yet learned to convert my pain and joy in experiencing the most forgotten things, the most ordinary relationships, the simplest, clearest feeling, into liberating action. I am still unfinished, still tied to my name, still moving uncertainly about in a fluid, as if I had not yet been born, or as if I were a child, ignorant, privileged, loved, but not there, Vera! You see, in the midst of this summer's heat I am longing for tranquillity, cold, snow, a chilly winter sky with motionless clouds (as if someone with a light brushstroke on a still damp sky could make the white paint spread softly in a long streak across the paper), life tuned down, the way I remember seeing it as a child sitting at the window. The janitor's wife, a black figure, walks across the yard with a broom, stops and looks straight at me; it is as if she wants to tell me something or threaten me with something; I withdraw from sight, my heart pounding. And they didn't know that the secure family ties, Father's and Mother's, had already broken and my face was slowly beginning to lean over that precipice called life—a precipice which we fill with words, intimate gestures, which I fill with you, Vera, your skin, your warmth. One spring day, in windy weather, you came; windows opened wide, anxiety straightened out like a white sheet, there was brilliant sunshine; I opened up my eyes and lived, lived. Yes, we live, we live!

Helena

Day in day out, on the way to school or on the way home, they wanted to walk beside me, watch me like a dog, hardly daring to touch me; they wove dirty stories or clumsy jokes around me, whispered behind my back; and the girls joined up in groups, their arms around each other, their ugly faces turned toward me for a moment and then away again. I walked as if they were invisible, indeed, reality itself invisible: the room where we were living, the "oriental" decorations, Mom's hysterical lifestyle, the men who came and sat on the lumpy sofa, drank crème de menthe and spit out cigar butts; the whole semi-shabby, furtive, peevish, fake life of lies, conspiracies, clumsy jokes, coarse words—all this I walked past or through as if I had a skin that no one could touch or penetrate. And still, when he pushes into me and touches internal apertures and long-concealed needs, I sometimes find the whole thing ridiculous, or ugly, naked, bare and vulnerable, and I want it, want to sink and be dissolved, I want to tear off my skin, want to close my legs around his back, be plowed, be sown. "You shine in the dark; you yourself are so dark that you shine in it": when he said it I knew he was right, knew that I had met a man I could not despise, that he could take me away from this city I had never seen, never experienced as mine, that I had walked through these streets, these rooms, these looks, that I had got my period, that I had grown up and secretly dreamed about being carried off, and that he was the one who could do it—not because he was more experienced than the others, or much more tender, but because he touched me not only with his hands but also with his words. As if a long silent youth, hard work on the farm, defiance against his father, loneliness, a kind of natural union with the seasons had made the hidden language inside him mature, so that when he met me he instinctively understood my muteness, my needs, understood that I was not cold, not indifferent, not derisive, but was only protecting myself. Then we moved here; I learned his work and my place, did not submit but adapted myself to his rhythm and his silences. We both longed for a child; I had myself examined, it was my fault, I had an operation, I lay still hoping fervently that I might be transformed, made pregnant, become fertile, but it seemed as if many years' repulsion, frigidity, and opposition had altered the very life cells in me, as if my body had let me down where I needed it most, as if ecstasy and secretions were not enough, as if my life had long ago been misdirected. Gradually the darkness, the long winter months on the farm began to eat into me; darkness began to filter out between us in the bed. I tried to escape; for a brief moment I found with Tomas that fear I missed in Bert, otherwise so much alike: the same distance. I harden, I burn inside, I make unexpected gestures, speak louder, my voice gets shrill, my beauty is covered up by hard makeup; and he, perhaps he seldom thinks of me, he

88

has given up and is at the same time tied down. It isn't my fault alone, it is all those who have touched me, soiled me and driven me away, all who have smeared me with their dreams of happiness and security. Security! It isn't in the silence, the roads, the fields, the table, his hand; security is something I have to build up from the inside in order to confront him and the world; I know it, I am gathering all my strength; I have to give birth to myself, do all the necessary tasks myself, cut the umbilical cord between me and myself, be reborn, with my past experiences as fruits—wonderful, life-giving fruits, not dried up, bitter, forbidden, indeed like fruits in my hand. And there shall be no fear between us, only this shining in the dark, no violently consuming blazing light but a cool one, like the cool light the other evening which never wanted to go out, that time, in another more peaceful world, seemingly safe. He stood behind me as I was standing in front of the mirror and he held me; it was like seeing a strange couple, that's how far we've come; and I answered the way I knew he wanted me to answer, and he replied the way he knew I wanted him to reply: very light, playful, tender, intimate words, the skin touched and seemingly mute, and we as if enveloped in the evening, while dusk penetrated into us and between us and slowly filled up the clear water, the way blood clouds and obliterates what once was peaceful, concentrated and pure.

Vera

Calm evenings and the candle barely fluttering in the light breeze, breathing calmly by his side, bright mornings as in my girlhood when I could see the beach rocks glittering through the water, speckled, alive, fleeting. Words uttered spontaneously, which made him calm and me glad. Martin who came because we wished it, because through him we were united even more firmly. The summers here when the birds grew silent and we were sitting on the porch talking, in the bright moonlight. Grandmother's face as she looked up from her book and looked at us, her loved ones. The fragrance of jasmine entering through the windows and mingling with the smell of warm skin and the perspiration of love-making. The huge treetops which captured the wind and, through their masses of leaves, black in the pale night, let solitary faint stars send their needle-pricks into our open tranquil eyes. The grass damp with dew. Tomas's restlessness which in the long run I wasn't able to subdue but which invaded me as well. The restlessness I had let go in order to observe myself and my contacts with others, a conscious, firm, early matured decision formed—unconsciously—already in the earliest girlhood years. Was the garden then as cool, as beautiful as I remember it? The mirror in my room reflected the light from the window. In the dim light the washpan and the pitcher glowed, fine light sand squeaked under the pitcher and moved in a few fast whirls as the cool water poured into the pan. Sleep was deep and calm; the skin felt warm and familiar against the lips, quickly tanned in the sun, while Helena got sunburn; her thin white skin erupted in splotches which I slowly rubbed with ointment while she leaned her face toward me until her dark hair covered up my light thin hair, her face searched mine with curiosity: "Why don't you ever get angry? How does it feel if I do this— or this?" and she rolled my earlobe between her long hard bony fingers until the pain made the tears come out. "Say something," she said. I shook my head. Later, when one morning Tomas told me about his night with her, I felt strangely calm: I knew that he returned to me still more yearning, that her heat concealed an emptiness, that her silence and frigidity were not a defense but a Nessus cloak, and that she would shrivel up without anyone's noticing it, shrivel up inside her beauty. She was not the one I felt sorry for—it was Bert; and noticed myself how hard I was. To the room with the white curtains and the clean mirror I cannot return. In Martin I am discovering Tomas's restlessness and fear, the same tendency to withdraw. I have learned from Tomas; I withdraw my hand; we are sitting silent in the grass when we hear Bert calling:

"We have to leave!" Now I'm overcome by an unexplainable fear: "Do you have to? Couldn't Martin at least stay behind?" But I know that they have to go, that they have to prove something to themselves; it's important. Tomas brings his face close to mine and whispers: "Stay calm." Odd words, comforting words, words which ought to be mine but no longer are. And he adds: "Go talk to Grandmother; she is probably feeling lonely and unneeded."

Man grows old while aging, dies while living, remembers faces, events, objects that seem familiar, forgets them, ages past them, past the trees and their greenery; every spring they rise again from the dead and touch the sky with their young leaves while he is slowly going toward autumn and winter never to see spring again, the bright days, the still pure, liberating promises of June. . . . A wind blows through the streets, the wind across the field picks up, the darkness is torn asunder like a worn banner, the fires spread; it all happens irrevocably, as if all were standing still.

As the car started and turned down along the road to the city, they saw a big cloud above the forest horizon. It felt as if summer had been restored by the white purity of that cloud. Vera and Helena stood on the lawn waving; they could just see them through the hedge gliding past, as if through diagonally flowing water. Everything was flowing at and past them: the road with its softly curving tracks, the screeching crows taking to their wings like a sudden shadow, the trees with their trunks alternating in quick jerks. They started talking, as if a suffocating silence finally had to be overcome. They shouted into each other's mouths; Martin hung between them laughing; the car was pulled through the curves; the shining hood sent a reflex; all they sped past stood mute and abandoned— "nobody is about because it's lunch break"—and Harald's house-corner sped past; they caught a glimpse of a face behind the windowpane with the red potted plants, or was it merely a reflection, a phantom, something resembling a mouth, a pair of eyes—they were past it. A cloud with a dark underbelly hung above the trees; between the spokes of the slowly turning wheel of the field they saw for a moment the church steeple and a strip of sea, as glittering white in the sunshine as a flock of metallic down or wings. They felt free—as if looking forward to an adventure; but the closer they got to the fork in the road and the asphalt highway into town, the quieter they became, the darker the shadows fell out of the great cool forest which now stretched along both sides of the car and only now and then allowed a weak unreal glow to illuminate the soft damp moss, the tall ferns. Suddenly water lapped between the tree trunks, rushed in like a narrow belt, divided the shoreline and joined it again, disappeared, then flashed once more; hot leather mingled with its cool blue streaks, as if the water were reflecting another sky than this whitish-yellow shifting sky where not a single cloud was visible anymore. The shadows lay like pieces of clothing and whirled away in the cloud of dust, the steering wheel trembled, and Bert's gripping hands followed easily, with small insignificant movements, the pattern of the road slowly winding in through their eyes, so that simultaneously they all leaned first to one side and then to the other while the silence slowly tightened in the rush of sound from the window panes. Bert turned on the car radio; unintelligible sounds mingled in a weak, confused, agitated flow; he turned the dial, and suddenly out of a hole of silence arose a few bars, a cascade of pure, slow, mounting notes, a fugue so dense that no human voice could match it; it glided and escalated, like a groove their even rhythm could not possibly follow, the condensed desperation of all passion, lightly growing, striving toward light, like the whirling treetops, like the minutes whirling past: mouths emitting the lament of violins and dark violoncellos and the flatly roaring base violins; a dream about desperation, born out of desperation, created long ago by mute mouths, hands that have felt the dead speak, eyes that have looked into the eyes of the dead. And here, at its highest peak, the music suddenly stopped, a deafening *ethersus,* a cacophony of—were they voices, mouths emitting screams, yells, or was it water, storms, the sound of landslides, stones, crushed *materia,* star fragments? Bert quickly leaned forward and turned it off. Sweat rolled from his brow, slid down the slightly protruding cheekbones; he turned his head toward Tomas, who for a moment looked into his eyes and then turned again to watch the road and the row of newly planted maples. The first buildings came into view, no people about, two trucks roaring at them in the gray-green colors of the army, army transports, then dry dust, silence. They glided into town and parked in front of the gas station; CLOSED said a sign on the door. From the bar next door came the sound of crockery and raised voices. They sat peering into the dusk suddenly afraid of getting out of the car: like people you see on the plains, strangers, settlers, faraway travelers passing through, with silently abiding faces, as if everywhere they dragged along poverty, rejection, insecurity, distress.

Gran

Here in the washroom it is dark and cool. I sit down on a bench and place my hand on newly ironed sheets in a stack next to me; I run my hand over their light surface; I can still feel their cleanness, although my body has given up on me long ago. I listen to those who are living and moving, running and talking out there, in the summer, and I know that already by listening I wish to live, to hold on, with the grip-claws of my hands, with the wrinkled skin, with the eyes that can still see the daylight through the narrow window slit, with the back still able to feel the cold wall behind me: two mute things touching, cool and dark in a lonely room.

Suddenly, blinded by darkness, with the headlights as tired alien remnants of light spilling out in an endless stream across the cold hostile wheel tracks, the roadsides, on the house walls flitting past, on the tree trunks—as if the summer day were drowned in the silence and frost of winter; and then suddenly there is a wall, a dark wall against which the lights spread out, reduce, in raging, heightened horror: silence, a heart which opens up the doors, an empty room. And through its walls the slowly felt reality, its tough, pallid daylight filtering through like pale muddy water, its content robbed of all beauty: signs, flaking roofs, roughly hewn telephone poles, an abandoned car, the blood which through its rhythmically repeated fear rejects the eye's images and repeats: here, here, it's happening here. And nothing happens.

Tomas

From every street, every bend of darkness and light, every junction of yellow soft silky sunshine and the smell of dust and old age from the wooden walls, the windows mute or mirroring the sky, farther away the high-rises separating the air into distinct blocks chewed off by the trees; from the driveways and the sudden sharp sounds of metal, cars applying brakes; from loud voices like pieces split off hard impregnated wood; out of the confusion of power lines which they only now noticed branching off everywhere, telephone lines, wooden poles with pointless, eroded anchorings, or the already mottled tall streetlight poles curving like swan necks, not to mention all the billboards, neon lights, with gaping mouths or frozen gestures, with blood-red shouts or horror imprinted in the walls, and beneath them, beneath them, dark or mute reflecting window openings behind which people moved about, as if previously or just now drowned, as in aquariums; from perspectives which revealed the quiet hot little parks with empty uncomfortable benches, the planted chestnuts weighed down by their too-large leaves, hands on a narrow slowly bending stem, the shadows underneath it hardly moving, the smell from the sizzling oily tar-drenched small craft harbor; out of and from all these surface-mobile activities, from the woman who stopped at the bar door and then ran around the corner and in the gas station door with the CLOSED sign banging against the window, swinging sideways back and forth, and a swarm of sparrows simultaneously sweeping out of the bushes in a chatter, hovering nearly still in the air, then diving again into the dark among the closely growing leaves; out of the air above the mute, wasted, trampled, hot asphalt ground there arose, like a faint mist, a hot mobile margin, like a moving wave of water obliterating the outlines, the secretions of human fear, the silences between the quick shouts, our own sensations of pent-up horror, fear barely kept in check, indifference, the hard-won workaday life, so that all colors, all distances became alien, meaningless, or totally other. We had seen this thousands of times, but only now did we see everything abandoned, broken or seemingly solid, a provisional refuge for those in need. All the stone walls, even the shadows, took on a faint reddish hue; the man walking past had a face which, turned toward us, dissolved and became firm again, like the sound of the flock of sparrows: empty, silent, or everywhere sound, a heightened chorus, a hurricane of sound like a block of silence, observed by our arteries, picked up in the blood and pulsating there, spreading this sensation of emptiness, insecurity, which made us stick together and the boy press close to me, this instant, dark like a pupil unblinking, before moving on, before we reject, forget, take the step, see the bar door slowly swing open. Someone says something to the food odors and the twilight, laughs uproariously; a fat man in rolled-up shirt sleeves and a panama hat passes us without looking at us, restores the city, the air, the colors and the smells to their right dimensions, arches above them the yellow sky with brighter blue streaks, and disappears into the photo shop at the opposite corner.

Bert

I have toiled on the land. I have been washed by the seasons like a man by waves, balancing over the deep with arms outstretched.

Slowly I have been carried ahead. Slowly I have come to the realization that all I see is here only for a moment. Trees, houses, roads: I have to push them aside in order to see ahead. There, beyond the fields, the forest and the turn of the road, the present lies waiting, concealed by rubbish or tall grass. There, beyond the waves, I can discern the shore, quite dark, and the white stretch of sand. There I want to be hurled and, like an explorer, wade to shore in order to find the familiar, what I have always seen and never discovered.

Gran

My arms along my sides. In the dark, only the water dripping from the faucet. The back pressing into the hard wall, my arms as if I were sitting on a porch, in a rocking chair, one evening after harvest time, somewhere far away, in the southern states, in some play far away. So few children are growing up around me. I had hoped for more, and more land, more soil, more fruits of the land, mild warm summer evenings with voices around the softly shining lamps like birds or flowers, all in the midst of the silently listening cool greenery. Land belonging to us which we tilled, interest we paid off—just dreams. In some play, not in a laundry room in the country, not after yesterday, not in such a June, and in such a country, and Hannes still living, his hand on my knee, so like Tomas's hand, Tomas so alike: he will die! No, he will not die, he will return, he will sit down at my feet; the cicadas, the smell of the mulberry trees, words to utter, lines written long ago, before the Exodus, before the fields lay so lonely and I no longer knew them, as if white dust had settled on the soil, worms burrowed, as if the people had closed the hard dry wooden doors and left, with their household effects, bulging bedding, worn gray things: a migration of lemmings, forever fleeing, along the roads, along ever-narrower roads, to end-stations, blind alleys, silent laundry rooms. So little remains. So few memories. So soon.

96

That day another hundred or so died of the after-effects. The bodies lay still along hospital corridors or out on the ground, in fields and in woods, closer together the closer to town you got. You had to step over them. Most were lying still and no sounds came from them, or sounds so low that they were obliterated by other sounds—ambulances, steps, low voices. Or is it so only in memory: total silence, the skin torn off, the eyes still alive, following those still alive or silently focused at nothing, in the swarms of insects?

Out of the gray haze, out of the clouds, a procession of youths slowly winds its way, in sparkling white shorts, in gaily colored T-shirts: MAKE LOVE NOT WAR, STOP NUCLEAR WAR, DO YOU WANT TO BE MURDERERS? Dust swirls up; at the street corner five large dark-green vans stop, loaded with blood plasma for the disaster zone; no police are in sight; some soldiers jump down and try to stop the march; they run in among the lines; the procession veers, makes a detour; the first raindrops begin to fall, big, heavy, warm, like fruits. In the soft shining warmth of the clouds the voices sound as if they had no echo; only the gestures interrupt the slow wavelike movement; the first van moves slowly forward and blocks off the corner; the vanguard of the march stops and looks around; the rain slowly increases; the tarp on the van begins to shine. The headlights throw a narrow pale strip of light across the asphalt, which starts at the corner and stretches like a broad abandoned rain-soaked band out toward the woods. "Why don't they go along and help instead of causing trouble?" The man raises his coffee mug to his mouth with cupped hands, perspiration on his brow. Concurring oaths spill upon the table within the circle of men; from the next table Martin looks at them with a candid pale face. "Go ahead and eat," his father says. One after another the vans turn and come at them and drive off past the window; the procession of demonstrators turns aside and disappears in the rain. Silver-white droplets are visible on the outside of the glass and their shadows faintly, rigidly, emerge out of the smoke and condensation; the waitress reaches up and turns on the television; the conversations die down. Sparks smothering, the smoke rises slowly; it's getting brighter outside.

Martin

While I drink a glass of milk, they sit and listen to an interview with someone from the disaster zone. The glass is cool and I press it against my cheek. The voice is rough and tells about people who just wander off along the roads and don't reply when spoken to. If someone stumbles, they pull him along or let him fall without paying any attention to him. Someone in the bar is coughing and the air is thick with smoke; no one looks at anyone else while the voice drones on and on. I am scared and bite my hand, feel the taste of skin. I want to go home. Everyone is turned away from the window; on the television screen there are faces, uprooted trees, parts of houses, people passing by not bothering about the camera. Or are they looking into this room where I sit among all these silent people? . . .
Outside it's getting darker as if it were going to rain. Daddy suddenly gets up; we hurry after him. The air stands still and the clouds gather and fly gray over the square, the streets, and the houses, all of which are unfamiliar.

Helena

She looked down at her hands in the dishpan. This she forced herself to do—all the simple tasks, all the steps through the rooms, the routine movements: fixing breakfast, making the beds, sweeping, dusting, going to the store, returning from the store, fixing food, setting the table, doing the simple bookkeeping tasks; the silence, the door, the bed, the mirror image; sometimes she locked herself in the bedroom, lay motionless, bunched up, her face in her

98

hands, immersed in the sound of leaves outside; Bert stood behind the door, tried to speak to her, became worried, succeeded in forcing the door, touched her shoulder cautiously; she stretched out looking up at the ceiling; he sat down next to her: "I was worried." "You needn't worry." "Are you ill?" "No." "You are alone too much." "We both are alone too much." And she: "I'm a stranger to you." He shook his head. "I am." He sat motionless. She started to perspire. Yellow on a gray foundation: her eyes began to wander along the walls, there was no anchor; she groped for his hand, it was there, silent, mute, without words; it said nothing, it touched her, sparks flew from her hair; she closed her eyes and remembered, pulled the plug in the sink and stared down at the whirling water; with a gurgle it disappeared, also the hands, the face, everything. It ate its way inward; like the eye of a storm it tarried above her breathing, above her heart: heavy and tired her body continued living, heavy under the thin skin, large under the thin dark features: "release me, release me!" Her lips were moving; she was standing still in the kitchen; it was getting dark outside, as if out of the ground a long restrained storm were rising, a forewarning rising out of the dark, a confirmation or a liberation—she no longer knew; a great indifference took hold of her and along with it a great relief: "they are gone." "Almost all." She dried her hands, sat down at the kitchen table, and looked out into the yard and the hesitant rain. Eyes open, the eye like a sex organ: the shanks spread out, everything revealed, the eyelashes, the pubic hair shaved off: blind, lost, cut off, the fetus removed, everything restored, neatly, without bruises, without marks, without trace, without a trace, relief and emptiness, as if everything, the blood, the nutrients, the sweat, the tears, the content of the bowels, everything had been forced out and had left her alone, at the table.

In deserts the wind obliterates all heroism with a fine layer of sand and the notes left behind are seared by the sun into an ever-clearer text, as if written down by a brain ignorant of mirages. In the mangrove thickets the wounded one collapses and no one hears his voice; only amulets are left behind, hard metal or bits of glass; but here in the country there are only fields between forests and forests between fields, roads in between, and the smell of mud and water. People here are observed for a long time before they die; they are kept under observation, they are cared for or teased, they are blown over, they suddenly fall inside houses or into ditches, or lie still in hallways. No sandstorms, no reptiles, the hands lie relaxed over the open eyes. Now people, cars, wagons, insects are beginning to stream in. Orders are dispatched like postal packages; they thump down on the counter and are sent on. But above the landscape the same cloud, the same pale yellowish-white light, the same sky, as if the globe had but a single sky to depend on! A single one!

Vera

This rough hair holds electricity, which makes the nerve threads glow. The wrinkles around the eyes are not mere laugh lines: they had already been drawn with invisible needles before Tomas came along. And as far as virginity goes, I was not a virgin. I burned, slept once with a virtual stranger, lived once as if nobody existed, and I was obliterated. In the car coming here it was as if I were dragging along a vacuum, memories where the furniture has been carried out and taken away while I followed it with my eyes from the window, at dusk, back then, in the white girlhood room which now is gone. It always comes back when Tomas strokes my hips: this other Vera, she who must never speak through my mouth. Maybe I am, as Rosa once said, a fallen angel; perhaps I am getting closer and closer to Helena; perhaps we will soon be sitting next to or across from each other and speaking, calmly and pleasantly, about the men, about the child, her child and mine, and about all that we have lost. Perhaps the summer will continue, warm and broad like an open bay, and will grant us the cool of evening. If we wait together, they will soon be back, everything will be restored, my body will regain its shape, the throbs of anxiety under the skin will disappear, we will all be together and eat the same food at the same table, perhaps even tonight. We must make preparations for it; then it will come true. They shall see how we love them! Calmly, as if we were all close to each other, and are. And have to be.

How do we know that the seed of the explosion was not hidden in the furniture? In the room with the heirloom sofa and the chairs placed so that two stood on each side of the table and one faced the sofa. Hidden in the dusty, disintegrating, dry excelsior that some workman long ago had concealed under the pink upholstery material, which was later covered in velvet—in order to be authentic! How do we know that the explosion was not concealed in the silence around the table, in the hand of the father turning a page of the day's paper, and in the children who sat there looking up at him during those brief moments when his face was visible between the pages of the day's paper being turned, loudly crackling, almost roaring? Families sat in every room, in every house, in every city, in every country; all over the globe chairs stood, sofas and tables stood still, dusk descended, the sun plunged red and cold behind roofs and invisible horizons. The youngest ones went to bed, then the teenagers followed, then the parents; the old people slept in their chairs. How do we know that the explosion was not concealed there, in the sleep, among the furniture, in the floor plan itself, in the measured movements, in the familiar routine, in the heavy draperies, in the twilight, later in the night? In the secret gestures, in the wife's whimpering, in the chauvinist acts, while the furniture stood there straight-backed and only a cold moon sent a ray across the heirloom rug and glowed on the tile of the beautiful dark-green porcelain stove? How do we know that the seed of the explosion was not hidden there, under the rug, or under the heavy blanket in the bedroom, or under the floor itself, under the house, there in the very turf they owned? In the blessed earth? In the trees growing out of this earth? In the tree which was cut down and made into furniture? In the armrests, in the slightly curved legs? In the four legs supporting the seat, the two back ones straight, the two in front slightly curved? In the shattered wood? There, perhaps the seed was hidden there, in the furniture!

Max

Max, you're like a dachs(hund)! As if I had heard and finally seen through the simpleton jokes, the open mouths, the curious eyes, the hate like a smoldering fire behind the grimaces. The point is that you have to keep your balance, walk the tightrope, without a net. As if I never left that backyard, that well in the yard, the light always dimmed in the room with the two lamps: the one glowing like a bloodshot eye in the ceiling, the other covered with a yellow cloth with a fringe; it was lit when Mother got up to do her newspaper route. Her shadow moved like nauseating dark spots on the wall, and Daddy groaned in his sleep. I always pretended to be asleep until she had left; then I got up quietly, washed quietly, all with bated breath. The body was something alien; that was one characteristic of those of us working our way up from down below, always at a disadvantage, trying to keep our mouths above the surface of the days in order to stay alive: our bodies long remained unfamiliar to us. Nobody touched us. And if someone did, the body contracted like a startled animal. It was shameful to show yourself naked. Intercourse was forcible, always quick, violent, a mixture of accumulated desire and submission, the whispered protests— "The boy is asleep, don't bother about him"—and I put my hands over my ears and didn't move. The dark was filled with red and green spots which were sliding, sliding through the minutes and the hours. I decided to cut loose. I decided to push out of my skin, to change skin and clothes, never be humiliated, never live in poverty. I had to be determined, to find a passageway into the street and the spring sun. How I emerged from the twilight, the smells; how I turned on the flashlight under the covers and started learning about the world around me; how the thoughts of adults, slowly, misunderstood, filtered through the fear and loneliness, there, in the childhood room, slowly stuck and built my frame so that I could grow up straight—I hardly remember but long to be back there! I stand looking at this green landscape and long to be back there. Thirstily I lived through each evening; I started where I'd stopped the night before; at times my head sank down against my shoulder, and the roof of the public library reading room with the dirty brown wood carvings seemed to stare at my back as if I were on the wanted list. I read myself through stone and walls, worked my way through the paper supply house as if I wanted to fill the bales with my own writing: I ACCUSE! But I kept quiet about it, worked myself up through the labor union and squeezed through the Depression as if some gigantic invisible force were waiting to take vengeance and throw me back down into those shafts of poverty out of which Father and Mother could never climb. As long as I had enough food and honesty to survive a day at a time! And enough physical strength not to fall ill. I've hardly been ill since. I learned to sift, wipe away—words and phrases as well—to focus on the end result. I learned to listen, to those of false honesty, the desperate ones, the resigned; from them I learned to keep quiet. I learned about machines and about human machines: how they function, how they fit into the general scheme, the pursuit of a reasonable degree of freedom, a life fit for human beings, men and machines together. When first Father and then Mother died, I stood in silence, as if at last I had been liberated from the past. I learned the rules of the game; I learned to live with machines and to sell them. I traveled, and everywhere I found similarities. I started collecting rocks, from different parts of the world: burning rocks or mute ones, gray or sparkling, crystalline or closed up, all different,

103

some like birds' eggs, others seemingly exploded from some unknown planet. But all of them hard, dependable, heavy, all with the same core: here I am, always the same no matter what you do with me, even if waves have washed over me for thousands of years, or I have been hurled out into the silence to be shattered; I lie exposed and yet always closed up, I live at your mercy but am free and independent, I have seen it all and have no further comments, I am the core that survives generations, wars, catastrophes, death. Here is the landscape, here the road, there is nothing else; Rosa exists, the constant giver, always outwardly colorful, inwardly searching for security. They are all searching for security, and I am not their pilot; I observe them, I sit in silence, I speak in the same manner to all of them, the same way I speak to myself, and sometimes I ask myself: have I already died; was something irrevocably cut off, way back in my childhood, in the hard battle with poverty? My sole goal was the core of the rock, to pass unscathed through all the difficulties, neatly dressed, to be able to speak, live, behave, create without being beaten, torn or humiliated. What did I lose? When I see Tomas I sometimes envy him his softness, his searching, his want of the core of the rock: for what is a rock? A rock is the unmovable, the rigid, whatever is mute and closed up but also open to the one who sees and knows the structure of the rock, its history, its prerequisites. And when I touch Rosa it is as if someone else were slowly filling me up, were touching me through her and through me her: I see, I feel, June is standing cool and waiting at the door out to the bay—the bay not visible here but within reach. They are all close to me because their lives are so short. My life is only part of a rock's life. And no one will survive but the rock. There is nothing else I can compare to the rock except a star. Gravel spread around in space, rocks falling endlessly, glowing meteorites slowly cooling off, cores of rocks, seeds of rocks, petrified wood: we can own none of this, nor mistreat or oppress it. We only live in this moment, in the touch, in the silence, in the oblivion. I have stepped out of the rooms, I have discovered myself; I know I am alone and therefore co-existing, participating, helping. "Mein sind die Jahre nicht, die

104

mir die Zeit genommen, Mein sind die Jahre nicht, die etwa
möchten kommen; Der Augenblick ist mein, und nehm ich den in
Acht, So ist der mein, der Jahr und Ewigkeit gemacht."⁵ Eternity,
the stone and we who shall die.

The Lute Player cannot be saved. The knee and the entire right side
with the crimson velvet drapery have been damaged by falling
plaster. The smile shimmers through the dust layer but could not
prevent the disaster. The sixteenth-century tapestry is lying halfway
down the corridor as if dragged there by mad servants, and in the
silence the smell of burnt metal and gas fumes is still more notice-
able. Here clean-up will take a long time, while the landscape
outside, with prone figures in more or less beautiful poses, seems
static, idyllic, forever green. But the water of the bay has shifted
color. It is like congealed clay, the shores as if someone had stepped
in a puddle; mud has splashed all the way up the museum walls.
Into the corridors filled with pictures, the remains of statues, beams
and broken glass, a pale sun blows air which rouses clouds of dust
particles. The day after the disaster no one has yet had time to visit
the galleries or even cautiously blot the face of the Lute Player
which glows softly in the dark. Luckily it wasn't a Rembrandt.

Martin

We entered the barracks which had a slightly arched ceiling and
lodged several hundred men. All sat down, close together, as in
church. An older man with a face like a dog's and a crewcut stepped
forth and said that he was the civil defense chief and that everything
was under control. He asked us to register, all those who wouldn't
be called up in case of war. "How about us, who will be?" someone
shouted. He continued speaking, but I was looking at a man next to
Daddy; he kept wringing his hands, he scratched himself, he
twisted his face as if he were crazy. There was a smell of sweat.

Another younger man came and spoke at a podium—that it was serious and that a mobilization order might come any minute if the situation got more serious. I was scared and so were the others; I wondered if their throats were aching as the fear spread? I knew nothing, just felt as if it were getting darker, and all the adults were becoming huge—like huge dwarfs, with giant hands—and I had to hold onto Daddy. The floor was thumping; there were lots of feet, and many kept getting up and asking questions. First they called out in ordinary voices, then they started shouting; somewhere a bench gave way and people fell and got up as if they had almost been sucked into a whirlpool, into a sewer. Many wanted to know how you could protect yourself in case there was a nuclear war, but the man said that was hardly likely, and he had to shout it in order to be heard. All the time there was a quiet murmuring which sought to grow and break out and burst the windows. "I want to leave," I said. "I guess you can sign up in town," Uncle Bert said. "I'm not going to sign up anywhere," Daddy said. "Do you know what that means?" asked Uncle Bert. Daddy said, "Come, let's go." By then the hall was already full of people who were standing and shouting. The younger man at the speaker's stand tried to shout into a megaphone; the sounds came out very thick. There was so much congestion that I started to cry. Daddy tried to lift me up; we were almost carried forward and out by the pressure of the crowd. I don't know how long it took; it was so hot. It stung; the lamps, the voices, everything struck and stung and frightened me. Outside it was absolutely quiet; silent people were standing outside; a loudspeaker had been rigged up in a tree, but crackle was all you could hear—as if the tree were on fire. It had stopped raining but the air was filled with smells, good smells. My body was aching, and what I understood was that everybody suspected war. I have only seen war on film; lots of people always die. Wham! then houses, roofs, everything falls apart, and all die, except the victors, who parade; it rains on the film or it's scratched, someone is always standing and making a speech or shouting, the sky fills up with black bombers, big cities lie still until everything suddenly crashes and roars; or there are barracks, like the one we were just in, but full of pale sick people, in striped clothes; they are hanging dead on barbed wire, I have seen it. They are lacerated. I don't want to see them. I don't want to see any war. "Are you feeling ill? Let's sit down," says Daddy. Uncle Bert goes to do some errands; we sit on a bench and Daddy holds his arm around me; in front of us is a row of small slender trees and wooden houses; a few solitary people hurry past; the sky is full of flying clouds, some illuminated by the sun; the rooks are screaming around the old church tower which rises above the greenery and the roofs; they are scary, black, they are dead people who have become birds! We will become birds and fly around, screeching; feathers will grow out of our skin, and we won't be able to speak anymore, just screech. I have to press my face against Daddy's jacket while spots are dancing before my eyes.

Gran

I don't know human beings well enough to refuse them help and will never learn to know them. When you ask me a question I want to reply. Indeed, next to me you are the oldest one here, and we can sit together in silence without disturbing each other. I am not sitting here because I feel abandoned but because I want to rest. I rest better in unfamiliar rooms. At times I felt more at home on stage than with Hannes where there were so many crisscrossing family ties, in spite of his best efforts to make them invisible. To make invisible: Rilke has written something about it; I can't quite recall what. It's part of old age to enjoy not only remembering but above all forgetting. To be an actress is of course also a kind of attempt to make oneself invisible—don't all of us want that? And by "us" I mean those of us who don't necessarily want to rule the world but want to make it go on existing in balance with ourselves, without things like this happening. Do you find these ideas too old

and old-fashioned? I've always held them. And it was no catastrophe for me when I had to give up the theatre. I continued to make
myself invisible, to immerse myself in Hannes and Tomas, perhaps
too much. Perhaps there wasn't enough left for Tomas to fight; what
he accumulated in such quantity was insecurity, the same kind
Hannes had which surfaced after the bankruptcy. Now, many years
after his death, it seems I shall know that fear—that everything is
sliding, that something one has fought for is becoming pointless,
that there is nothing of value to remember, and that the truths one
has espoused are mostly lullabies. Pretty? Yes—as the rustle of the
wind in the trees, but what does it tell me anymore? I get worried or
depressed because the years—in my experience—make a person
more and more vulnerable, and to age is to fight against this increasing sensitivity and to resign in the end. Not to give up, but to
resign yourself. And resort to those reserves of humor one has, if
any. Then there is another prerogative of old age: I can reject reality
if I wish. I can wander into some family album and stay there for an
evening, among people who are dead and whom I perhaps don't
even remember clearly, except that they lived and I lived among
them. I have been building up reality ever since I started walking
and now I feel that I have earned the right to do with my reality
whatever I please. My work mostly consisted of looking reality in
the eye, of always distinguishing between it and fantasy, and by and
by I learned to see not only that the borderline was fluid but also
that what people often called "reality," meaning what they could see
with their own two eyes, was only a part of the world of the senses,
because sometimes they didn't hear even the clearest and most
distinct sounds, they didn't see the simplest colors, and smells
would pass them by because they didn't recognize them. They
thought reality ceased when they went to sleep at night. They
thought that the evening prayer they memorized as a child was
some magic incantation which could be left behind the way you
discard a streamer when the party is over. When the sunset was so
beautiful as to seem hand-painted they talked about unreality, be-

cause it did not fit into their world; and their feelings, forebodings, silences or whispered words, their dreams and daydreams, they did not want to admit as reality. Is there anything that cannot be admitted as reality? Have I talked myself into a corner? So, you mean that if reality is seen as that wide, then it cannot be rejected either. No, you're right. I can reject all that I feel is not pertinent, but it is not the same as rejecting reality. I may feel that the only important thing is to be able to sit here in the laundry room, here where it is cool and fairly dark, and carry on a monologue—no, not that, we are conversing in spite of the fact that I am talking a bit more than you are. But you have just as important, if not more important, a part; you are able to make even the silence fertile and you can support them by being with them, while I am starting to glide off, I am no longer seen as quite an equal, I am starting to revert to my childhood and, if I can conjure up a smile on their faces, something has been gained after all. No, no, I am not escaping into old age; I am only trying to get along with myself. The others have to manage, and no doubt it was important that Tomas and Martin went off together and could show their togetherness in that way. Tomas has a kind of toughness in him; he will still grow. You are worried about Rosa? She is at that age when she can feel deeply rejected and maybe panics at the thought that she might actually be rejected, but her roots are too deep for her to blow over—or have I misjudged her? Because there does exist a form of disillusionment which can hit you in the neck so that you almost keel over: life is not a game without purpose; the purpose is there waiting, as a black angel or a white one—time will tell. You can't tear down heaven and earth; more likely they will tear you down until only the essence remains. What is the essence? I don't know; does anyone? To know that life is rich and important, that we hold onto life with all our might and suffer from it, and that only when we have become used to the idea that it may leave us any moment, only then will we see it, will we see its features, its lined features, the rivers and the deserts and the sweat on the brow and the eyes, and we can rejoice that at least something is left and that some hand will be groping around the blanket feeling lost, the simplest things, hunger and a glass of water, and that one has been abandoned—by God? I have felt God only in absolute silence and solitude; standing in a forest among the sunspots you can create him in your mind; you have need of someone to talk to who only answers with a kindly silence, a childhood guardian, a comfort in the direst moments. He won't still the hunger and doesn't make the poor rich, but He makes a man out of man before he storms on like a torch between heaven and hell. And this I will tell you, that fairy tales, they are the closest thing to reality I know; they are like the deepest soil we require in order to live; out of imagination all trees emerge. The visionaries, as Hannes called them, and whom he considered the first and foremost. Perhaps he felt he was something of a visionary himself; he sometimes fell so silent when we were out walking, in nature, and sometimes, but rarely, he told me one of his dreams: they always had to do with how good people were and with miracles. About how the seed of evil might be hidden inside an egg, and how it could be destroyed by the prince hurling it at the chest of the evil one. And what if the world is such an egg? What if it has to be crushed so that something better can begin to live? This earth, it is the only one we have. How can anyone believe that there will remain even one streak of light, any life at all, if the earth is crushed? God does not hold us in His hand; it is we who are holding Him. He is in the sweet smell of apples that was in these walls when I was newly married and Tomas not yet born, and my father-in-law was living and already thought that most of all I resembled an eagle. An eagle! To hear this from a walrus mustache, and me a young girl trying to divide my life between Hannes and the theatre, and succeeding! Do you know how? By early on using my eyes as a kind of digestive organ and what I saw as a basis for experience. You cannot think through things without having first seen them, really seen them—all the rough spots and how they function. I saw the women running in their long gowns; I found it

110

not only grotesque but also in an odd way confirming what I had always suspected: there is nothing in itself remarkable, ugly, upsetting, unnatural, cut off from everything else. People were running, they fell like ants, blood flowed out of their mouths, the square was strewn with bodies, snow continued to fall, people were screaming. I saw it, I learned to see it, I learned to speak inwardly, so that now I hardly know what I have been telling you and what I have been telling myself; what I probably want to get across is that a certain sense of unreality is necessary for us to live in reality, and that Tomas is about to find it out, right now. It is like meeting a god, your god, and finding out how bitter and at the same time necessary it is. Perhaps some white dove will someday rise from our ashes—like a mirage, a quite real, seen and experienced mirage, a miracle, a dream.

Tomas

Why didn't the heavy-set woman in the flowery robe pull up her stockings; why didn't she bend a bit farther down so that the wall might have caught the worst of the heat that welled in through the window and hit her where she was sitting, deep in thought, suddenly blinded and screaming? Why did the boy run out of the cool archway just then and encounter the wave in the street which picked him up and threw him against the toppling wall? The streetcar driver turned his head to the right, and everything blew apart. The child the obstetric nurse held by the feet cried out and was silenced again. The tanker *Victoria* spewed oil like a burning banner across the harbor: the metal melted, the greenery was sucked up and blackened. Why? It's Saturday and the questions come too late; the cries were emitted yesterday and they encountered a void or the finest dust, spread like sand throughout the atmosphere: a moving mass of grains of sand, facts, impulses, gestures: all already in the

111

past. Now all that remained were imprints of shadows, used-up bodies. This won't happen, you say. It will never happen. There can be no mistake of such magnitude: mistakes are made below top level, chance figures its randomness, the human hand doesn't tremble, the doublechecking is controlled by a thousand impulses. You won't burn, you won't die, you will run out into the day, no one will see you, close your eyes, no one will see you; there is no pattern here, no devilish plan to blacken the park, no punishment to the body sprawled across the bed. Try to find a pattern in these shuffling footsteps! Try to find it, in the pause right after, before the screaming starts and deafens you! There is no bestial plan, no living devil, there is not. Indeed there is no one here to give an answer. It is too late, the rooms are empty; there is only a sound echoing through the ether, shattered, as if someone from another planet were transmitting a death message; there is crackle in the ether, it is like needle sparks, as if the optical nerve of an eye were quickly picking up and spewing out as words fragments, parts of lives, lives which could then more calmly, more forcefully, more indifferently closer to the periphery continue to pacify, admonish, explain. They heard it, on the car radio, the forest gliding by, the roads circling on: "The Security Council has been called to a special meeting tonight to sort out the incidents which in the course of the past twenty-four hours have led to the death of thousands of people. A general alert has been proclaimed in large parts of the world. The Prime Minister . . ." and then disturbances, a repeated sound, like Morse code, staccato, and while Tomas felt he was sinking away from all living things he saw for a moment the road, the landscape, the branches, the leaves, smelled the car engine, smelled leather, saw Bert's hands on the steering wheel, saw like a camera everything in negative: hair, eyesockets, everything radiating out into the darkness that burst into flames before his eyes until he started living again, until life returned, June stood in full flower, and he turned around and looked at Martin and saw in the boy's eyes his own fear, and became calm.

112

Bert

Three checkpoints along the road. I see them as through the aim of a gun. I explain, Tomas is sitting silent next to me, the boy has fallen asleep in the back seat. I have the liquor in the shopping bag, the bread, the butter, the meat, all we were supposed to buy. The pipe tobacco, the vegetables, the salt and the sugar, the flour. How can there be gulls this far inland; why are they screaming as if they were circling over a gigantic garbage dump? Perhaps they are right. I explain to the police, everything is OK, tree trunks fly past. On film the wheels always go backwards. Synchronization. It may still rain tonight with that dark cloudbank across the yellowish-white sky where the clouds are passing, pregnant, expectant, birthing, soft like women. Sometimes she is like the edge of a knife, or a cut in the skin; she has to be met quite openly, firmly, while there is still time. The advantage of living as we do is that so much of the turmoil becomes merely echoes, unimportant and comical, violent or grotesque: everything is squeezed inside the television screen, while the evenings grow darker and proceed along their customary path across the fields and along the roads, of which I know every turn under any conditions. Each change a confirmation, a repetition, a habit, a sense of freedom. How quietly the car glides along the white road; it seems a bit darker already, the long hours until we can sit down to dinner. The middle of the day, at noon, that's the best time, or early in the morning, when only the birds are following the tractor, or the evenings by the sea, in the cottage, with the lamp and the table and Helena reading; then I can enter into my book, into tranquillity, be forgetful and forgotten myself, light my pipe, contemplate my life. I still feel something akin to growing pains, as if I wanted to review some more, calmly sort out confusing paths, woods that flow together or apart, secret covered drainage ditches incorrectly crisscrossing the terrain. And I want to calm her down, lie still by her side, glide into sleep along with her, inside her, and she quite tranquil by my side. Fancies! Cars rush toward me, suddenly an entire column; they tear up dust from the road, enormous colossi, gigantic, army vehicles, what are they doing here? Here! Their roar dies down and I turn onto the secondary road home. The eye follows the turns of the road, sticks to the road constantly, and that's good. The way the seasons stick together and follow one another. And we stick together and follow—or are alone, absent, away, like houses one has never seen. Tomas, tonight we will sit and talk together, we will prepare a simple feast; soon it will be Midsummer and everything is blossoming around us, don't you see! Yes, let's live as if it were the last Midsummer—as if there were no sorrows and no wars.

Helena

Anxiety was like a physical pain at the midriff. She supported herself against the sink, looked blindly inside the cupboard; there were jars, bags, to the right the dishdrainer with a few plates, the cups from this morning. Through the window came the sound of a car; it wasn't theirs, it was a heavier car, a truck at high speed, it was greenish gray, it was shaking along across the potholes; a dust-cloud reluctantly dragged behind as if risen from inside the road itself; the rain had not restrained it. From between the dissolving clouds the sun peeked out, the forest stood black. There was something wrong with her eyes: they were unfocused or magnifying; they altered the colors, pushed aside the clouds or woods; the fields they covered with an alien membrane, the air they filled with unknown particles; and did not the entire house smell of smoke from a fire? It was like the time when the houses buried in greenery suddenly burned, her home too burned, the summer, the canoe; Mom screamed when the lace curtains burst into flames in a quick hot swirl and the windowpanes exploded. Everything was concentrated in such moments, impossible to decipher, filled with a kind of confirmation: I am one of the chosen, I am one of the fragile, one

114

of those who will be thrust into the fire, but not immediately; no, first I have to be forced to understand the nature of fire. At twilight, among the tall dark trees that resisted catching fire, the house burned down in a few hours, like a roaring landslide; the things they had had time to remove were standing exposed on the gravel in front of the house. The first summer of peace, the first concrete feeling of unreality, the body maturing in leaps and bounds, the limbs stretching out, bony, the dreams confused, borderline dreams between childhood and adulthood. That was when she started wearing her hair the way she still does, combed back. They moved farther away, farther down, into poorer neighborhoods; the father had rages, the mother withdrew inside her shell, painted her face, decorated her room, turned away from reality; she had to share in it, she got her mother's share, there were cuts, blows, bloodlettings, secret, internal; she changed. There was the street, the trip to and from the office (she dropped out of school early), the vulnerability. Early on she developed traits of hardness, repelled more or less brutal propositions, met Bert at a gin-drenched party, went with him, fought him, alongside him, ignited suddenly, was unable to stop herself, screamed, wept, and went to sleep turned toward him, peacefully. I don't understand myself; all I need is to construct a clear, firm, binding scheme, a program for my life, in order not to fall and kill myself, she thought. Bert is part of that pattern. He cannot cause me to fall; he will catch me. But no one, not even Bert, could meet her fanatical demands. She had to stifle them. She walked alone and repressed them, suppressed her rebellion, turned all her efforts toward the child they were expecting. It was as if she had sucked all nutrition out of its body, used up her own child so that it could not be born; Bert was mute, touched her mutely, and she turned her face to him: "Do I still shine in the dark, do I? No . . . never more. Marry someone else. I am used up." He just held her, rocked her; she found it silly, offensive, as if she were a child: to that she could never again return, never. She turned around and supported herself against the sink with both hands.

"Are you in here?" Vera asked at the door, softly, as if she had not wanted to ask. "It wasn't them returning?" "No," she replied, "not yet. Don't worry." She looked at Vera: how she has aged—a worried matron; something derisive welled up, as if she had wanted to reveal—reveal what? Perhaps she knew about the brief unsuccessful encounter between her and Tomas. Vera sat down heavily on a chair by the kitchen table. "The radio," she said, "is speaking of a general alert all over the world—this is something bigger, more awful—and of the salvage effort; it goes more slowly, the risk of radiation. . . ." "The risk," Helena interrupted, "the risk, it's everywhere, in our skin, in the water, in the air, everywhere. It has been there for a long time already; didn't you know, just look around! This world has cancer, didn't you know? How awful it must be up north, all the dying, all the suffering. At Hiroshima they waded out in the water, stood there dying, their skin came off. . . ." Helena didn't answer, wiped her hands repeatedly on the towel, raised her hand up to her face; it smelled of washing powder. "Who is talking down there?" she asked. They listened: Max's and Grandmother's voices were barely audible, mingled, dropped into silence. As when Dad and Mom quarreled, closed the doors so she wouldn't hear. Her skin felt hot, her heart pounded; would one of them kill the other? She saw them lying in pools of blood; she sat up in bed hardly daring to breathe; the lamp buzzed beneath the red shade; her narrow corner was like a lonely ship threatened by black torrents of rain, by storms, by pirates; you couldn't be safe from anyone. Even the ties to Dad and Mom broke off; all it took was Mom shouting to her: "You always take his side!" And in her wilted face she discovered an alien, cold, violent glimpse of hate because she had locked herself up, remained mute for several days. In the silence only the screams of the swallows could be heard; they flew like shadows across the graveled area and were gone again in the pale afternoon. Vera sat silently, her face in her hands. Helena went and stood next to her, stroked her blond hair; it felt quite dead and rough. The dog came out into the kitchen, looked at them, turned

116

its face to the window, then lay down with its head between its paws. "Will you set the table?" Helena asked. Both of them could hear the faint sound of a car engine; Vera looked up, they looked at each other as if they had simultaneously exposed themselves: all their anxiety, all that they had in common, everything that had filled them when they thought they were at their emptiest—it all rushed in, a longing, a need to be close, to live. They called out simultaneously, hurried to the window; it was the right car, it was an ordinary June afternoon. "We have to set the table!" they shouted, "we've been wasting time!" They rushed past each other; from the stairs Max's steps could be heard, already tired, old; they took out the dishes, started setting the table; sunspots, shadows were hovering, the front door opened, a fresh wind swept through the room; beneath all this lay their anxiety like a heavy treacherous foundation. It wasn't possible to explain. It was mute. It took no time, because it neither required nor used up time. It was there, like a disease just taking hold yet fully visible. Like something crawling about in the room, on the skin, on the cheek. To those who hadn't felt it, one couldn't point at it and say: "look, there it is again, reborn, in its entirety." No, it couldn't be explained. Not to those who had never cowered in a heap. That is why the dead were silent and shared the silence with the dying, the living. Surprisingly few were complaining loudly in the midst of all the stink, the dirt, the broken rubble. No, most of it was mute. There was nothing more to say. If one had grown up with it, one might say: "there it is, I recognize it." But most did not recognize it, did not listen for it; it came, it grew clandestinely or quite openly—the hate, the conviction, the strength. There were no forebodings here, no contacts like a scream in the dark, no explanations. It could not be explained, nor did it need to be explained. Few were listening. Mostly all was mute. Only the insects—the flies, the mosquitoes, and the other bugs—were making a lot of noise, as if they were wild with anger. In large dense swarms they sang, as if jerkily rushing on, carried by their own movements, like clouds driven by the strong wind. Their

117

existence could be explained. The dead did not defend themselves. The dying did not defend themselves. That was all. Nothing else. Mute. The defeated knew it: that they had been defeated.

Rosa

How strangely and catastrophically outside appearance and internal secrets have collided in me. What I am I do not know. I am the certain knowledge of these two images. It's dripping, it's flowing out of me, out of my large mouth, out of my broad body, out of my small eyes, all that I have seen and experienced; it assumes odd colors, it makes me laugh or secretly cry; cynicism is like scouring powder for my soul: if I rub off the pig's bristle a shining staring doll's face is revealed, with curly hair, with stuffed stitched limbs. The one who occupied my bed far into the teens, like a kind of proof that I could never really grow up, didn't want to grow up. And was forced to grow up, and enjoyed being forced, and stored up everything: all I saw, all the trips I took, all that Max offered me. There was a wealth in everything—in the teacup, in the clothes, in the intercourse, in the fear, in the love. At times this multifariousness disgusted me, but that was what nurtured me, made me see clearly, too clearly, and hence forced me into the part that became mine: that of the red rain, the quick colorful capers, the mild philosophy of life dressed in attractive bitter cynicism. Max saw through it, all the way down to the girl with the doll face, the woman in the maze, the battle between the desire to possess and the perfect, pure, placid chastity that no external force can touch. Thorny rose, sharp wind, sea: I have the agility, not in my clumsy body but in my soul. Whatever the soul is: perhaps a glance, perhaps somebody else's, perhaps a bird shot in flight, perhaps the dew in the meadow, perhaps the beauty in ugliness. Perhaps it feeds on disasters. There are pyromaniacs who torch themselves. With his hand Max gives me solace. By existing he gives me faith. I will grow old ungracefully but digni-fied, like some old dancer of Toulouse-Lautrec's, and I will die quite chaste, happy and pure. I have dispelled from my body everything nasty such as rejoinders, grimaces, cynicisms, to the wide and colorful world where I am like the shadow-play under an enormous glimmering tree. They believe I say just what I think. But behind the picture there is always another picture, that other one, the silent one, the receptive one. Circuses, bread: the circus as bread. The only thing bothering me is my awkward body. I would like to be a tightrope dancer, show physical agility (oh! with Max I can do that, too) to a horrified, trembling, laughing, enthusiastic crowd, but a measure of exhaustion has entered into me, my foot slips, I fall: it's not showing under the makeup. I wouldn't at all have minded playing against old Grandmother; in no time I would have caught up with her twenty-year advantage in technique and experience. Yes, you must be quick, inwardly quick and ready, have a quick tongue, have a quick eye, be quick in the giving, quick in the taking, quick in the forgiving. Stop, go on, use your eyes carefully. See Max at the window, the ugly tapestry on the wall: "The Lord is my shepherd, I shall not want." See the words, see the Lord, see myself as a lamb, see the wool, see the meadow, hear the bleating, be calm and happy. Follow the wind, but be aware of its direction. Be able to stop. Be able to leave everything behind but the heart. My heart, as if I had two, one under each breast, both alike, one for him, one for the world, the world with forests and seas and living, suffering people, the world with hunger and death, with children, with everything, with good food, good drink, friendship. Calm evenings, evenings for listening. Flowers, white fragrant jasmine in an old brown glass jar at the window. Sleep well, without dreams.

Max

The years, it seemed to him, were utterly mixed up in his life, so that he barely remembered when he got married, when he lost the

119

child, when they went to Tanganyika, when he lost the last vestiges of faith, and yet continued living, continued to show tenderness—the only thing. Derisive yet mild, hostile yet coolly indifferent, life was tugging at him from now one, now the other direction, tossing him from one extreme to the other, yet permitting quiet observation. How had he got here, so far from the ancient origins, here where he stood looking at Rosa? Everything seemed to him without order yet predestined, pointless yet with some hidden purpose, as if he had all the time been standing by his own deathbed listening to his own barely discernible breathing, and had known that he was going to survive them all, all of them!—as long as he kept silent, as long as he realized that he was dying every minute, that every action revealed a glimpse of his skeleton, the cranium, the seams of the skull, and that beneath he had it all stored away: the vaguest memories of backyards, of hot dark rooms, the slush on the hard school steps, the fear, the shame, the humiliation, the love: cool waters glittering between silent tree trunks, somewhere at some shore, but when? when? where was it? whose was the living arm around his shoulders, perhaps now dead, turned to dust: he couldn't remember. He remembered the clear May morning Mother died, her quick breathing, quicker and quicker, the sudden silence: a roar of voices all around him; he wanted to fall down on his knees and pray, to whom? The Lord Our Shepherd? Yes, to him. Silence, emptiness. And through the tears all the scruffy treetops blowing and thrashing about against the sky; there was an echo, life was offering its day, the echoing hallways at Diedrichsen & Co., where the light always seemed to go out, the smell of carbon paper, the odor, the stench from all those who had been shot and were lying in the snowy slushy streets, the big engine house full of oilspots and the cable system, where each step had died or had the hard sound of metal. And outside: the light, the day brimming over, every beach a discovery, every rock a sign—it wasn't so long ago, it happened yesterday, he had gone down to the beach; it would still happen, he stood so close to his childhood, like two horses in

120

a green pasture; down on the beach the children are playing and Rosa is getting out of the water; she is pregnant; she is lying still, free of all anxiety, calm; she opens her eyes, looks at him: she is unfamiliar, close like all the rest, mixed up in memory. For this, to reach this, for this moment he has lived, exerted himself, struggled on, bent over the drafting table during dark lonely nights, produced inventions, been victorious, won, served, deserved, loved, mourned, been silent. Here, right now, he experienced a fervent sensation of loss, the loss of those who had died, the life that had been lost, and facing the future he felt only emptiness. What was holding him here? Rosa? He looked again at her face, a faint smile, the eyes closed: this, too, he could give up. Was there besides himself, his skin, his limbs, his pumping heart, anything else keeping him here? The eyes, the heart, the limbs, the thought like a needle attached to the eye: was that all! It was a matter of indifference. The mouth that spoke the words, the hand that touched and caressed, the thoughts that meandered: indeed he was without a self, without needs, free; a reflection upon a wall, a voice disappearing, a path into an autumn day along which no one walks: no, there was a child he was trying to protect, who looked through his eyes out at the road, who was growing old inside him, unchanged, continuing to live, a rock in his hand like a sign, and he, walking that road, in memory or beyond memory, focused on the living and because of this focus calmer, less afraid, less and less attached to himself, his voice, his life only a temporary disguise, the anguish only a figure on the sidelines. Soon, soon he would glide off, like a boat gliding off at night, unfastened by whomever, disappearing, empty, under the sky.

Martin

I stick close to the wall. I am carrying a machine gun. There is no other way out of this. I zigzag between the drums and keep firing. I throw myself into the car when it has already started moving. We drive quickly out of the city; the street corners we round on two wheels. We see the road reeling in and out in front of the windshield. "Faster," I hiss. Slowly we leave the pursuers behind us. I look back: only a truck rattling along and growing smaller. Might they have arranged a roadblock? Yes, there! We slow down; I sit and stare rigidly ahead. They are in disguise. The men in the front seat are in disguise. I am taken away. What if I threw myself out of the door? No, it's too late. I will be thrown into a dark room with a stone floor. They tie my hands. Slowly I lie down on the floor; there is a smell of gasoline. If someone put a match to anything it would go up in flames, shrivel up. I don't want to grow up; I want to stay the same, always.

Tomas

He remembered her voice. He remembered her tense neck, and the way Helena had turned over on her stomach in the dark. He remembered how she had cried out at the moment of orgasm, and how he had lost his desire, had withdrawn, lain panting, sick, inwardly moaning, with angry lightspots dancing before the open blinded eyes. "Did I startle you," she asked. He didn't answer; he lay imagining himself away from everything connecting him to this room, to this bed, and he tried to eject her from his consciousness, eject Vera as well: this was he himself alone; there was nothing to fill him, only the contact with Helena's body, the sweat, the silence in which both were lying and both realizing that this was their sole, revealing, casual, never erasable encounter, indifferent, filled with loneliness, passion, and thirst for tenderness, now just an episode from which he—above all he—wanted to escape. The next morning he got up as if he had finally awakened, cleansed himself, and he dived from the landing into the water, down into its depths, as if the bay, the coolness, the morning could wipe out everything and make him new and whole. The morning had never seemed so clear, so worthy of love, and even Helena, now forever placed on the

122

outside, seemed closer to him. In the evening they sat talking together; it was a quiet conversation with long silences, and they understood that they would never again be so close, and they were overcome by a tenderness for each other; they were satisfied with the words and the silences, went to their respective rooms, slowly lost the memory of each other, so that the face he was trying to recall remained just a dark splotch. Only the eyes he could remember distinctly: their smile, the hesitation, the isolation which was part of her and which she would never be able to accept. Or perhaps now—facing this; faced with pressure, force and extinction, perhaps then. Was this necessary in order for them to realize the fragility of their own limits and the fact that they were needed by a wide, ever-widening circle? He had always known it. From the raindrop, from the grain of sand, he told himself. From there. From the smallest. From tenderness for the part, tenderness for the whole must start. From the observed, the experienced, the seen, what is picked up in the blood, from every act with a simple, forgotten, vital meaning—the mother offering the breast, the man placing his right hand under his cheek as he goes to sleep, the grandmother slicing bread in the kitchen in the evening, the boy running home along the street, the swaying lanterns with their dull cold shine— from the lips that move, the movements of the eye, from the hand rummaging in the worn purse, the trembling head of the old woman, her face as lined as a world, the globe, shaking, shaking, all alone: they could change it, change everything, and nothing could frighten them anymore if only they emerged from their compartments. Was it so? The moment he opened the door, he was afraid that not Vera but Helena would be the first one he met. It was Vera; they embraced quickly: "Have you heard . . . ?" and he replied, "Yes." And he added: "We must stay calm; you and the boy will have to rely on me." He didn't hesitate; her body responded, as if she had heard it through the clothing. Startled, they smiled briefly at each other.

123

Pulled out of an aching womb, wiped off, washed, nourished, rocked to sleep, slowly taught to see, walk, slowly seeing, thinking, dressed, helped along, addressed, answered, sent off, brought back, comforted, provoked, calmed down, directed, forgiven, abandoned, humiliated, strengthened, elevated, forgotten, rediscovered, accepted, ignored, exposed, loved, despised, hated, declared unfit, pushed aside, isolated, condemned, killed, buried, obliterated, out of nothingness, into nothingness.

They were sitting together until evening came, each one talking with the others and with himself, or silently contemplating the reflection of the four white candles on the bottles and the glasses. On the table with the dark blue tablecloth were set white plates and high sturdy transparent glasses. The frost on the vodka bottle was becoming striped; the herring jars were emitting a sweet, appetizing smell which mingled with the odor of warm potatoes, dill and candlewax. The thin white net curtains had been pulled; behind them one could faintly make out a pale, deepening sky and the treetops. On the opposite side the door was open to the porch and the sea. After dinner they had slowly prepared for a late evening together. They had packed the necessary stuff into baskets, had loaded them into the cars, and about eight o'clock had driven down to the beach. Martin was elated; he carried baskets, blankets, and rattling bottles until his thin arms ached. Down by the shore the tree trunks, tall and silent, had a warm red glow; the grass grew tall, the bees were still buzzing, and a pale white sliver of a moon swayed like a sharply chiseled cloud above the islands and the bay. They took both rowboats, spoke in a low voice, and experienced a wordless, warm, calm, kindred feeling: everything in this landscape was close and familiar to them, every pull at the oar well known, every landing place habitual from years ago, every hand movement obvious. They disappeared into the shadows on the island, reemerged close to the cliffs, turned in toward the cottage, and unlocked the door. Bert went in first; Tomas followed. The women sat for awhile on the porch catching their breath. Grandmother was placed in a chair, and everyone inquired about her health. Older people have white faces, lined and tired, Martin thought. He took the air rifle, broke it expertly, put in a bullet, and took aim. The old tea jar stood there from the summer before, on the edge of the big oak stump; at the center of the stump red meal had collected; Martin held it in his hand; it was like planting-seed, and still warm from the sun. In the dell darkness was growing out of every barely visible branch; it climbed up the tree trunks, tried to catch the birds: some sparrows, a few noisy crows, farther out to sea in the light from the water the screaming or silently gliding gulls. He took fifteen steps back and aimed. There was a twanging sound; the jar fell down in the dry grass. Daisies grew there, small and pure like white eyes; he bent down and started picking. From the cottage voices could be heard, a door closing, a warm flickering light from the oil lamp which threw large black shadows up at the tarred roof. Grandmother was looking out across the bay thinking of all the summers she had spent here with Grandfather, with Hannes, how he had come silently rowing after midnight with the catch of the evening, and how they had sat on the cliffs together cleaning the fish: roaches, perches, maybe a pike caught on a ledger-tackle in the low waters that were now so quietly catching the depths of the sky. Everything felt oddly close and unfamiliar, something gone forever and yet painfully continuing to live: she had to swallow. Vera and Helena spread out the blue tablecloth; Rosa had lit the oil lamp with no shade in the kitchen and was inspecting the glasses from the summer before, wiping them off with paper. Each with a pair of buckets, Tomas and Bert walked down to the well. The dog which in the boat had sat absolutely still looking at the open sea was running around in the grass with its nose to the ground; Max came with wood for the open fireplace. "Don't carry too heavy a load," said Grandmother. He stopped and smiled. They listened: inland, from somewhere in the dark woods, the cuckoo could be heard. It cuckooed eight times: "a lifetime for both of us," said Max. "Or a day," she replied, the old woman, her face deep in shadow. "Yes, a day," he said as quietly. He went inside, came out again and sat down; tall and taciturn, he leaned against the log wall and watched the sunset. Down in the dell the reeds were standing so tall they hid the sea. The water in the well felt cold against the wrist; Tomas brushed back his hair with a wet hand; deep down in the well the falling water echoed. "We could have immersed the bottles down by the landing," said Bert. "This is more convenient," said Tomas. "Hey, we didn't bring the radio." "No," said Bert, "we forgot it." For an instant they looked at each other. Two heavy, already aging faces, marked by nakedness, certainty and answers received. Bert bent down, picked up his buckets and led the way back to the cottage. I have been walking this path as long as I can remember, he thought; I might have worn it down more than anyone else. I have come out here, alone, on cold winter days when the trees were standing oddly bare, and the driving snow whirled around summer's hidden skerries: now everything is familiar again; summer is my season, I want to die with it. No—not die, live on. Uphill Tomas saw Martin and called to him. He had nothing much to say to him just then, only wanted the boy to stay close to him, asked something unimportant. At the same time his eye was receiving an uninterrupted stream of impressions, colors, smells all around him: he longed for the hour when twilight and light balance each other, when the voices are muffled but retain their tranquil rhythm, their connections: thus life ought to be—a conversation carried on at dusk among people close to one another. Not that they couldn't be strangers; he recalled a moment when his entire life seemed to depend on a single visual impression: how once a boat was passing; a woman sitting in the aft looked straight at him and he at her; they followed each other with their eyes. He was maybe twenty; he knew that she meant everything to him; he could still remember her light dress, but he never found out her name. He lived, he was active; on evenings like this he remembered her, like an image, a longing. The unattainable! He no longer sought it, he looked closer to home; now he was happy at the water splashing on his foot, the sound of

126

dry leaves under the oaks, Martin's light voice answering, all those close to him moving about in front of the fluttering candles on the set table, beyond the window which had captured the sky, the red clouds, the pewter-smooth surface of the bay. Like shadows of screams, the noise of the gulls rose out of the broad billowing reed fields at the mouth of the river; from the other side of the island they could hear the snort of a motorboat; then it died down again. "Well, my silent angel," Rosa said and placed her hand on his shoulder, "where are you dreaming of escaping to now?" "Nowhere," he replied. "I have escaped and come all the way here, and here I'm going to stay." "Don't you also doubt the safety of this place, all the tranquillity—the people, the water, even the sky treacherously beautiful, or what do you think? Doesn't it make you worried? You have always been the one to get up suddenly and leave the table; as a boy you used to do it; we never knew where you went, what you were thinking; you returned and seemed unchanged. Isn't everything unreal, shadowy and swiftly disappearing?" Rosa asked. She added: "That sounds solemn, but I am in that kind of a mood tonight; I want to play that part tonight, I want to be myself, I want to ask questions, chat, reminisce, as if I were forcing myself to hold on"; she looked away. Vera called to Tomas from the cottage. "Wait a minute!" he replied and said to Rosa: "What swiftly disappears isn't unreal, shadowy. Precisely because it is quickly erased it lives, here, close to us. Look around you. We know every stone here, and rocks—ask Max—live a curious life: mute on the outside, full of life on the inside; unchanged, eternal, layered life. Sure, it's treacherous and fragile; it mocks the entire world order. So let us also mock the world order: if we can't change it, we ourselves can at least steer another course, straight into evening, straight into the sunset." He stopped talking. Fanlike, the waves flowed out behind the black motorboat rushing into the dark space between the islands and disappearing; soon the water rustled against the rocks on the shore; Martin stood with his white legs in the lapping waves. How small he is, Vera thought as she came out on the porch and passed Tomas; they said nothing but felt each other's closeness. At the sink Helena pushed the hair off her forehead; she had loosened it, and it fell over her face. Tomas pushed it to the side and gave her a kiss on the cheek. Helena turned around and smiled: "ready for supper?" "Yes," he said, "and hungry as a wolf, in spite of dinner. Should we have heated the sauna?" Helena turned down the lamp wick; it became dim and quiet, and both remembered their encounter, their lack of success, the loneliness they shared. They knew they remembered; Helena held his arm briefly, then went in to Bert and Max in the big room, where they sat talking in a low voice. "What are you talking about?" she asked. "About farming," replied Bert, "about planting seed, new methods, about our mutual mother earth." "The earth," said Max, "must sooner or later be allowed to renew itself, not by chemical means but by being allowed to rest in a sensible way and then having natural manure mixed in. I once invented a plow that had movable rotating plowshares—a crazy thing which might have been a hit at an art show in the twenties." He stopped talking, looked out the window. "There are no cows left," said Bert. "There're fewer and fewer fish. There are hardly any horses, and sheep used to graze here on the island fifteen years ago, but not since then." "You certainly are earthbound," said Helena. "You have to cut yourselves loose, gentlemen. You have to learn to fly; you must accept that the earth is fragile; we have to be able to find shelter up there, on the moon." She pointed; between the dark treetops the moon was rocking to and fro, pale and small, immensely far away. The dog entered quietly, walked around the room, and then lay down by the door and watched them. "You have to help me with the jars," said Helena. "I am being quite useless," said Max; "may I?" "With pleasure," she replied. Bert went out on the porch, lit his pipe slowly and painstakingly. Martin was standing there, thin, with bare legs, the bunch of daisies on his arm. "Everywhere they are on the run," he said; "the field mice have dug tunnels all over the island; suppose water will slowly seep into them and the island will sink like a sponge?"—he laughed. "The island won't sink; on the contrary, it rises," answered Bert. "When Daddy and I were boys, the water almost crossed the island and there was only a narrow isthmus joining this part with that one over there. Ask Helena to find a vase and place the flowers in the middle of the table; they are beautiful. Daisies, wild chervil, those are my flowers. And also lilacs." "And limewort," added Martin. "Yes, limewort," Bert answered. "And wild roses," said Grandmother. "Earlier there were enormous thickets of them, on the way up, by the big cliff. Where have they disappeared?" "The wild things disappear, Grandmother dear," said Rosa; "nature becomes civilized, fits in with the architecture; confusion is replaced by order, crooked roads by straight ones; only among people is confusion allowed to reign, confusion, disruption, hate—no, let's not talk about that. Not on an evening like this. Look, the Evening Star, if it is the Evening Star. Happy and blessed you are, in Heaven among the stars." Her voice seemed to break; for a moment everyone was quiet. Martin turned around, started walking down to the landing. "We'll eat in a minute," Vera called. "Don't go far!" Martin turned around. "Star!" he called, "Star! Come!" The dog came through the door, ran softly down the stairs, and disappeared at his heels round the cliff. Vera and Helena went inside. "Tomas," said Grandmother, "do you think the boy is scared?" "Who isn't?" said Bert, "and the one who isn't I feel somehow sorry for: he is blind." "Martin has inherited my anxiety," said Tomas; "it didn't come from you, Grandmother, rather more from Father." "I was only scared on opening nights," replied Grandmother. "Only of them. But as soon as the curtain went up, I became calm. I thought: we have to make it. I have to make it. Come hell or high water." "Did anything go wrong?" Bert asked, "did anything ever go wrong?" "Certainly, certainly it did," Grandmother replied; "some little things went wrong, but never anything crucial." "When you stopped, didn't it go wrong then?" asked Tomas. She hesitated, then said: "No . . . I knew what I was doing. I gave it up for something more important." "Let us," said Max, "let us then one day give up all this—people, togetherness, summer evenings, calm bays, bird calls, experiences, dreams, glasses and bottles—let us give it up, for something more important. Perhaps there really is something more important for which we will give it up. Perhaps we will be making room for something totally new, growing out of the bedrock, something we have forgotten and lost and betrayed; perhaps we have to go in order for something new to grow. Like a seed from some seed pine being carried on the wind, whirling around in space, perhaps from that star, and the seed falls upon the scorched earth. . . ." He stopped speaking; they sat in silence. Two ducks flew silently along the water's surface, alighted with beating wings; the water barely made an audible splash; they floated in among the shadows of the reeds. Helena stood at the door: "Come and eat! Everything is ready. Would someone find Martin?" Tomas got up, walked down toward the landing. Martin was sitting there with a fishing rod, the dog beside him. "Are the fish biting," asked Tomas. The boy shook his head. Both of them watched the floater, which in the faint breeze seemed to be always floating farther away among the leaflike narrow wave shadows, as if all the time lazily carried off by a giant fish; an optical illusion, reflections. "Come!" said Tomas, "we are going to eat." "I'm not hungry," Martin said quietly, his hair shining pale above the thin neck. "Come, we want to have you with us at the table," said Tomas. "Why?" asked the boy stubbornly. "Don't you want to?" asked Tomas and stroked his hair, left his hand on Martin's cheek for a moment. Martin struggled to his feet and followed him into the shadows of the island where the light from the windows shone pale, honey yellow, and where the voices emerged as if interrupted, echoes, shuffled by some hidden Player holding their cards. He shuffles us, he deals us out, thought Tomas. What have we done, what has the boy done to be discarded, to be put aside, if that will indeed happen; what kind of revenge is this? He stopped, pulled air into his lungs: no! I can already feel the rough warming taste of the shot of vodka; that is enough. The evening, the twilight, the screams of the gulls, Vera by my side and the boy, that is enough. "Wait," he said to Martin. "Wait for me. Let's go fishing later, after eating?" "Don't I have to go to bed?" Martin asked, the narrow oval of his face pale in the slowly fading light. "No, you won't have to. Not tonight. We could try it before the nightly north wind, out by the peak." They saw through the window the others already sitting at the table; they were talking, their shadows moving, hands passing plates; for a moment Tomas and Martin stood looking in. Then Tomas pulled open the door—fluttering candles, the smell of food, the welcoming voices; here were their places, two empty chairs by Vera; they sat down quickly. It's almost like Christmas, or Midsummer, Martin thought. We are having a party! He was filled with a strong, quick, sudden feeling of bliss. It was like a gull suddenly flying, straight up, straight at the sky, in order to hurl itself again to the water's surface, and rise again, quick as a flash. Tomas looked around: when we live, we live in these moments, these evenings. He raised his glass to the others; they smiled and the meal began. They passed plates; the dill spread its warm June fumes around them, which mingled with the reflexes on the glasses, the frothing beer, the vodka in the small green goblets; their eyes started to shine; Grandmother began reminiscing about the theater. "Poverty, growing pains, loneliness—those have shaped me," said Helena vehemently but stopped when Bert placed his hand on hers. Between their feet, under the table, lay the dog; now and then a low growl could be heard, a sign of contentment. "Disasters come conveniently for us," said Rosa; "we will escape from something bigger, something more awesome." "What? what?" asked Vera. "Your body," Grandmother answered dryly. "Yes, it too. But not only that. We will escape from faith, certainty, duty, distinction. Why not say it outright?—from God," said Bert. "I approach God only when alone, or on rare occasions when someone has written a word that hits home." "Hear, hear," Helena shouted, "Bert is giving his Sunday sermon." But Bert went on: "Do you recall Zosima's older brother who died at seventeen—his faith, his rare joy, how absorbed he was in everything, how humble, how guilt-ridden, how forgiving?" The conversation faltered; Tomas continued Bert's train of thought: "Markel, the brother, dies like the summer does, is revived like the spring. Vera, if no more spring came, would you regret your life? Would anyone?" "Yes," Helena answered, "I regret that I was bitter for so long, without help, and that others stay bitter for so long and don't get help. We are sitting in our shimmering glass world, the wind is picking up outside, listen! The trees are billowing; soon they will be pulled up by their roots, soon they will be whirling around; darkness will sweep through us, through the room; half-empty bottles, the dirty plates, and your pipe smoke will disappear as if it never existed; we will be carried off in a whirl." She sat down, bent her head. "Come," said Vera, "let's go outside to cool off." Helena shook her head: "Let me be." "You mentioned *The Brothers Karamazov*," said Max, and his tall dry agile body leaned forward; the shadow on the wall behind him shrank; beyond the window Tomas could see stars like sharp pricks of a needle. "Do you recall Ivan's declaration of love for life?—'Even if I lost my faith in life, even if I lost my faith in the woman I loved, in the world order, even if . . . even if instead I became convinced that everything is damned—no, in disorder, damned, maybe in devilish chaos— indeed, even if I suffered all the horrors of human disappointment, I would still want to live.'" "But Ivan is speaking of the thirst for life before he is thirty," Tomas shouted; "after that he doesn't want to live any longer." "It makes no difference," said Max. "To love life more than the meaning of life, that is faith not tied to age. To love, despise, hate, grow close together in the flowerbed of life and breed more life together. Listen!" They stopped talking and listened; close by an owl was hooting, the island owl: a black hole in the cool whisper of the trees. It seemed to Martin that he had slept intermittently and dreamed, and he watched the fluttering candles, then leaned heavily against Tomas and asked, "when do we go fishing?" "Now!" said Tomas. As they wound their way down to the shore, they saw the women sitting next to each other, chatting in low voices. "Of course I understood that he was unhappy," said Vera, "that he was trying to break loose. . . . It wasn't only that. Like me he thought that sensuality was a value in itself, that only through experiencing could we—well, liberate ourselves, experience the world around us as new." "What fancies!" said Helena. "We didn't get close to them. We didn't get close to each other. We only got close to ourselves. I'm nauseated by the picture. It also frightens me. But if I watch myself closely, perhaps I will be transformed, acquire wings and feathers, spread out in all my splendor, distribute my beauty freely." "I have so seldom dared," said Vera. "It's too late; I can't change anything. I can't disturb the heavenly order; others do it better. To be, to act . . ." Their eyes followed a dark bird soundlessly gliding across the sky. Martin saw it too: "Look!" Tomas looked. "It may have been a hawk," he said. "They sometimes glide on the wind, circle around and around until they finally hurl themselves down to catch their victim." And he thought of Ivan, what he had said about the children, about their suffering, and the fact that if truth had to be bought at such a price it wasn't worth it. What harmony can there be if hell exists? What kind of love can there be if such hate exists that all love, all the small despised human ties are severed by—by whom? By God? God's will, or that of men? This self-destruction, beyond all balance, this hate, this wish to torture—he had felt it himself. He felt it himself. Christ felt it. God—who was he? But Christ experienced it, the pain, the rebellion, the humiliation, the poverty, the derision, the persecution, the vinegar, the ultimate solitude. And the resurrection. Who would move aside the stones from the front of their unknown graves? He shivered, told Martin: "Come, now it's time for bed." And he called to Vera: "Martin has to go to bed!" While he walked up toward the cottage with the boy—always the same path, the same light shining, the same voices welcoming them—he mumbled to himself, again and again: "All is confusion, except in me. All. Also in me," he said half-aloud. With wide-open eyes he gazed across the landscape, the bay, pale as milk, the silence filled with a high, barely audible, mighty and vast note. "Do you hear it?" he asked. Vera listened. It was as if someone were calling—they did not know who or from which direction. Whether for joy or in peril, they did not know. They turned and went inside. The wind picked up, bluish-black waves among the shore shadows, agitation among the rocks, across the bay a window where the light went out. Helena stood still for a moment, her face turned to the wind. Bert came out to her. "Say something," she said. But he did not reply, just pulled her close. "It isn't enough, it isn't," she mumbled, her face against his chest. "What isn't enough?" he asked. "Look around. Listen to them speaking inside. Is that not enough?" "No," she replied, "it isn't enough. It doesn't stop anything. It doesn't change anything." "And if you now had a child, wouldn't it distress you even more?" he asked quietly. Helena closed her eyes, crept close to him; the tears welled out, slow, hot, reluctant. The night turned, unnoticed, into day.

The lamp calmly burns on the long table made of broad dark boards. Near dawn its light pales and soon can no longer be seen. But no one sees it; no one is sitting at the table anymore.

SUNDAY

It makes no difference where I start, because I shall return there.

Max

Max went out. The voices floated like shadows out into the summer night. They rose and sank. He stood by the tree thinking that an old man does the best he can. He shakes his large organ. Slowly life is running out of him; no semen runs in anymore. The heartburn can be felt all the way down. Yet I'm only a few years past sixty. My self-pity I will hide between a couple of oaks on an island. All, all of us deserve to live, are worthy of it. He bent his head back and saw through the branches isolated weak stars. The earth was swaying a bit. His thoughts glided by; he was unable to hold onto them. "It's late," his mouth said quietly. Late. Martin, I feel so sorry for Martin. If I could bargain with you, a life for him alone, I would do it. Great Avenger! Aren't you tired of sacrifices! He lowered his eyes, took a few steps in the grass, fell heavily down on his knees; no words came out. Nearby a duck took to its wings with a quacking, along the water's surface. He listened to it until the sound died out.

The world at dusk with its treacherously soft contours, its surface of beauty, its grass, is floating through limitless space: a star, a weak signal in a sea of hard-to-interpret, searching, faraway voices. Loved, hated by those who lived there and prepared its fate, it lived for a moment in eternity, then went out like an oil lamp when the wick is first turned up, then slowly lowered, until the room with those keeping vigil is only darkness, silence, and night.

Tomas

The night is calm, as if it were holding its breath before an expected violent eruption. Tomas stands for a moment alone in the dark looking out at the calm bay, the strips of pale water like molten tin between the tightly growing reeds, and closer to the shore an area of water mirroring the tranquil sky. Soon we won't be seeing this anymore; someone else (maybe Martin) will walk in the grass, will remember us for a fleeting moment, then return to these same rooms, perhaps to the same smell of cigarette smoke, open beer bottles, half-eaten tins of sardines, while the oaks, the birches, the alders along the shore slowly move their branches and leaves—for whose enjoyment, for what receptive senses? Or are my middle-aged nervetips only now, and at rare moments, sensing all that has not yet been completed, feelings that have been hidden and, with an undercurrent of melancholia, are searching for a response among the silent patient movements, those of the winds, the people, the earth? He went back inside. In the open fireplace hard brown oak chunks were burning with a clear ring. Vera had located an old transistor radio; emanating from it in a weak, burry tone was some unfamiliar, romantic, unidentifiable, songlike music based on old folk-music themes—maybe Russian?—performed slowly, fiddlerlike, by a quartet or quintet. Vera was listening to it. Tomas sat down across from her; they looked at each other, looked into each other, as if here, now, they wanted to tell each other what they had never before been able to shape into words and what even now remained unsaid; they would remember this moment as physically real, more physically real than the moments of intercourse and lust.

136

A voice was speaking, he caught the words "Borodin," "special news report," "the extremely tense situation all over the world has led to a series of mobilizations which, according to the U.N. Secretary General, has brought the world to a threshold beyond which it would be catastrophic . . ." Sudden silence. They waited; the silence continued. He turned the dial, found only weak confused echoes, voices from a faraway alien world, a world living inside them and filling them up, a world they fought and sometimes forgot. "We have to rest," Vera said. She got up, touched his cheek with her hand and disappeared into the dark dressing room. It's late, it's early, he thought, early, soon dawn.

Gran

A few warmly dressed children stood in the square watching the Punch-and-Judy show. It was cold. I approached reluctantly; they turned around, glanced at me without expression, then continued to stare. They were dressed in felt boots, in coats that appeared to have been dug out of old army surplus stores; out of closely wrapped scarves their faces were sticking up like cabbages. I turned my attention to the stage. Two deformed men, almost giants, doing battle: oh, how they were hitting each other, and from the invisible director came screams, moans, shouts. What a fistfight! How attentively we all watched. People quietly crossed the windy square with its narrow rills of blown snow; all of us stood silently watching how with a stranglehold one of the giants slowly forced the other to his knees, flipped him backwards, and then, with a big knife, cut off his head—all this dreamlike, farther and farther away.

Tomas

The Reaper, the Gardener, the Man with the Scythe—what kind of forlorn, shabby creatures are those struggling up the dry grassy

137

slope toward me, breathing hard and shouting: "Wait for me! Wait for me!" What kind of ridiculous worn-out clothes are they wearing?—clothes that seem oddly familiar, my own discarded ones. The Gardener in some kind of golf pants from my teens, light brown, almost grotesque; the Reaper squeezed into an old blazer from my student days with holes on the cuffs and the elbows; the Man with the Scythe in a broad-brimmed hat, like a make-believe vagabond. All three give the impression of impoverished amateur actors; and their tools are rusty—an old hoe, a scythe held together with wire and not in touch with a grindstone for decades! They waddle along as if straight out of a nightmare, with the unsteady gait of old men, trouser seats drooping, faces unshaven, panting, emaciated: "Wait for me! No, for me!" I haven't asked them here; I don't know them; I don't want to have anything to do with them; I hate their insistence, their filthy beseeching yet threatening countenances. If I were a giant, if I were God the Giant, I would pick up a boulder and crush them, the way you crush insect pests, vermin. . . . I do not know them! I turn around there, on top of the hill, and return half-running; I increase the pace; I hear their puffing and panting fade out; I run between the first tree trunks into the dark forest where my steps vanish soundlessly in the silence and the coolness. Only my own breathing disturbs the peace, the almost solemn high devotion. I sink down in the moss close to a clear dark spring; I look at it blindly. Suddenly it becomes lighter; I look up: a cloud, an enormous cloud covers the sky, as if a membrane were drawn across my eyes, and I jerk back and look into nothingness, see nothing. Faintly I sense that branches are breaking; I hear confused voices, familiar panting, close enough to paralyze. I sink backward, as if someone were twisting my face and pulling it down toward the silent cold ground; mustering my last resources, I open my mouth and seem to shout, "This way! Here I am! Over here!" and I see them bending over me, observing me, as if they always knew that I would call them; they wipe the sweat off their brows; they bring their faces closer to my face; it is as if they were trying to follow the movements of my lips, while my eyes look past them at the cloud, the cloud.

The recruits are far too young. First they think they are seeing a Western; then they throw up, become useless, have to be carried off along with the bodies. And the older ones . . . did they think this was a continuation of the Second World War? Where all this damn mud is coming from the Devil only knows—a muddier lake I have never seen. And not a single one is really prepared. What good are civil defense courses if nothing works when it is needed? What's the point in piling blood plasma, blankets, and food in a field while some damned study commission struts around in protective clothing taking notes: "Most interesting"? The few doctors we have are exhausted. There is not a chance of saving even a fraction of those who might have been saved.

He turned away; the journalist stopped writing; the stench floated in through the barracks window like a rag against the mouth and mucus membranes.

Bert

"I wish," he says, "that it were winter. That we were coming back together from the sauna just as the sun is sinking red behind the dark edge of the forest. That the snow were white and clean, like your body. That we were alone here. That you were calm and happy, alone with me. In the city I was overcome by such a fierce longing for it. It was hot, pointless, and confusing. I wish everything were clearer, cooler; then it would be easier. Do you remember when we skied across the ice, out toward the open sea? How suddenly there was a rumble beneath us, and we rushed back blindly toward the shore? Only a rumble, hardly a mark on the snow, the birds screeching farther out, the sun burning in our eyes.

Just to ski on, get lost, in the whiteness. No, I'm not making it up. Dreams—one may have them if one is firmly enough anchored in the here and now, in the ground. One can be so in various ways. Tomas is starting to be. But you . . . you are floating like a bird, a peregrine falcon, above reality in order to find the right spot, absolutely the right abode. Can't it be here? Must you go all the way to God in order to be able to return; must you choose between heaven and hell? I can only give you this path to the sauna and back, always just as beautiful, don't you think? You who are my dark conscience. No, I'm not sleepy. Come and sit down here, look and you will see: the birds are swimming in the sky, the shadows of the reeds are trembling slightly; there was no storm after all; see how beautiful the cloud over there is: a dark leaf. Not many stars are visible. It was a good idea to stay down here. Say something. Perhaps June is better after all, with the light and the first heat of summer, like the warmth you give off. Cool, clean-scrubbed skin. All is forgotten, isn't it? Isn't it? Hey, it's Sunday. I have a premonition . . . it's too quiet. Are you asleep? It's too late to talk, I suppose. This earth is too beautiful for us to get to keep it. Soon no one will till the earth anymore; the fields, the ditches will grow over; the water will become toxic and the streams filled with mud; the grass will wilt; each tree will slowly prepare for its death. Only we are swift. I support the rifle with my thumb and forefinger, elbow against my body. It's getting dark. To kill, take aim carefully, first prepare, plan, leave no detail unchecked. Those swarms of scientists, if they were sitting like me now facing the silence, the bay and the twilight . . . each of them has seen it, forgotten it. I aim the gun, I pull the trigger, click: the trees go up in a whirl, the earth shakes, the water flows down into cracks and crevices, the colors burn up, the skin is scorched and flies to paradise, or hell. No, we'll stay here. Nothing will change. The snow will come and cover up everything, and it will all be cool, clean, and forgotten. We will forget. We will forget that we once lived. That we carried so many crosses. Do you want another drink? Only clear aquavit, snow and clear aquavit, cooled down in the snow. That's life."

Helena

Lips against lips, so soft, so moist, so violent; eyes closed, as if the body were striving to escape its prison, into another one where no one knows his proper name, where skin meets skin, the mouth formulates shouts, common to all of us, yet yours alone, nobody else's, no one's; and the world will not be wiped out, time will not be wiped out; they will sink deeper down as if they were part of the circulation; the legs, the thighs close around your back, stars erupt under the eyelids: we have made a child, I know it now, I feel it, it has to be so; we are strangers, close, exhausted; we turn our backs on each other and go to sleep, while the twilight pales, pale as the skin.

The old woman was sitting up by the stove. She hardly turned her head when the relief crew in protective clothing tramped in armed with Geiger counters. The walls, the ceiling were intact; only the windows gaped with fluttering curtains. On the floor, covered with rag rugs, a child was playing. They hadn't seen anything like it for quite awhile; perhaps one of them recalled a faint childhood memory of some summer in the distant past. "It's God's wrath," the old woman mumbled, chewing on the phrase again and again. "God's wrath." They left again. They had other things to do. In the surrounding woods randomly toppled trees lay here and there. The air was at the same time clammy and oppressive, sharp and acrid, scorched and autumnal.

Tomas

He turns a corner. There is no corner to turn around. He encounters a mirror and his own image: the body is cut off, his lower torso walks one step behind the upper, the cut surface blinds him like a scream! He falls directly inside the street and acknowledges that sooner or later this had to happen, sooner or . . . ; and supports himself on his arms that tremble in the dark as if they had been injected with moonlight and the shadows of moonlight. He had seen them already as a child. All is unchanged, his alone; he cannot talk about it. He sinks back.

They open their mouths, close them again. They love and withdraw within themselves again. They live out their years, dream their dreams, in the end lie down in the place indicated. Of the one who indicates their place to them they dream; him they love or hate. Him they bless or deny. Or they neither see nor hear him, he does not exist; what exists is the dripping faucet in the kitchen, the banging barn door, the flag line beating against the pole, the breathing that stops and starts again, suddenly, in the averted face.

Max

Lava was running out of his mouth, burning lava! All the dark figures in the background pointed at him; perhaps they were shouting; their pale faces were turned toward him, and he bent down, took the lava in his hands; it was cold! He started pulling it out; it was heavy, pliable, it glowed in the dark; he pulled and pulled, emptied it out of himself; the flow of lava from inside him grew thinner and thinner as if there were a giant spoke around which this vital hose had been wound, first in a broad band, then more and more painful and thin, finally becoming a thread that cut his hands, until with an overwhelming effort he broke it off; a sharp pain shot through his hands and his stomach, perhaps the way a fish feels when the too-deeply-lodged hook is pulled out by force. He sat up in the bed, with wide-open eyes; he felt a shooting pain in his chest;

142

it was half-dark in the room, Rosa sleeping with her back to him, like a large dark mound under the covers. I'm no savior, he thought, no savior, nor any catch; leave me be, let me live for awhile longer. Cautiously he lay back down again; some cool draft swept across his damp forehead, and in the room, in the gray light of the morning, in the world, there was no firm anchoring place; everything was unresponsive, empty, as empty as he himself. Dawn broke; the shrill beach magpies pierced the silence with their loud screams.

Vera

There can be no shadow without light, even if it's hidden. She lay thinking about it, about what Tomas had said. So what? she thought. The truth is that the shadow usurps the light, is heavier than the light, harder, more ruthless. The shadow wins; it is the shadow that remains. Can we then call it shadow anymore? Perhaps we will be calling it—light? the hidden light; it is a dream. It is faith, it is Our Father Who Art, the desperate hope. Tomas, nor can I be without it. Do you hear! Deep inside I do believe, not only because of Martin, not only because of myself, not only because of you. Because of all the living things. Because this bed, this room, this pale dawn still exists; because children are still being born, children, everywhere, every minute. Because people are dying, every minute. No one can be so insane as not to see it. Feel it. I believe that if one could get every person to picture for himself that the blind heat, the light without a shadow, death, is part of the senses, the intestines and the skin, to experience disaster as a shooting pain, a suddenly-torn-off nail, something familiar, simple and awful—if each one could picture it, have a realistic dream about it, don't you think that then . . . ? She turned around, quietly, lay looking at Tomas's withdrawn, sleeping face, like that of a child. Somewhere there was peace; she was headed there.

143

Rosa

The moon is tumbling through the clouds as it did when I was a child. Time and movement have no connection. The moon tumbles, it crashes, it reaches nowhere. It stops. Who carries it? How can it float up there? Who created gravity, motion? Who will undo it so that the earth will actually crash, scorched, or will change its air, change it into a gas, which in turn will ignite; the air will consume itself, the earth its beauty, the people their lives until all is laid waste—as up there, on the moon, where people walk around digging and leaving traces, people who along with the moon are tumbling through the clouds? Soon no one will see the moon. Back when I was little, the eye was flying along with the moon: time and movement were united. . . . Now, yesterday, an eternity ago, the moon and the woods were standing still. Time and motion had taken different paths, away from me. . . .

Gran

When Jesus reached the rocky ledge above the lake, he looked back. The landscape was buried in a violet haze, but night was already falling among the mountain peaks in the East. Pale stars stood still in the sky. I saw all this, though as if from a hiding place. When Jesus raised his left arm, a black raven came flying and sat down on it. It looked at him and then, quick as a flash, stabbed him in the wrist. Then Jesus closed his right hand around the bird's back before it had time to escape and hurled it with both hands like a stone down into the lake; it fell without using its wings. A pale silver membrane covered the Sea of Galilee; the bird sank without a trace. I was overcome by a great feeling of relief. At that point I woke up. This dream is one of the few I can remember clearly, but I have no explanation for it.

Like every flower shooting its stem up from the dry clay soil. Like the secret springs and water veins pushing through the earth on their way to the sea—nourishing, mute, deep inside the earth. Like stones never touched and always slowly changing, stones which suddenly erode, disintegrate, or slowly rock with the waves in water-smooth silence and solitude, beyond all human desires. How the clouds glide and the grass is bent by them, by the wind and the rain. How the lower species wake up at dawn; how the sand patterns itself, without anyone having stepped in it. How life begins and is extinguished; the fallen tree becomes silvery, cracks, loses all its soft parts, becomes petrified, ceases to breathe, no longer moves. How the horizon remains unbroken; only the solitary bird calls, hardly any of them even; the day, twilight, night, and twilight again. The ice-blue water, the cliffs, the sky the color of blood at sunset: all gone, all hidden, all in darkness. To remain, neither dead nor alive, neither with nor without, an object, a movement in eternity, a dream, a rest, a silence. Only the faint sound of waves, soon more distant, disappearing. A deep silence, and then sudden darkness.

The dog stood still, listening. The forelegs firmly planted, the hindlegs ready to leap. The eyes as if squinting sideways, in order to catch a blind spot. They followed the screeching crow which rose from the top of the alder and disappeared. The woman, too, was standing still. The smell of rain-wet greenery was heavy, like metal. The sky covered in haze. Inside the tent the man was having a dream about a ship which is sinking through ice, deeper and deeper down; it's sinking and he is closed up in a world where no messages can reach, only the piercing, hard sounds of splintering ice-floes in the all-engulfing darkness.

A motorcycle courier is tearing up clouds of dust along the road. Behind the helmet's plexiglass a face is discernible; no one knows

145

whose. The birches hasten to assume a static, darker green shade. The fields tilt like screens against the sky, which begins to be crisscrossed by light red trailing clouds. Hesitantly the sea touches the shores, withdraws again. It is as if dirty water were running down the map from the disaster center. Roads marked in red become dirty gray. An index finger with a diagonally cut nail is pointing at a map somewhere, underground, in some headquarters. Someone says something and looks up. It is summer; the earth is pushing up its flowers and its green trees; perhaps the trees don't want to live, the roads don't want to be roads; perhaps the water in the wells wants to go up in steam, the shadows want to be obliterated, the veins to run dry; perhaps the people don't want to be people anymore, squeezed inside their tight skins, chained by their limbs? The silence is full of contradictory voices; they can be recorded, like the screams of bats: behind the voice giving the orders, the courier can hear them as a hum, like stardust in the ether.

Helena

She saw herself lying dead, thrown across a chair like a piece of clothing; her skin was glowing in the dark, painfully exposed to all eyes. When she awoke, she lay for a long time with unblinking eyes and listened to Bert's breathing, which now and then stopped; she rose up on her elbow, touched his shoulder, but he did not wake up. She settled back, let the reluctant, slow tears fill her eyes and slowly run down her cheeks. Not a sound in the night; the white fields lay silent.

Bert

In the middle of the night he woke up and remembered—as if it had been the reason for waking up—a picture, one of the last ones of Father. He was sitting by the fire; Bert saw him through the porch door; he was sitting with his fly open holding his penis in his hand. Bert remembered the tired, upturned face in which a weak reflection of some ancient gratification was mirrored like a tired and bitter memory. All the signs of old age were assembled there, in the old face of this man who was a stranger to him. He turned and went down the path and thought: No, no . . . without really knowing what he meant, his eyes blinded by tears.

Helena

She felt she was one of those people who, when they want some sun, are shaded by that single, solitary, tiny cloud to be found in an otherwise clear and cloudless sky; and in spite of the fact that Bert gave her everything in his power, she considered life unjust, unjust to her personally. She had long held onto this idea. Studying it now, she smiled: she had progressed a bit. She turned over and went to sleep.

Martin

It is cool, early morning. Martin goes down to the beach. All the others stay behind—Grandmother in the room adjacent to the sauna, Tomas and Vera in the tent, Max and Rosa up in the attic, Bert and Helena on the long benches in the livingroom; and he who has been sleeping with Grandmother quietly creeps outside; from the tent not a sound, only the birds are screeching and carrying on. He squats on the landing; it feels cool against the soles of his feet; the water is cool and clear. The clouds move on the surface of the water. If I fall in, I will disappear without a sound, like a stone, he thinks. He inches back. He gets up, walks toward the cottage. The pajama pants are getting wet from the dew in the grass; he bends down and turns them up. Far away the faint sound of an airplane can be heard. His heart starts beating faster; he remembers the day before yesterday, the trip, the fear, the mounting roar. He looks around. Isn't the greenery turning black; isn't it getting a bit darker; isn't it awfully quiet? No one is there to see it; they are all sleeping. His mouth tastes of blood. The ether vibrates with a deep singing sound. The sun has clouded over.

Sunday morning the astronomer sitting with his photographs suddenly gets the notion that the great mirror-telescope is in danger. From his nightmares he has carried along a faint echo, as if the big lens had suddenly, explosively, cracked, producing a long, continuous, coldly ringing sound, and the entire frame had toppled over and fallen through the observatory wall leaving a big, gaping, irregular hole out toward space. He enters the observation room, looks up at the cupola. He is alone. Perhaps someone, long ago, on Tau Ceti, did away with the fear of death. All there, even in the nerve constellations, is subject to the laws of nature, under control, calm, as calm as timelessness, or sleep without dreams. The high room gets darker for an instant, then brightens again. With a simple hand movement he can open up earth's biggest eye on space, on the galaxies, the nebulas, the solar systems. What use is it now? He shivers, goes back to his darkroom, closes the door.

See this proud organ: the wrinkled purse with one testicle lower than the other, in its net of skin; the acorn reddish purple with its slit of an eye, the penis brown with veins, meatier, less firm than the skin elsewhere, higher up the scruffy bush of hair and the pale shield of the stomach; and this organ is rising slowly, nodding, as if it wanted to brag about its lack of beauty, and then quickly, as if in pain, push in and hide in the warmth of the womb, as if it wished to find the body's core, the innermost secret of sensation, as if again and again it wanted to hurl itself at something hidden that both he

148

and she are closing their eyes to, a secret dream behind blind eyes, an obliteration of all that is "me," "mine"; this organ which is searching with its eye for the heart, attempting with the anguish and love expelled from its eye to alter the life of this other body, its circulation, its thoughts. This body wanting to return to the womb, the mere sensation of shrinking, of light: an odd averted darkness in which a heavy searching, thrusting body inside another responding, longing body was trying to escape, from everything—from the body, from the lovemaking, from the touch, from their names—in order to be drained, become naught, die; and how this organ then, like the trunk of a disappointed elephant, withdraws, a tiny nozzle; how for days and nights it remains hidden, swelled only by fantasies, visual impressions, pictures of faceless bodies; this organ, a little god, forever blindly demanding; this nose, a caricature, slowly used up, once shining! in secret union with the purest, the most passionate: slowly, slowly it reverts, mostly rests, pale, bloodless, finally to merge with earth along with the rest of the body, be quickly obliterated, while its seed somewhere on the dark earth continues its proud upright stride, its naïve boasting, its drum-major gesturing in the bright air, its oaths to the flag, its progress, straight as an arrow, red with eagerness, the ruler of the world with its screwed-up eye, you, cyclops!

Tomas

Is there a force that binds the stars together? That carries on a conversation when the wind is down, outer space receptive, all the while that we are sleeping? No one on earth answers, or can reach up to make contact: we can imagine the force but do not see it. How is it with other stars? Perhaps a quiet, uninterrupted conversation is going on between some live, highly developed planet and the force it has begun to pin down, slowly to be sure, but still a force it can take the bearings of, analyze, tame. A force to answer. And we, we aren't even mentioned; we live in an unknown or indifferent sphere; the force may know all about us, the star may know all about us, but we are of no consequence to them. We do not answer or answer unclearly; we do not know them, and perhaps they—the force and the star—are observing us with their kind of compassion. At night while Vera and Martin have been sleeping, I have at times arisen and quietly gone out on the porch and observed how light has returned, the stars have paled, and the damp grass has made my feet cold. Last June . . . a silent bird glided across the sky above me, a hawk or a falcon, unknown to me, as if it were searching for me with its eyes—a sign I could not interpret. I have seen the stars quickly devoured by the dawn, the air masses, the distance. I have listened holding my breath; the only thing that exists, the only thing there is, I have told myself, is what I can perceive with my senses. Whence then this anxiety and this thing I cannot under-stand but which may exist, as anxiety, as a suspicion, a possibility, a necessity: the voice behind the voice, the sense of vertigo in life, stardust and distance like a secret dream injected into the blood? All these galaxies, bunches of rays, stardust, paths, black holes, gas nebulas, falling celestial bodies, infinity, hurling itself at ever-greater infinities—are they talking to each other; is there someone who binds them together, someone who will evict a body out of its system if it becomes too destructive or attains excessive or ques-tionable power? Or is it we, the inhabitants of the star, who our-selves choose the year, the day, the moment of our extinction? Is it our own will? What wind of rage blows us all into a heap or blows us away, out, like splinters into the gaping void? Only what I can see is keeping me alive! Only the voice of my beloved is keeping me alive, and the bird, a chicken hawk.

Vera

To be bedded down, cry of exhaustion and relief, lie between cool sheets while Mother arranges the bedside table, places on it a soft reading light, and brings refreshments, books—how I long for it: to give up, be cared for, be able to dream free of responsibilities for once, rest and dream, and sense life at a distance, indifferent to its noise and sacrifices. Helplessness—indifference—surrender—peace. At last to be able to rest from everything.

On the third day people are still walking around stepping on those who have been thrown into the streets. You wonder what they are actually looking for—probably relatives. They look with rigid eyes past you and drag themselves on with unbelievable effort; they don't complain; they are probably in shock. What a contrast to the leadership at military headquarters: crack people, aware of the situation, the room dim, the big position map illuminated, radar paths, radar bases, a faint odor of something—celluloid, male cologne, a faint roar from the air conditioning apparatus, dial tones, the alertness of the quick hands as they move across the instrument panels, somewhere, hidden, blasted deep inside a mountain, not for every man to know, not an area for just anyone to tramp around in, drag himself into; this knowledge is reserved for the trained, the uniformed, the admired, those with a focus, those focused on death, on death! There is not this disorder above ground, not any of these with their skin torn off, legs bare, eyes blinded, lungs scorched, these sprayed, trimmed, trained, classified, from service rejected, discarded, collected, broken, moss-covered; indeed, you ask yourself, what are they looking for, what are they dragging along, what is driving them around this burned-out lake, as if they did not see the special forces, the saviors in their protective clothing, the privileged saviors? Somewhere on the three-dimensional map a lamp lights up, a low voice speaks into the microphone in direct contact with the administration shelter; it is impossible to distinguish the words; clay covers the open mouths; walls continue to collapse even if there is no wind; it is quiet, cool, the calm of death.

151

Helena

Moments of horror? Except for yesterday, I can recall only one early gray morning at Skeppsbron pier.[6] The ship put in with the stem a bit forward, and fourteen large white majestic swans strayed between the ship and the edge of the quay. I was dangling above their certain death but couldn't get a sound out; I saw them already crushed, a mass of white feathers, blood, broken necks—would they scream, moan? The gulls were just flying around; the traffic roared eternal; a guard with a uniform cap came running, and with a stake he prodded them backwards and out; they glided calmly, without haste, in the narrow corridor, in the dirty oily water and swam out. I felt as if I myself had been on the point of being crushed. That is all I can remember. I was paralyzed. I was alive, I had escaped—everything except the picture, the memory. My wrists still ache, or wounds open up, like blows from inside, and pale again—the way the rising and falling sound of air-raid sirens still makes me stop working and look out the window at the wall across; my eyes are searching for a strip of sky, my thoughts are thinking: oh, so now it has started, my body sits numb in the chair, my memory brings out the taste of darkness and war, of cold and fear, the sudden flight from the blinding white snowy day to the miserable lightbulb of the air-raid shelter, the muffled detonations, my body crouched, everything turned inward and fragile, like skin which quickly, in one fell swoop, tears off, revealing the pulsating, bleeding inner organs. Just a short moment, like a reminder: do not forget the fear, it is vital; no one can be unimportant to you, we all bleed, we all have to receive together, just receive, digest, in order to be able to get up and continue our work, in order to be able to see. Yes, to be able to see.

Bert

Someday I will wake up and not be able to take off my pajamas. The room is in semidarkness and there is no one to speak to. I tug at the jacket forcefully and a tack flies on the floor like a spark from a roaring fire. Now I notice that all the material has been fastened to me with tacks or with nails: where wood and cloth join, dark narrow bands run, glued or nailed all over me—as onto dry drift-wood. There is no point in sitting like a big log on the edge of the bed trying to tear off these products of handicraft nailed into me, draping me, keeping me prisoner. I lie down (fall on my face) and am carried off by the rain. Hands by my sides, my skin bursting open and twisted like tendons around the iron-hard internal frame. I moan, I must get out of this! Finally I hit a big dark dam-lock; it opens with a bang, the water rushes out, is sucked up by the sea which receives it with indifference, puts its weight on the unruly waves and slowly spreads a cold clear moonlight across the black surface. I lie looking straight into the dark; there is nothing but darkness.

They are lying in a separate room, in semidarkness, unconscious. They exhibit symptoms the doctors hadn't expected—eczema, breathing difficulties, cramps—that do not correspond to the normal pattern of disease for those wounded in nuclear attacks. Four doctors who have touched them have been infected. They have been isolated. More protective suits are needed, perhaps also facial masks which can better protect the skin, the lungs. Outside it is strangely quiet. A birch is dropping its leaves. The third morning one of the less affected doctors points out the window, at the tree. The doctor on duty follows his pointing arm, his eyes. He remains standing for a moment, then quickly leaves the room and closes the door quietly. The air sweeps through the rooms as if filtered through a large tortured lung.

Max

He wasn't thinking. He saw. He saw objects and landscapes, he saw faces, he saw nothingness; he was changed by what he saw, he did not contemplate it. He participated by seeing, as clearly, with as much concentration as possible; but when he wanted to articulate it, to himself or to others, he became blind, and the things fell apart, like ashes. The connections were cut off; only the eye, seeing, remained and was altered by what it saw: how everything was gliding off, how everything was limitless, dead or alive, without anchoring, without reality, yet not unreal; it existed, it could be seen, he could touch it without it withdrawing, but it was totally alien, it spoke, it thought, it was covered by woods or hair, bark or skin, it drank air through leaves or lungs, it stood still in the dark like himself. Could it see? He did not know. The wind blowing came from a vacuum.

The old office building with its sturdy brick walls still stands almost unscathed. The few working there all managed to survive, many with insignificant burns. Also the nuclear shelter under the new television relay station survived the shock, even though it was undersized and provided shelter for only thirty of the two hundred people employed. However, the air purification system broke down.

Rosa

This fear, anguish: was it a fear of having one's name obliterated, one's "I"? But the nameless objects, the world which also didn't have a name, the deed that was not named and hence most free, the gesture in the dark, the stranger on the road who passed and smiled at me, the water, the trees, the sky: what names did they have? Why was I afraid? Why did I remain in my heavy body, my painted, cleaned, groomed, self-assured, overflowing, picture-emitting, picture-demanding, emotion-demanding, temporary, loved, hated body? Sometimes, sometimes I long to be cut out of all contexts:

154

unknown, without having to watch myself, I sit in a room without objects with a free view of my life, and I say: it makes no difference which course I take; nobody can see me. Nobody. But somebody always does see me, somebody fixes his eyes on me; it is a compulsion or a dream, hell or heaven, or something in between: a certainty, quite unfounded. Like someone close in the dark when there is no one. As if someone smoothed out my features and the heavy lines, bleached my splotchy skin, and then handed me over to namelessness, me-lessness. Like undressing and then, light as the wind, rising in splendid colors, being transformed, disappearing.

Tomas

I can still see him before me like a dark shadow in the whirling snow: he stops, looks with gray eyes at the rickety wooden sheds with their heads in their arms, crouching under the wind, full of moaning, sleeping, fleeing people. He has a steady grip on the brown suitcase with a strap around the middle, filled with the assets of the bank. St. Petersburg 1917! They sent him because they knew they could trust him: he moved about in life as if he had been given a commission of trust for eternity, a jacket to wear and care for no matter how worn it might look in the unflattering light from a cold light source, a direct light source, eyeballs following his every move. He was twenty-seven, but parts of him had aged, his frame and face hewn into deeper furrows and folds than necessary. Yet this childish gaze, this inviolability and the unconsciously clumsy movements, a body—heavy like mine—bent slightly forward. They had not sent anyone else. He went to the railroad station, where one of the last trains was standing amid a cloud of smoke; he got on; there was a smell of charcoal, darkness, damp homespun cloth: he noted it, he remembered the traces of blood in the snow, the streak of unreal white skin above the stocking of the woman who wanted to sit on his lap; he had pulled back. He used to tell us

155

about it, his eyes looking past us; he was smiling. Snow was falling outside the tall windows, not unlike those he sat behind; the red plush glowed in the light from small sconces; it was freezing outside; the horses had frosty muzzles, people hurried past like bundles, the darkness was as oppressive as a threat. He was repelled—just as I continue to be repelled—by this world of beauty and violence, riches and hunger, vomiting from overeating and vomiting from exhaustion, hunger, lousy dogfood. He owned one suit; he was sitting in his hotel room cleaning it. In the full-length mirror he encountered his own image: he looked like a servant. He was a servant serving big capitalist interests. He went to the party to which he had been invited; the bank managers turned around, placed a few polite phrases on a silver platter, gesticulated with their white gloves lightly and derisively, or drank themselves round, staggering, ruddy and loud. He had identification and could take out what he was supposed to; he packed the banknotes in the suitcase, placed on them the nightshirt with the red border and the monogram his mother—I never saw her—had embroidered on the breast pocket, spread old newspapers on top, sat on the lid and subdued the old worn leather suitcase, and left with the taste of caviar as a stale deposit on the tongue. Groups of people, heartrending goodbyes, shouts, all slid past like tattered banners, were reflected in the dark windows, until a vast, empty, white landscape filled the railroad car; only then did he sit down. On the bench across from him a woman was sitting in dark hat and black mourning veil, with a girl, then fourteen. I have seen a picture of Mother as a girl, already a beauty, dark hair surrounding a pale placid face with big eyes, shaded by a straw hat with a ribbon. They were sitting in silence; they looked at him and then turned their eyes away. Three marines carrying rifles with mounted bayonets came to search the car; suddenly the woman leaned forward, thrust into his hand a package wrapped in some kind of gray litmus paper; her eyes were wide open with terror. He put the package in his big leather tobacco pouch; everything happened quickly and smoothly, as if they had been acquainted, recognized something in common; above his head the suitcase lay like a big leather grenade; the guards looked in, passed by. The woman started talking in a low voice, but he sat looking at the girl; she looked back at him; they created a silence between themselves; the thirteen years separating them were yanked away by each clanking seam in the track; they sat like children across from each other, and he was overcome by tenderness. I can feel that same tenderness in my own body; I remember his hand touching me when I was ill, only when I was ill and lying in my bed looking at the ceiling, far above, it floated off. Hannes: a name which slowly has been filled with meaning for me—memories, a gesture, a figure, the hand opening up and explaining, the mouth moving—but I cannot hear what he is saying; the roar from crossing railroad tracks obliterates their first encounter, his and Mother's. The water bottle jingles monotonously on the wall; behind Mother's face I am still looking for the face of that fourteen-year-old girl toward whom he is just now leaning and showing something: perhaps the gold watch his Mother gave him, the one lost in the bomb attack in 1943; it could be wound up and contained a microscopic chiming heart which chimed twelve times; she smiled as she pushed aside her hair with her thin hand. Her mother, my grandmother, was observing them. Sometimes Father would similarly study Mother's face, which was covered by a thin membrane from the parts she had played on stage. It is as if slowly and only now as she approaches seventy has she glided into that world in which she lived the happiest and most free eight years of her life until the crash, when poverty began, and the dark apartment with the high windows was filled with strangers, while he withdrew, became stooped, sat in a corner, barely looked up, read, or followed her with silent, furtive eyes. And no matter how she tried to convince him—I recall that he seldom replied—he blamed himself for having forced her to give up the theater, a life she herself had fashioned before he approached her in earnest. For ten years they kept company, he waited, she matured early, at twenty-four

157

she married him. He was thirty-seven then. Three years later I was born, between two opening nights. He sat in dark boxes and watched her practice, saw how she fought hard, bent, was hardened; her internal life she saved for him. They were married in a snowstorm; there was always snow everywhere. They came here, probably by horse and sleigh; perhaps I came about in this room. She had wanted a child, right away! Her career was not interrupted; I have a vague memory of her on stage in some children's play; someone is bending over me and saying: "there is your mother!" I look up with a candy-smeared face; there are many lights; children are running around in costumes; a face appears in a capote, painted, the smile like a bleeding wound—that's not Mother! I wept. I was removed; she came to me before I went to sleep, the darkness fragrant and rustling. Now, over hers, father's face is superimposed, eyes closed, the tears slowly running down his cheeks. He was easily moved, could not control himself; also his deafness was increasing. The big heavy frame collapsed, he sat at his desk with temporary work, tax returns he assisted with; the green desk lamp threw a pale gray light on his skin and the dark stubble. When I enter he looks up, then continues working, conscientiously, tired, as if he no longer has anything to say to me. Only later did I understand how his deafness must have plagued him, how he did not want to admit that he was getting more and more isolated, how the silence was eating at him from the inside and could only be alleviated by Mother who now cleaned house, washed the dishes, walked me to school, took care of practical matters, rented out rooms, who walked through the rooms as if across a stage, swiftly, nervously, it seemed, but with internal toughness, the dark beauty still shining out of every movement and gesture, as if she had discovered hidden wellsprings. Perhaps Father had simultaneously found an internal hearing to replace the hearing he had lost and could tune in to sounds the ordinary ear cannot pick up; sometimes he would seat me on the sofa, place himself on a hard chair in front of me. I looked up into his face as at

158

a vast landscape with unfamiliar waterways, crevices, mountains, and valleys. He talked to me, told me about the approaching war, related no horror stories but reported calmly and in a way hard for me to understand about persecutions, Hitler, pogroms, political constellations; he gave a picture of hunger, rebellion, and want; his room became a room for trips into hidden matters, indifferent to most people; Mother sometimes came in and listened. The streetlights were swinging to and fro; I may have been only six or seven. Perhaps Father had the sensory capacities and nerve system of a bat? He slowly yellowed away; his hands lay big and motionless on top of the cover, like mine now, mine that are alive, that can touch Vera. How did he experience her life in the theater—like a world outside the world? No, like the innermost of worlds. He sat in the empty auditorium and knew everything: the stage decor, the backdrops, the dreams, the constructions; the lines, the gestures, the smell of cloth and dust, the smell of the great world stage, the smell of rust, the smell of blood. This they shared; she knows it; she continues to live with the knowledge of the mechanisms, the silence, the curtainfall. From both of them I inherited the sense of disaster, groundless, mysterious, intriguing, and inarticulate. It hid in the big dark corners of the room, moved like spider's webs in the ceilings (where there were no spiders, only dust traps); by distancing each image it confirmed the experience they had imparted to me, and with their eyes I saw the world filter in through every crack and reality like blood running through the thickest, sturdiest walls; that existence was put together out of scenes; the wind existed in order to swing the two streetlights through my nights and dreams, the sea roared in order to test my perseverance, the dark hid unsuspected snares which had to be coped with without looking right or left. They had—with their silent generosity—given me an inheritance to look after: use your eyes, take a step back, stand still in times of persecution, move cautiously, go up in your work as into something holy. I collected photographs; I sat in my room behind the kitchen and studied the details of foreign cities; I was astounded that colors, people, driving clouds, mountains, and water could be captured outside myself and still I could share in them, study them, and in my imagination recreate the moment it had all been captured in the picture. My hot dreams merely confirmed the coolness, the distance, the need for work, focusing the eye, the hands, at a single goal: endure! endure! Endure like the rock, become invisible like it, become mute like it, its heart, its core which is the rock itself. Max's idea! Someday, some moment I would understand everything: Father's and Mother's life, my birth, the years that trekked across the floor like streaks of sun and shadow and that his eyes followed to the end. He must have remembered summer mornings like this one, all clear and calm, and beyond the roads at rest, the haze above the meadows, the light greenery, he must have pictured all the changes, forever repeating: the darkening treetops, the ground congealing under icy partly moldered leaves, a red sun indifferently burying itself beyond the black edge of the forest; and in the landscape the people, their helplessness, their thin arms, their faces as if disinterred, or quickly spilled into the gutter, into the streets, and behind silent housefronts—backdrops all! Always, behind every landscape, every person, another landscape, another person, like the reality in a picture before it is thrown on the fire, twists, shrivels, turns to ashes, dies, a reality just as impossible to obliterate as the fire, as hard as the stone, as wide as the water's surface, as permanent as the doubt, Tomas! Was I given this name in order to doubt the testimony of my senses, the only thing we have? I observe with my skin, I see with my sexual organ, I grow out of my words and smell the salt of death on my dry lips, I see the wounds open up beneath the skin like flowers or the marks of blows; people are dying and you turn away or proclaim! demonstrate! theorize! With a tender gesture he leaned forward and saved them, touched the hand of the girl; the train cut right through their lives, he wasn't afraid of being found out. All that was worn out, tattered, exhausted: I saw it behind the paragraphs, it opened its petals in silence like the night rocket, its heavy fragrance followed me along the way between those who own the world and those who turn away from it—all are parts of the world, both the one sitting under the lamp and the one watching the one sitting under the lamp, at night, on the porch, in the dark, in a "happier" era. Subjugated passion, subjugated passion for work, a slow maturing process, slow satiety, slowly to fill out your own physical frame, approach someone, mature, be disappointed, love and not love, be loved and not be loved, the attempts at fusion, the heavy movements, the weak rejoinders, the relief, the seriousness, the joy: was all this part of becoming myself! Who is I myself? I would like to be nobody, nameless and mortal!—to merge with my deeds so that what I did would be as natural as the changes of nature, the growth of the plants, the course of the clouds, the bright arch from morning to evening. Did I become myself with you? Certainly I did: I lost my name, merged with my senses, grew as an emotion grows, with finely veined leaves, quietly in the cool morning air filled with the song of birds . . . and the open mouths, the erupting skin, the dying, the pointless pain and its bloodstains, the voices far away, are echoing in me.

Martin

My name is Martin. I could be someone else, but who? I became me; I am lying here listening to Grandmother's whistling breathing; there is no one else but her, but those who are now living on the island, the others I can only recall, and they do not exist; school, the teachers, where are they? My name is Martin, and I am the only one awake, the only one who lies looking at the morning sun, here, on the island, which is a cloud floating on the water and the only one in the world. If I will it, I shall never die—but those who had to die, where are they? Will their skin, their flesh disappear? Are they lying unprotected looking up through the earth, or are they floating somewhere between the stars? I could never have been anyone else; who am I then? Perhaps I could have been a plant—or the streak of morning sun on the wall, or the bird which yesterday glided across

161

the deepening sky with a faint crimson border on the horizon. It was a black bird; perhaps it saw me, perhaps it said something to me; I followed it with my eyes. Martin: that's me, my arms, my morning; now I shall go quietly outside, down to the beach; I will swim on top of the water like a bird in the sky, and if someone wants to find me he has to look, everywhere.

The international control commission arrives by air and grabs a quick lunch at the airport. The speeches have been cut down to two. One of the cars in the procession later collides with a tractor on its way to the fields. Most of them are sitting in silence. Mostly these are uninteresting fields, forest edges, ugly farms and buildings.

Vera

She felt his fear and found that by loving him she could make this fear change course, that tenderness and ecstasy put both of them at a loss for words, calm. She noticed that her name was not important to her, but his was. They did not talk to each other; they glided into sleep as if they had sanctioned each other's solitude, silence, freedom. They slept; the world around them resounded with cries they did not hear. Just before she went to sleep she knew it: Tomas was going to leave. She forgot it the same instant, wanted to forget it, sank as into cool clear water. In the dream he spoke to her, and she replied. That, too, she had forgotten when she woke up, when it was morning and the tent flapped with gliding, oscillating shadows. She moved closer to him. His breathing seemed to have changed, he seemed no longer to be breathing; for a moment she thought he had died, then he turned toward her, his eyes still closed.

On the training film the doors of the furnace recall a turn-of-the-century dirty bakery. The inductees are chewing gum or talking in a low voice. Hitler's shouting face: a comedian. The mass graves, the piles of eyeglasses, hair, shoes: they have seen it all before on television. Let the dead bury their dead. On the way out they start to tease the fatso of the company, who is perspiring profusely. Tomorrow they will be traveling north: cleanup work. "Hey you there!" they say and trip him. He struggles up; he has lost his glasses. "No messing around here," shouts the sergeant major. And it's supposed to be Sunday.

Tomas

"Helplessness," said Tomas, "eats its way out from the inside. I have had enough of it. I have lived long enough in the shadows. I have minded my own business, I have been considerate, I have listened, I have worked, and I will never think of it as pointless. I have tried to learn something, gather information, tried to learn something from my experiences and, as far as I've been able, tried to help others—these are fundamental qualities in me; I shall try not to let go of them. But at the same time, I have felt a helplessness which has kept on growing: I can do nothing, we are playing pieces, the mighty make all the decisions, so one might just as well try to escape. . . . There is more than one form of escaping. There is escape that signifies wisdom: an old Chinese proverb claims that 'of the thirty-six ways of avoiding danger, fleeing is the best.' But there is also escaping from oneself, from what one might be, and that escape tastes like blood in the mouth. As if one were hollowing oneself out. What is the point of peace, beauty, all one can see, all one can feel, your warmth, Martin's trust, if at the same time I am seeing myself in reverse perspective, through the wrong end of the binoculars, a shapeless figure running, or trying to hide this fear. I have made a decision. I have to go back. Tomorrow I will drive

163

home. I'll return next weekend, if possible. In any case, I intend to sign up. I believe that it will strengthen our union as well. Last night when you came to me, I experienced something extraordinary. As if that strange woman, that memory, the picture of something I thought was unattainable and hence desirable, had suddenly disappeared, had begun to feel like an unnecessary appendage, a stupid passion, an advertising trick by the memory; that back then, in my youth, when that moment would linger and remain, it fulfilled a function in my life, an important function. It gave me a certain sensitivity toward people and a pair of eyes that were getting sharper through practice. It also gave me a front, and behind it a sometimes violent, unexplainable feeling of terror: now I have been unmasked! Now my duplicity, my ignorance, my indifference is in plain sight! There I am standing, as in a nightmare, without my trousers, caught—perhaps by you. I never want to experience that feeling again. Insecurity, fear, we have to live with them and must live with them in order to be prepared, in order to be able to help. I will never lose my sense of disaster. But I have to remove the sludge from it. The running away, the falseness—no, don't interrupt me; I know what you want to say; indeed you are partly right, but partly wrong, and hence wrong: there is quite a lot we have concealed from each other. You have been bothered by my fear, I know. I have been bothered by your—how shall I say it?—your 'anchoring,' which I have often felt to be false, your lack of tenderness, this feeling of yours, as you have sometimes complained, of being a vacuum, a neuter, that I admit. If you have felt passion, it has been external to you. And if I have felt passion, I have suppressed it. The only way to grow is to liberate ourselves from ourselves, as best we can. This observing I do is no release. It is one thing to feel removed and to need this distance—when one is building something, creating something, participating in something. It is another matter to feel the distance as a paralysis. I intend to get up and go. I intend to try to make my way up there, if it's possible. I shall get as close to the lifeless as possible. I feel it under my skin that there are people up there who envy the dead. No, now I'm exaggerating. I don't feel it under my skin, but I can imagine it, part of it. I can even see it. I can also see how beautiful this morning here is, the water, the grass, the purity, all of June around us, the birds, the mild wind, and the fragrance of your skin. . . . No, this world is a world of poisons, threats, excrement, accumulated death, cynicism, hate, stress, arsenals of weapons, a world of destruction, terror, massacres, suffering and death. And always it is meted out to the innocent. How much peace of mind can we afford? I cannot answer that question, no one can, not unambiguously. I do know that a feeling of peace must exist; we have to be able to afford so much peace of mind that we can—act, help, live. We have to live with at least enough faith—some form of faith, freedom from self-abasement, a feeling that it isn't merely my own egoism that propells my drive for self-preservation, and that this drive for self-preservation is not always satisfied only if it can survive, squeezed into bunkers, behind walls, in escape positions, only if it is rigidly contemplating its own fate, always mirroring its own fear. Fate! Fear! Feel, feel here how beautiful you are! Tell me, what does it mean to be a coward? Birds use protective coloring. Is cowardice a protective coloring, so that you are not visible, so that you think you are invisible. Perhaps it's the opposite; perhaps you emit a peculiar odor, an odor like the sweat of dead bodies; perhaps you are condemned in advance. They fish for you with spear and torch at night; during the day someone stands behind the door watching you. It's better not to think yourself privileged. If we stop feeling that we have a greater right to security than others, perhaps then we can help each other, adapt to what might be in store—suffering, death—if we are able. I know, you are thinking of Martin. We are not important, but he is! I refuse to offer him up as a sacrifice for something I do not know, something I despise, something I can't see! I must see it! I have to see those who are dying face to face, I have to see my own face! Yes, I know, I'm hiding behind words; I hesitate; I rush in two directions and may break, or become more assured. I am going, I will sign up,

165

I'll see what happens, I'll keep in touch. It's just as important as it is for Bert to continue his farming, and for you to be here, close to Martin and Grandmother, and to help Helena. And if there is some problem, if you need advice, go to Max; he embodies so much in his silence. It's only a matter of days, after all. I'll leave, I'll return, and if there is security in the act itself I shall find it and bring it back with me. I shall find out what I can do. I am going to throw myself into something that will make the stomach contract as in a cramp. Why don't I stay here? What is preventing me? I don't know. But last night, after you had gone to sleep, I lay listening to the wind in the trees outside, to odd sounds, and to these sudden silences that come and are peopled by our own imagination with devils and murderers. And while I was listening it was as if I had stepped outside my body and at the same time had left in there, in the shell, all my anxiety, all my fear, all my anguish: I looked calmly at myself and at you sleeping; you had such lonely hands, such an unfamiliar face, and that made me feel somehow confident. That we are here, that nothing can be changed, that thousands of people have slept in this way, with their eyes closed. And died. Confidence. That is crazy, I thought, since we are forever tumbling, head over heels, day after day, down; we are being battered against ever-harder rocks; we get more and more fragile, more and more vulnerable, and around us light after light goes out. Whence then this feeling of—peace? It just came, it just is, I cannot explain it. It was as if I had reached a point I have been avoiding all my life, as if instinctively I had turned a corner and suddenly seen my entire childhood open up before me, in the perspective of the old familiar street: the twilight, the swinging streetlights, the quiet housefront, severe yet illuminated by the warm glow from the windows, all that I have been looking for since I became homeless, since I began building new homes of my own, never the same. Do you follow me? I felt as if I had reached the calm behind the poverty, the joy behind the fear, the moment when the candles are lit and we are sitting in the family circle: it is

166

Christmas and someone has been born; someone is always being born in order to save someone else. You see: fear and joy, loneliness and closeness, faith and lack of faith, life and death stand so close to each other! Can you tell them apart? I have tried; I cannot. I have to learn to feel my way ahead, to exercise my imagination, make myself nimble, think like somebody else, act like somebody else. Big Somebody Else, be me, come inside me! And if I later discover that what I pursue tomorrow is a purely egotistical passing fancy, another alley to stumble in and turn back from, a childhood backdrop to be dismantled finally, reckonings with the same familiar, fleeing, ever-dominant 'me,' then I shall return and ask for help. But I don't think so. I shall daydream myself there, express myself there, and, while expressing myself, shall be creating myself and my chances—I shall be creating us! I can leave and know that you exist and that I live with you. I can't see you and yet I see you, Martin, everybody. To be open for an instant—there is a foundation. We have no other foundation. Let's rest a moment longer. Look at those shadows on the tent wall. It seems as if not the wind but someone else moved them. Always when observing the play of light and shadow on a tent wall, I feel empty, empty and free. Or when I stop on a forest path on a totally gray, soggy, sad April day smelling of runoff water and I listen to some lonely blackbird, or in the evening in a snowfall, as I ski homeward, you know, that sense of freedom, as if nobody needed me but I needed everybody, and as if I were changing every moment, as if I were slowly starting to resemble myself, the one I've always been but never knew, that hidden element which I have in common with you, yet is my very own alone."

Hunger, poverty, suffering, fear—there life was searching for you. It forced you up against the wall; it forced your arms apart. When you

167

saw someone dying, someone dead, then you wanted to live. Summer emerged from there, from the darkness of the wasted ones.

Helena

Bert comes to me; it's morning. I can't stand my fists anymore, my demands, all this tense, hard, blood-tasting search to realize myself. He is here, I help him; it isn't important for me to be satisfied; I try to explain that to him. I cannot go on living in a continual cramp. He lies still, as if he had known it for a long time, felt it, known me better than I did myself, and had only waited for me to arrive on my own where I have now arrived: to the point of exhaustion, a new attempt to find security, in the midst of catastrophe. We die without having been able to accomplish a fraction of what we intended. And he says: "We die alone. So what? It is this bruised life that frightens us, not death." And I recall how at home when I was a child we were placed in a row on a mattress on the floor; our faces and shoulders stuck out like cabbages in a dark cellar; it smelled of blanket and linoleum. Buckets were carried in and out; the years were carried in and out with their leftover potatoes, gravy and leftover potatoes; how could I forget all that bitterness? Life stood at eye-level and rolled roaring into the room early every morning. Father lay in the sofa bed, under a gray blanket with a crimson stripe. He could sit silent on the edge of the bed for hours. The yard was gray and full of shrill voices; there I grew up thin, my shoulder blades sticking out, like candidates for wings. —I notice that I'm smiling and that Bert smiles back at me.

We must see the world as if for the first time, or the last. We must focus our attention, our eyes, our sense of touch, our words as if everything were new and fragile. All still alive and not yet condemned to extinction. Everything pure, or twisted, changed, trans-

168

formed. Everything loved, and hated. As if we were seeing it for the first time, or the last.

The dog came running across the meadow as if pulled by an invisible rope. It was running parallel with the edge of the woods, like a shadow broken off it. No sounds could be heard. The dog turned, came running in a half circle, to Martin. It leaped, Martin held it, the sunlight shifted, shadows glided across the greenery, and the two of them wandered off in the tall grass, filled with secrets.

Those who ransack the grocery stores in the periphery have remained totally unaffected by all warnings about the risk of radiation and toxicity. They are a tough, progressive people; they go on living, their spirits burning like household spirits.

Rosa

Rosa turned around on her elbow, heaved her heavy body, looked with clear shining eyes at Max. "I keep getting heavier," she said, "soon I'll sink like a stone into the ground and be gone." "No," he replied, "then I will be the spit that strikes at you; the sparks will fly; I am like a stake in the ground, and god knows if I don't send out shoots one day and start to grow, my roots will twist around you." "They already do," she replied. "They have for a long time." He did not reply. "Odd," he said, "how thoughts will wander, without any clear path. I just had a mental picture of a city where the cemetery and the zoo were side by side. Have I seen it, or is it something someone has told me about, long ago? In the silence the dead can hear the lions' roar and the peacocks' call, and perhaps the animals in their turn can, at night, catch sounds from the beyond: 'come let us out! You whom we cannot see, you who live in freedom there on

169

the other side of the wall, come and free us!' The lion roars, the zebra walks back and forth in its cage, the polecat runs frantically back and forth in its latrine trough, the monkeys rush chattering up and down their wire walls. . . ." Rosa swung her feet slowly out of bed and got up. "What lesson shall we learn from this?" she asked; she went to the narrow attic window and looked out. "None," Max replied. "Not that I can see. But the picture is attractive. The zoo, the cemetery."

The meaning of life is perhaps hidden in the sensuous thought, in its connection with emotion. Everything contributes to shaping a person's landscape. Skin, hair, words, and touches which are unspoken words: you remember, someone is right now remembering something from the past, or the future, as if everything were an unfinished dialogue in an eternal, ebbing, flowing conversation. . . .

Gran

In her face the years have only seemingly settled down. She comes out of her room as if she were living in a luxury hotel; she is as stylish as a ship with an oaken frame, and she smells as autumn smells: of grace and decay. It is her steps you hear, in cemeteries, or in small but tidy rooms, and her silence is pure, almost virginal: "We loved each other, up to the day he died," she said yesterday, "and I don't mean just spiritually. But it is uncouth to talk about old people loving, almost dirty in your sacred young ears. Just wait, your turn will come." She embodies a toughness which tends toward small cruelties, small ironies. In her, the skeleton is covered by dark skin; out of her still youthful face two very clear blue eyes peer from under dry graying hair. She and Martin look at each other; both live in their own outsider's world and hence stand close, don't even need to talk much with each other. They walk among the shadows of the trees; he runs ahead; she has to catch her breath and stops, slightly forward bent. From the bay a steady soft wind carries a smell of clay. The trees under which she stands are so big that they keep their coolness, the same coolness that always flows toward her when she visits Hannes. Suddenly she sees his face before her: a pair of hands is covering it, then moves aside; something white, shapeless—a mouth trying to say something, the face of a clown, a mirror wherein the lights go out and only the face remains and shines in the dark. She sits down heavily in the grass. I was born crooked, I will die crooked, she reflects. Then they straightened the limbs, cleansed and opened the eyes, turned the face straight out at life and the audience; the legs were limbered up, the joints and the limbs learned to dance so well. Just an ever-quicker, ever-quicker swirl, gestures, calls, supporting actors who have disappeared into the shadows, the silence along the barely discernible soft carpets behind the stage, the smell of dust and wood, of cloth and grease-paint. Only an instant, only a short triumph, only a few years, then the curtain came down, the body collapsed, the gaze was averted, and another, lonelier, more difficult dialogue began: the dialogue between her and Hannes, the dialogue with the sick man, the dialogue to cover up an impoverishment. It was like learning to smile in the dark. Hannes, Tomas, Martin—they melted together into one face; it bent over her and said: "live! go on living! get up! old witch!" and she did; she got up, walked cautiously along the path she had once together with Hannes worn into light grass, just as light as this. "Grandmother!" Martin called from the shore. She went in that direction.

In the darkroom he is putting the finishing touches to the calcula-tions of the experimental sequence. The new bacteria culture has been a success: the crowning achievement of his research career.

171

The infrared screens are faintly mirrored in the highly polished steel frames. He bends down over the electron microscope. He puts on the facial mask and enters the culture room. He doesn't hear how quiet it is outside. A few minutes till noon.

Vera

There, beneath her hands, his skin was alive, his arteries, his thoughts: how little she knew about her son! His eyes turned to hers; she could read fear in them, concealed or half hidden, so that she would see, feel, pull him close to her. Indeed she had carried him; she had called him up from the blind dead darkness, she had given him birth; and now she was closely examining his skin, his hair, his neck, his thin arms, the big eyes in the narrow face, the cowlick in his hair, saw how he slowly, hesitantly, uncertainly, eagerly, took a few steps out into the still cold water, how he stopped and looked out toward the sea, then turned around and smiled at her. She smiled back, spread her feelings for him into every part of her body; the air exuded this feeling, the feeling took a leap, into the shadows, into the sunlight, into the quickly passing minute when she was still carrying him inside her, close to her, a picture of Tomas and her, a union that was wordless, unerasable, at its innermost core happy. If only he would not be left alone! He sat down next to her; he was freezing, she could feel it; she put the bath towel around his shoulders which were sticking out like those of a thin bird, like little wings—no! not wings! no angels! no death! Death did not exist, not now, not here, must not exist; she forced it back, away; she held her hand around his shoulders, felt the warmth of his body, but his thoughts she knew nothing about; his expression was somehow averted, the feet were moving in the sand, and a voice which was smaller than usual asked: "Is Daddy going away?" "He is going back and forth to the city; he will soon be back."

172

She, too, now felt the clear, cold wind that penetrated the sunlight like an invisible shadow.

The bulldozer pushes aside the wrecked cars, then takes them to their burial ground, pushes the twisted remains into a surprisingly big heap, a cemetery for burnt rubber, beams, crushed glass. As if a blowtorch had passed through them, one after another, looking for a sign of life.

Max

He remembered the countless ones leaning over their machines, the halls with windows overgrown with soot, bodies that had adapted themselves to their tasks and been shaped by the movements required by the tasks so that they had become part of the machines, the ovens, and were moving in a pattern unfamiliar to the observer. Had he adapted, too? He was part of a world of habit. He saw Martin running down the path. He held his hands in his lap, like an old man. The morning sun shone in and warmed his skin. His eyes were like windows behind which he could picture light, during those long years in England.

Gran

Rosa has hands like little pillows. She comes in to me, talks about the boy, how she and Max have been thinking that they—being childless—and what she's thinking. And I think: it's too late. It hurts; I sit bent forward, she stands by the window, I in my granny's chair, bent forward; we are unreachable as if we were suffering from stomach cancer, as if we were being consumed, before our time. I see the window, the foliage, trees that have been growing there for hundreds of years: happy, independent; that have strengthened their roots and sucked nourishment from all the dead stuff hidden in the ground. No, this world scene will be inherited by no one. The curtain will be blown away in shreds; the play can't even be brought to a conclusion! And Rosa is talking about making a will! I feel so tired; I might fall on my face and remain lying there, invisible.

Bert

She leaned on him and said: "This time, maybe this time; yes, I believe it. You will see, I will give birth." And he held her tightly, pressed the dark thin face against himself—the way you push away something that might make you happy, he thought: No. No dreams! He saw Tomas sit down next to Max and the boy pass Vera with the dog obediently running behind him; they disappeared behind him; they disappeared behind the corner of the house. A gust of wind shook the treetops, the air seemed to belong there, in the tree. Grandmother came out on the porch with Rosa. He felt Max observing them for a moment, Max the seer, the comprehending, Max the mute. He didn't know what to say and whispered: "Yes. I have the same—the same feeling. You will see." Vera turned around, went inside. He felt Helena turn away, impetuously, get up; he did not make a move, but remained sitting. Helena looked at Tomas, passed him, and Tomas sat down next to Bert and said: "I'm leaving. Today. I don't know why I'm doing it, but I have to." Bert glanced at him: a narrow face, a kind of introversion, determination mirrored in the face, in the eyes that no longer were gliding anxiously over objects and faces. He said: "You do as you wish and have to. We will be expecting you back. But if you hesitate, then don't do it." Tomas turned to him quickly, looked him in the eye, saw a quick flash of fear: "But that's exactly why—because I can't run away; I hesitate but I no longer want to choose escape, always choose escape." "Always?" he asks. Tomas doesn't answer. "Don't do anything hasty," he says. Tomas replies: "No. I've been thinking this through, all my life. I didn't know it. It feels—difficult, unpleasant.

174

Not that I have to prove anything to myself. But it feels like something inescapable. I will—I hope—return next weekend." Bert heard it in his voice: hesitant and hence determined; fearful and hence unafraid. Perhaps that's how it is, he thought, out of context: the wind emanates from the tree itself. The earth is preparing for its extinction. Certainty tastes, like salt tastes. He sat looking ahead, with blind eyes. Each one went in his own direction.

We discovered it too late: we could have turned away from ourselves. Not so that we would have joined in the surface violence, celebrated moving on just for the sake of moving on, run ahead of the younger set in order to prove our own youth. But so that we would have striven toward creativity, action, helping. We were the ones who knew what hunger and death meant; we did not tell the others. We suppressed it. We had kicked ourselves up these narrow dirty stairways to a view of Security. But Security is a barge floating on blood. We kept quiet about that. We looked with disgust at well-nourished burgher's sons talking about poverty, their red masquerade costumes artfully draped around a lack of compassion, a lack of conscience: that's why they had to procure one. We turned away from them. We knew what death was, and every moment we turned away from it, denied it the way you deny an old childhood pal who has become insolvent, has fallen on evil days, and is hanging onto your jacket sleeve puffing his disgusting breath into your face. We started thinking with our stomach; it swelled. It followed us faithfully into the heavy sleep of guilt. Had we not done our share? We knew death; had we not sacrificed enough to it? Let those who wish taste blood and join together in an illusory freedom: we knew that foxy game! We recognized it! It hadn't taught us anything useful. Luxury, tranquillity, satiety. Tranquillity. Satiety. There on a railroad sidetrack some child was sitting, burned and crying. We saw the pictures, pushed them aside. And if anyone knew the mechanisms of the gas ovens, that was us. We saw the pictures, pushed them aside. We knew them all, the eye sockets, the

175

remains, the shots in the neck, the frozen limbs. There was no point in constantly reminding ourselves of it: we had suffered enough to merit forgetting. Our goal became to live well, to look away. Death, poverty, suffering—that's nothing to tell others about; it's something you want to forget.

Like water falling from jutting cliff to jutting cliff. Something clear, distinct, unavoidable, something pure. Falling, crashing blindly, in cascades, coolly dividing, always the same, the same element, the same movement, down, through the silence, through the clear air, through the uncertainty, toward uncertainty, twilight, darkness; and he who once imagined, dreamt about dying, like music playing in the night is muffled, dies; this roar, these mutilated limbs gushing down—that's how it was. And over everything a clear, pitiless, indifferent light, concealing nothing.

Helena

In indigent homes eventually everyone looks past the others, contemplates the bread or silently observes the yard, leaves his seat at table after a softly spoken "thank you," disappears in order to go outside and away. It makes no difference whether you have stepped down from riches or stepped up from poverty: at twilight all sit in their one- or two-room apartments waiting for nothing. I don't want to recall that time; that's why it is short, just an episode in my life, something to leave behind, to step up from. Yet I feel like Father's mirror image. Two mirror images produce a nothing. "Remember, Helena, never make the mistake of trusting another person." That was his legacy.

As in a Russian movie the whirling treetops of the parkway take time away, restore time, a road opens up and closes again . . . ; as when a silent water surface slowly changes from the lonely, floating leaves of autumn to snow, white expanses leading to heaving dark water . . . ; as when the spring sun slowly touches trees and gulfs, the snow glitters crystalline against an uneasy blue sky and the ice rings around the reeds melt, shadows of fish move across spotted red beach rocks . . . ; and suddenly it's summer, the treetops bend in the wind blowing over the skin, over the closed eyes . . . ; as when everything is happening in sequence, the lips hardly have time to shape the words, the hand hardly has time to touch the face of the beloved before dusk falls, before fall is here, first with golden crowns of leaves, then quiet, enveloped in mist, with vast fields where a train slows down as it approaches the station: a bell is chiming, you catch a glimpse of people with pale faces, they do not turn around, the train stops . . . ; you can smell charcoal and moldering earth, poverty, and you think, home at last! and feel the taste of metal on your lips; in the dark which suddenly has fallen you focus your eyes upon a solitary star visible above the forest silhouette; you don't know whether it is the Evening Star, you know that you won't be going away anymore, that the eternal circular movement has come to an end, inside and outside yourself, that you have arrived.

The only real, shared thing: speech, words, conversation. What was said alone nobody heard, unless it went through the tabletop, burned a path along the floor and hit you! you! you who are the shared in me and the antipode of nothingness.

This god who inflates the globe and wipes his mouth with the back of his hand while holding onto the short umbilical cord with stout fingers. Another go at it. On the surface thin lines open up, crevices, canyons, dark precipices, streams, areas of dark watery magma miles wide, strange light phenomena, blue vapors, floating mists! Now, now it's floating off, with woods and mountains, with seas and everything, with people, with bodies, with a swarm of invisible life, with a hurricane of voices that reaches outer space like a great, immobile silence. Perhaps the note is so high that no one can perceive it! And the globe is floating; it glides among the stars, it slowly turns around its circular path. But instead of shrinking it is swelling! There is something like a halo around its surface. There, there is the thinnest spot! There, above the surface, the needle point can be aimed! Thousands of arms are guiding the tip of the cone toward its goal. The wind starts blowing; people close their windows and continue sleeping. Half the globe is sunk in sleep. The other half is sparkling with life beneath the red-hot sun. Oh, could we be like it! Could we get its powers! The point has been aimed; we wonder what will happen! Turn on the television! See the super-sensation of the year!

Max

I look with a cold eye. At a distance they are close to me. Close up I cannot see them. They live for an instant, extended into a lifetime. They are close to me because they die and live as if unaware of it. They are close to me because I cannot protect them. One of the few who knows this is Grandmother. "I worry about them," she said just now. Does she? Do I? We both are beyond a certain borderline. Odd: once we were children, once we struggled, heard only our own voices. We thought security was happiness. Objects, like this island here, the beach, the women at the water's edge, the boy looking up at me, or at his father—all this is temporary. Look at them, don't abandon them. Describe them as if they were part of a violent, secret, unavoidable dream. Look at the cloud, swelling, fanlike,
the landscape unbearably still, for an instant, the leaves of the trees black against the slowly growing light, the heat, the boy shading himself with his arm, the interrupted conversations, the voices I

have heard in dreams, repeating: it isn't a matter of no concern. It is the fear, the anguish, the limbs, the clothes, the sweat, the secretions, the wounds, the pain; nothing glides off easily. It is my terror, my nightmare, the echo in my own eye; God, let it be so, let the children come to me, come, gather here! They hurry, they crawl this way. The trees stand black; I open the door and run to meet them.

Gran

She feels it coming; the heat touches her face as if it had been hiding there a long time already, in the skin folds, in the wrinkles: now they suddenly emit a glow as if illumined from the inside. Please, please, she thinks, take all these tired parts away from me. And at the same time her eyes with the heavy bags underneath look at Martin, as if they were imploring him to understand, just for a second: he lives, he will go on, so it is and no other way, so it has always been. Her mouth is moving uncertainly. She tries to get up from the lawn chair but cannot.

The hand is struck aside. The flags are torn off their poles; the poles themselves crack. The housefront facing the river plunges into the river. The meeting is interrupted and spreads out into the streets, intermingles with rocks, plaster, beams. Plaster, chairs, human limbs: the entire central park is like a pile of twigs. The eye barely has time to be raised at a cry before it is torn off! Farther away, beneath the yellow sky, there are only vast wheat fields burning up. Nobody is there; I listen: nobody. Everything is collapsing inside the eye, soundlessly.

The music soared out of the rubbish as if all the time it had been hiding, in the beams, in the concrete pillars, in the ground, in the water itself, in the air, and now slowly rose from the cracks, out of the mud, out of the caverns, out of the dust. It rose first as a low, then a slowly soaring note, was again blown away but returned like a stubborn echo, no, not an echo: a voice, a small chorus of voices, a grayish-white wind, but quite soft, among the still tumbling, flaying, frayed fragments of life. Human throats could not produce such a cold, high, final, pale yet obstinately lingering series of notes—like a weak echo of the alarm sirens of the Second World War, the old people thought: a voice like fine particle dust but at the same time clearly discernible, like a shadow that never leaves the light, a part of the earth, a sign of an eternal treason. Those who heard it saw it too: like a bleached-out version of life itself, a thin sky beneath a sky, a wail shaped into a corona, the wreath of death. But why was this music crying, composed of alien voices into a single instrument, a single pure note from the beyond? Indeed, this was the triumph of death! Why was it rising like a wail out of the ruins, this song which was no song but a guttural sound? Indeed this was its landscape, what long ago it had foretold, in lonely nights, among lonely people; indeed, many had heard it long ago, heard the music, seen it as rising whirls of dust in the tumult and noise, in all the signs of violent, overflowing, unhappy, hateful life: this note, this voice which already had pointed out the road toward an ever-heavier, ever-more-fragile, ever-more-encumbered, ever-more-vulnerable world: a music for cities and their inhabitants, a music for precipices and those living at their edge. Hadn't this music then been triumphal, baroque, swelling, colorful, imperious? Why was it rising with such a lonely wail out of the cracks of the earth? Why was it crying now? Why was it like a mist out of the mouths of those who were already dead and could no longer breathe? It soared and remained, it dropped but did not disappear, it remained—not an echo but the very voice of all that had been crushed, the core of the splintered rock, the cry of the fire dying down, the pale, thin, lingering, undeniable song of every-

180

thing abandoned, the song of the dead willow, the litany of our lives.

Three waves, the last one a tidal wave which beneath the white sky covers with a silent roar first the outermost islets, then the higher skerries, the woods disappearing into the whirling water, the coast with roads and houses, with people smaller than ants who hardly had time to stand up: everything covered by the heavy water above which only a tattered, dead flock of birds is carried out and away at great height: dead remains of a poisoned moon which someone way up high is observing, before he makes a sign.

At the end, all pass through that somber gate of memories into their childhood home to bid farewell.

NOTES

1. A Finnish custom on New Year's Eve is to melt tin, drop it in a bucket of cold water, and read one's future from the shape produced.

2. Civil War: January–May 1918, after Finland gained its independence from Russia. The Reds tried to seize power, perhaps with the assistance of Russian soldiers left behind in Finland after the collapse of the czarist government. The Whites, aided by a German expeditionary force, won the war.

3. Winter War: November 1939–March 1940, between Finland and the Soviet Union; the latter won.

4. Almqvist's Songes: poems (*songes,* Fr. "dreams") written and set to music by C. J. L. Almqvist.

5. "Mein sind . . . gemacht": Andreas Gryphius, "Betrachtung über die Zeit," *Epigrammata,* 1:76. See translation, p. xxxii.

6. Skeppsbron pier: a pier in Stockholm where steamers from Finland used to dock.

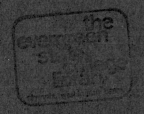